...prior to that was ...ealth advocate in a
... hospital. She also worked with sexually abused
... ...ers and taught psychology in both schools and
colleges. Born in the East End of London, she now lives in
Essex.

Praise for *Last Rights*:

'Nadel has made a sizeable impact on the crime and
mystery field with her fascinating series of thrillers set in
Istanbul ... Her new series, set during the London blitz,
ably navigates different psychological waters; it conjures
up a moving character in Francis Hancock ... A great
depiction of the period and a touchingly reluctant new
sleuth' *Guardian*

'Gripping and unusual detective story ... vivid and
poignant' *Literary Review*

'Nadel has created an atmospheric setting and a fascinating insight into the lives of Londoners struggling against the
Luftwaffe's nightly onslaught. The book's intelligent
original theme and empathetic characterization make for a
compelling read' *Good Book Guide*

'Excellent' *Birmingham Post*

Praise for Barbara Nadel:

'The delight of the Nadel book is the sense of being taken beneath the surface of an ancient city which most visitors see for a few days at most. We look into the alleyways and curious dark quartiers of Istanbul, full of complex characters and louche atmosphere' *Independent*

'This is an extraordinarily interesting first novel' *Evening Standard*

'*Belshazzar's Daughter*, with its brilliantly realised Istanbul setting and innovative protagonist was a hard act to follow. But she pulls off the trick triumphantly' *The Times*

'Inspector Çetin İkmen is a detective up there with Morse, Rebus and Wexford. *Harem* is the fifth in the series, and the most compelling to date... Gripping and highly recommended' *Time Out*

'One of the most intriguing detectives in contemporary crime fiction... The backdrop of Istanbul makes for a fantastic setting' *Mail On Sunday*

'Unusual and very well-written' *Sunday Telegraph*

'Intriguing, exotic... exciting, accomplished and original' *Literary Review*

'A bewitching style... a story that carries the reader forward willingly along until the well-sprung denouement' *Scotsman*

'As before, Nadel presents a gallery of richly created characters along with the superb scene-setting we have come to expect from her' *Good Book Guide*

Also by Barbara Nadel

Last Rights

Barbara Nadel

headline

First published in Great Britain in 2005
by HEADLINE BOOK PUBLISHING

First published in paperback in 2006
by HEADLINE BOOK PUBLISHING

A HEADLINE paperback

4

ISBN 978 0 7553 2136 0

Typeset in Caslon by Avon DataSet Ltd,
Bidford on Avon, Warwickshire

Printed and bound in Great Britain by
CPI Group (UK) Ltd, Croydon, CR0 4YY

Headline's policy is to use papers that are natural, renewable and
recyclable products and made from wood grown in sustainable
forests. The logging and manufacturing processes are expected to
conform to the environmental regulations of the country of origin.

HEADLINE BOOK PUBLISHING
A division of Hodder Headline
338 Euston Road
London NW1 3BH

www.headline.co.uk
www.hodderheadline.com

To my dad.
Although he's been dead for almost four years now,
I couldn't have written this book without him.

Acknowledgements

This book was an entirely new, unknown and scary venture for me and I have been fortunate in having had a lot of help from a lot of people. Ron Hart, Publicity Officer of the East of London Family History Society, was a great help. He readily shared some of his wartime experiences with me and put me in touch with others who also had great tales to tell. Foremost amongst these were Sylvia Ramage, Ivy Alexander and Eric Vanlint. Ivy and Eric were also kind enough to give me copies of their books *Maid in West Ham* and *While Pigeons Cooed in Hackney Wick* respectively – both of which were most useful. I would also like to thank Sharon Grimmond from the New Deal for Communities and her very welcoming History Committee.

Michael Grier, Community Relations Manager at Tate and Lyle was kind enough to show me around part of the plant and allow me access to the company archives. Steve Maltz of London Jewish Tours was also a mine of information as well as being a very entertaining fellow walker. Susie, Philip and Pam at the Spitalfields Centre have my undying thanks for introducing me to 19 Princelet Street – a truly life altering experience. I also have to thank the Newham Bookshop for the help they gave me when I needed it and just for being there with the right books when I didn't.

Brian Parsons PhD is a funeral service educator and author of the book *The London Way of Death*. He answered many often badly couched questions for me and was a mine of funeral service information. Thanks to him.

My family, both the living and the dead, were crucial to this project. Thanks especially to my mother for her memories, to my son for his vision and my husband for his patience. Finally, thanks also to my agent, Juliet Burton and my editor at Headline, Martin Fletcher.

N.B. Readers unfamiliar with words or expressions used in this novel can turn to page 336 for the Glossary.

Chapter One

Ever seen a man's face smashed in? It explodes. I've seen it done with bullets more times than anyone should. Going up, over the top, mud in your mouth, your eyes, your ears. The bloke next to you pokes his head over and then, bang! A bullet, one of Jerry's, one of ours sometimes, it hardly matters when his brains are all over your battledress. Not this time, though. This time I could see it was a fist. Burrowing into his nose, a big, hard docker's fist, pushing straight through to the back of the poor bloke's head.

I screamed. Bombs hammering down all around us, Canning Town, Silvertown, Custom House – every bloody inch of London's docklands – but they heard me. Men with faces like sweat-slicked potatoes. They turned and saw a thin, dark man in the shadow of one of the trees, a man shaking from his hat to his boots.

You hear some people say that war is different now. They say that with all the bombing it's not the same as what happened in the first lot. They say it's worse.

Depends on how you see war, I suppose. For me there's no difference. When I was in the trenches in the Great War, people died. Now people are dying again. Not only soldiers this time, I'll grant you, ordinary men, women and kiddies. But at the end of the day I wonder what's the difference. People talk about the old Kaiser being better than Adolf Hitler and I don't know about that either. I was twenty when I went off to fight for King and Empire, just a nipper in the scheme of things. I grew up, grew old and most of me died out there in the mud.

'Who's there?' one of the potatoes said.

Somebody ran over to me and looked into my face. I couldn't move, not with the terror on me. He was small, the one who came over, and even through my fear I knew I could have had him if I'd needed to. But then he smiled. Middle of the night, but I could see every inch of his leathery old face thanks to all the fireworks down at the docks.

'Aw, it's only the Morgue's son,' the old man said, with a dismissive wave of his hand.

'What? The wog?'

'Yus.'

And then they all laughed. Because it was funny.

So how did the 'Morgue's son' come to be shaking in his boots on the edge of a bare-knuckle fight in a graveyard in East Ham? I don't know any more than anyone else. All I do know is that ever since all this bombing started on the seventh of the month, this is what I've had to do. I'd

2

known it was coming. Ever since Dunkirk I've woken up shaking. Seems almost unbelievable all that happened only back in June. Even the weather's gone off now, as if we've suddenly crashed into winter before autumn's really out. Thrown down into the darkness . . .

But, anyway, this raid started and I had to get out same as always. My mum, my sisters and our apprentice boy Arthur went down the Anderson shelter in the yard. But it's like the trenches down there – bombs going off in your head, blood dripping down the side of your brain. I ran. I had to get out of it and I ran. It's what I've always done. It's what I do.

That I ended up in a graveyard was funny. St Mary Magdalene's is an ancient, creepy one too. Half the tombs are broken and sinking, and in places there are weeds up to your neck. All dressed in black, my top hat with its veil on my head, I must have looked like something out of a ghost story.

'Your dad buried my mum,' one of the potatoes said, as he took his cap off his head to show respect. 'Done her handsome.'

I tried to thank him but nothing would come out. When I run like this, my mind sort of goes back to the first lot, and while I'm there I don't know what I might be doing here. And even when it stops, as it had done when the men spoke to me, I'm still not right. My sister Aggie's old man used to say I was a basket case – and that was before any of this madness was even on the cards. Sometimes he'd say it to my face.

The man whose mug had caved in came over to look at

me. He was holding something up to his nose to catch the blood. I think it was a vest.

'Blimey,' he said. 'Gone bleedin' white by the look of him.'

The men laughed again – and so did I. You have to.

'What you doin' out here, Mr H?' It was a familiar voice, although I couldn't for the life of me place it at the time.

'I-I-I went for a walk,' I stuttered. I hate it when I do that.

'Funny time to go strolling,' another voice cut in, 'in the middle of a raid. Do this often, do you?'

'Y-yee . . .'

'Does it all the time so I've heard. Barmy!' someone else said, and they all laughed yet again.

Barmy. Yes. There's so much about me that is barmy. Funny, really, when you look at it. Francis Thomas Hancock, old soldier at forty-seven, undertaker, wog – out of his tiny mind.

There was one of those long whistling sounds then and a breathless moment before the bomb hit something close. Like I imagine an earthquake, like the endless pounding of the guns in the trenches.

'Blimey, that was close!'

'I think that's going to be that for tonight, gents,' someone said.

Men, some of them bloodied, started to walk towards the cemetery gates. The old leather-faced geezer, still in front of me, said, 'Come on, Mr H, get you 'ome. Don't want to have to answer questions from no nosy coppers or none of them bleedin' wardens, do we?' He took one of my elbows in his hand and led me on behind the others.

I'd heard that bare-knuckle fights sometimes took place in graveyards at night – you pick up whispers about such things in my trade – but I hadn't expected to come across one during a raid. Not that I'd ever really thought about coming on one at all. I'm not a betting man myself. There's enough risk in life without courting it.

When we got out on to High Street South, the old fellow let my arm go and pushed ahead. Suddenly I was totally alone. I stopped. There had to have been at least thirty men at the fight, but as I began slowly to walk back up towards the Barking Road, in the general direction of my home, I couldn't see a soul. Funny that, in the middle of a raid, no one about. Of course, most people were down the shelters or hiding under their stairs. You would've thought you'd see police and firemen and wardens about, though – at least, that's what I'd thought before the raids got going. But there couldn't ever be enough of them: the fires and the destruction are like the end of the world, what can they do?

When I think about it now, I suppose I don't know what I thought it would be like coming under attack from the Germans by air. In the first lot you could see their faces, frightened just like ours, scrambling to their deaths over the top of the trenches. But at such a distance it's different. Faceless machines come, drop bombs, people die. And yet in spite of this you get up, go to work and carry on – at least, that's what we've done so far. But not in a normal way. Normal ways for me used to include going to the house of the deceased, sometimes,

sometimes not, laying them out and then burying them – not being given a head and a bag of bits by some copper telling me to 'Cobble this bloke together for his family, will you, Mr H?'

And they call me mad . . .

It was only a matter of a couple of minutes later when I met him. Lurching, just like I was, over piles of something that had once been someone's home. The sky was red and yellow with him silhouetted black against the beauty of the bombing. If he hadn't been waving his arms around so much, I wouldn't have taken any notice of him. But he was, and even though I don't always stop and help – you can't – this time I did. Perhaps I thought he was raving. There's a sort of bond between madmen that almost forces you to get involved. I was in a couple of hospitals during the first lot. Gassed twice. But I knew who my own were in those places. They were the ones who ran like me, who howled and screamed like this chap now.

As I got closer to him, I could hear that he was shouting something. And even though I knew he wouldn't be able to hear me any more than I could hear him, I said, 'It's all right, pal, I'm coming.'

I don't know how old I thought he was at the time. Flames always, in my experience, draw the features down making people look much older. What I did know was that he was in trouble. He kept clawing at his chest as if there was something in there he wanted rid of.

'What is it?'

'I've been fucking stabbed!' He was a Londoner, I

could tell from his voice, and now that I was next to him I could see that he was dark. Black hair and a long, thin nose. I thought that maybe he was a Jew – either that or he was like me, us not being unlike each other.

'Stabbed? How?'

It was bright now, the ground lit by I don't know how many fires, some madness going on in the sky. Like daylight some of the raids, like the world melting into white heat. He was dirty, covered in brick-dust, and his hair was reeking of cordite, just like mine must have been, but I couldn't see any blood on him.

Mad.

'Look here!' he said, and he moved his hand away from his chest. 'Look at it, there!'

There wasn't much blood. Not like an artery hit or anything like that.

'Nasty flesh wound is all you've got,' I said.

One thin, sinewy hand reached out and grabbed me by the collar. 'She fucking stabbed me, I tell you,' he said, through gritted teeth.

'Hold on!'

His breath smelled of beer and there were gaps in his mouth where some of his teeth had once been. A fighter, maybe even one of them I'd just come upon in the graveyard. I didn't recognise him, but I wouldn't have recognised any of them at the time had my life depended on it. What I wouldn't forget, though, even in my dreams, was the look of hatred on his face as he turned away from me with a curse. 'Fucking whore!'

And then he was off. He pushed past me, skidding

down a pile of bricks, heading for Beckton and the real heart of the inferno. To be honest, I didn't try and stop him. I knew he was hurt, but he was in the grip of something too – and I know all about that and how unwise it can be to interfere with it. Sometimes helping those in the grip of madness can be worse than just letting the thing take its course. But then sometimes you read the situation wrong and it all goes phut. So I made my way home. I didn't see the man with hate on his face and beer on his breath again until two days later when he turned up unexpectedly at my shop.

Chapter Two

Hancocks have been burying people in the London Borough of West Ham for two generations, three if you count me. Apart from the Hitchcocks' firm, which also has premises on the Barking Road, I think we're the oldest undertaker's shop around these parts. My grandad, Francis, who I'm named for, started the company in 1885. Back in those days Hancock's was a building firm as well as an undertaker's, but Francis got out of the bricking and chipping around the turn of the century. So when Grandad died in 1913, my old dad took over the burying of poor men and women for a living. Because our shop is, and always has been, roughly at the centre of the borough, we've always got business from all over. And although in more recent years other firms have opened up in Stratford, Plaistow and further down towards the docks around Canning Town, we've managed to stay close to the people we serve.

Tom Hancock, my dad, was a lovely chap. All the old wags round here used to call him 'The Morgue', but he always took it in good part. When I was a nipper at school you couldn't count the number of lads whose dads took their belt off to them. Not my dad, though. He loved us: Mum, my sisters Nancy and Aggie and me. He didn't care what people round here said and they've always said quite a lot about most things.

Before Dad joined Francis in the business, he was a soldier and was posted out to India. He liked it there – partial to the heat Dad was – and when he met a local girl called Mary Fernandez, he liked it even better. They met in Calcutta, Mum and Dad – she was working at a convent that looked after orphans. Dad, Tom, wasn't exactly honest when he told his parents about her in one of his letters. He used to say, 'I wrote it like this: "I've met this smashing girl. She's a good Christian but a little bit dark. I'm going to marry her."' Then he'd laugh. Gran and Grandad nearly died when they saw Mum for the first time. Nancy was a year old and Mum was pregnant with me when they first arrived in West Ham. Grandad was nice about it, but Gran always called us wogs – all except my younger sister Aggie, the only one of us who took Dad's light hair and fair skin.

All through my life I've been called 'wog'. Not by everyone, and not always in bad spirit. I've had some very good mates in my time, still do. But some of these names and comments have hurt my sister Nancy who is the darkest and, in truth, the most Indian-looking of us all. I know this has held her back from maybe finding a bloke or bettering herself in some way and I must say it does make me angry at times. Although not that often now.

There's worse things than names in this world. I learned that on the Somme; I learned that when my mates dragged me kicking and screaming back to our trench that first time I lost what was left of my mind and made a run for it. At the time I hated those lads, called them every name a man can lay his tongue to. But they saved me – Ken White, Stanley Wheeler, Georgie Pepper and Izzy Weisz. The top brass would have done me for deserting as sure as eggs is eggs. Then I'd have been shot – not blown up like Stanley, not drowned in mud like Georgie and Izzy: shot.

What none of them could have known, though, was that running was going to become a way of life for me. Loud noises, violence – it all makes me want to do it. The Great War started me doing it and I've never stopped running since. Ken, who was the only mate of mine to get out with me, knows. We talk about it on occasion. It's as if my head, sometimes like that night at the knuckle fight in the graveyard, is bringing my body along with it – running. From life, from my own thoughts, now from bombs and guns, from women's screams and men's cries of despair – Mr H the undertaker runs and runs and then when he gets back to his shop he hides among any bodies he might have out the back. We're one of the few firms who can take bodies on the premises round here. I even know a bloke up West who embalms for a price – not that there's much call for that in West Ham. We're a poor borough. People here, even before rationing, have never had much that wasn't essential.

Of course, where you've got poverty you've also got

ignorance so quite a lot of people in the borough believe in ghosts and spirits and all that rubbish. But not me. The dead are gone and can't harm anyone – perhaps that's why I like to work with them. Innocent. I make sure the dead get where they want to be in spite of the actions of the living. I've seen it all. Widows digging in their old men's pockets for every last farthing, drunks burying their kids in paupers' graves, and now the Luftwaffe bombing the departed up into the light again, spinning their shredded grave clothes into the yew trees. The cruelty of the living is something that has no end.

I was back in our parlour with a pot of tea almost brewed when Mum, my sisters – the girls, I call them – and our lad Arthur came up out of the Anderson the following morning. Nancy went straight away to look to our horses, who had bashed themselves silly against their stall again in the night. Poor creatures, there's no knowing what they'll do to themselves once a raid begins. Aggie, as usual, was more concerned about what she looked like. She has a pretty, heart-shaped face with big blue eyes, the image of Dad's. Not that she's satisfied with what she's got. Stood in front of the fan-shaped glass in the parlour she pulled faces at herself, mucked about with her hair and went on about how 'rotten' everything was.

'I hate this rotten war with its rotten food and rotten muck all over the place,' she said. 'Blimey, I look as if I'm about Mum's age!'

'What? That young?' I said, trying to be playful.

Aggie turned towards me and glared. Then, when I told her I'd made a rotten pot of tea, she stomped off into the kitchen, her harshly bleached-up hair, full of brick-dust, flapping behind her like a dull mat. Poor Aggie, with her husband gone off with another woman, her little 'uns evacuated away somewhere in Essex, all she wants is a little bit of fun, but every time she looks in a mirror she gets depressed. Little or no sleep doesn't do a lot for anyone's looks, including Aggie's. There's a shadow of loneliness that hangs around her lovely eyes sometimes too.

Mum poured out for everyone into cups and saucers she'd come straight in and slowly washed up at the sink. You never know whether or not you're going to have water on after a raid but on this occasion we did. Aggie carried her tea up to her room while Arthur took his own and Nancy's out to the yard. Mum, her cup trembling on its saucer in her hand, looked at me as I stood against the door-post and said, 'I'm going to make you something to eat, Francis.'

'I'm all right.'

'No, you're not, you're skin and bone!' Her eyes started to fill then, but she held it back gamely. Mary Hancock, my mum, nearly seventy years old and still beautiful. Tall and slim, like me, she has the most amazing black hair – she uses no dyes to my knowledge – pleated up into a long, thick roll at the back of her head. Nicely spoken, with an Indian accent still, and a real lady. Like a duchess, my old dad used to say and he called her that too, just like I started doing after he passed away.

She took some bread out of the larder then, with what little Stork margarine there was left.

'Sit down, my son,' she said to me, as she pulled Dad's chair out from its place at the head of the table.

'Duchess . . .'

She walked up to me, limping a bit like she does when her arthritis is bad, her long black skirts swishing against the lino as she moved. The Duchess has never worn short dresses in her life or anything other than mourning since Dad died. Her dignity, as well as what she always calls her 'convent training', just won't allow it.

'Sit down, Francis, and please do eat,' she said, as she ran one knotted brown hand across my forehead. Her arthritis had started young, when she was about thirty. Our doctor, O'Grady, said at the time that she needed to go back to the dry, hot climate of India if she was to have any chance of beating it. But she didn't even want to mention that to Dad. She didn't want to make him give up his business and she would never have left him or us children. But she suffers for that decision. 'I wish you didn't have to run all the time,' the Duchess murmured, as she placed the bread and marge in front of me. 'I wish you could have your health back again.'

I didn't answer her. What was there to say? Some time, sooner rather than later, the raids would start again and I would run. Sure as night follows day. We both knew it.

I started on the bread and marge, more out of duty than hunger, but it made Mum smile, which was the object of the exercise. Then Nancy, or Nan, as we all call her, came in from the yard and, frowning as she almost always is, took over the tea with her usual well-meaning bossiness. 'You've got to go and pick up Mr Evans at eleven,' she said to me as, unbidden, she refilled my cup with tea and sugar.

'I know,' I said, as patiently as lack of sleep would allow. As if I could forget to pick up the deceased who, if indirectly, was paying for us all to go on existing.

'You conducting?'

'Yes.' I always had, ever since Dad died, which is fifteen years ago now. Out in front of the hearse, my wand in my hand – the conductor, the master of the final earthly ceremonies. The wand or cane, which is what it looks like to most people, doesn't serve any purpose these days. In the past it was used as a weapon to ward off grave robbers and as a sort of magical tool to keep away evil spirits. Hence the dramatic and mysterious name.

But I knew what she was getting at and I knew that she meant well. These days there aren't always enough men to carry a sizeable coffin like Gordon Evans's. Sometimes a funeral has to go without a conductor. But not this time.

'Joe and Harry Evans are going to bear with Arthur and Walter,' I said. 'They want to do it for their dad.'

'Yeah,' Nan said acidly, 'all very well as long as Walter don't fall over.'

Mum and I looked at each other and smiled. Although never a part of the business, Nan has always taken what we do very seriously. Ever since we'd lost our cousin Eric to the navy, she had been concerned about how we were managing. Eric had driven for us for a number of years and was a strong, sure-footed pall-bearer. But he'd been called up so I'd done what I could, which was to employ Walter Bridges, a single bloke with badly fitting teeth who, though getting on a bit and, it must be said, partial to a drop or two, is a good enough driver and not too bad a bearer. There is also Arthur, our boy, fifteen and nearly six foot tall in his stockinged feet. Dying to have a go at Jerry, Arthur can put a good gloss on a coffin, provided he doesn't drop fag ash over it afterwards. We also got Doris Rosen, our office girl, as soon as Eric and another of our blokes, Jim, left for the services. Had she been well enough, the Duchess could have managed the office and the bookwork, but most of the time now her arthritis is so bad she can't do much. More often than not Nan has to feed her, put her to bed, turn the pages of her book, take her to the privy … That's Nan's job, the Duchess – and the cooking and cleaning. Apart from feeding the horses sometimes, she doesn't have time for the shop and its doings, however much she might want to be in there, however much I know she envies Doris – who, in spite of being married, is a lot freer than Nan. In some ways, this war has freed a lot of women to do things other than look after men and kids.

Aggie came back in then and rolled herself a fag on the table. Nan watched her all the time, her hooded eyes, so brown they're almost black, scrutinising her younger sister for each and every sign of what she would call 'coarseness' – heavy makeup or too much perfume.

'I'm going to work,' Aggie said. She was indeed heavily made up now and her hair was encased in one of those net snoods the girls like so much. She looked, to me, as if she would be more at home in Hollywood than London. To my way of thinking, it takes courage to make yourself so bright outside when you feel so rotten within.

But as Aggie left, I could see the word form in Nan's mind – 'slut': written all over her face it was. And what a face. Bitterness is a horrible thing. It's not her fault. Again, it's to do with the way she looks. People made comments when she was a youngster and she hid herself away, looking after first Dad, then Mum and me and Aggie's two little 'uns when they were still at home. Aggie might be glamorous now, but Nan, with her long black hair and tiny delicate features, had been beautiful. But that was a long time ago. Now she's a spinster, a bitter one, and although I've always loved her, her spite is difficult to bear. I hate the way she disapproves of any fun Aggie might have. It's not wrong for a girl to wear makeup or even like a drink once in a while – especially not in these times.

'Oh, well,' I said, after I'd finished what I hoped was enough of the food to satisfy the Duchess, 'I'd best get on.'

I went downstairs into the parlour and spent a bit of time knocking brick-dust off the black curtains in the front window. A lot of windows had gone out opposite so there was a lot of glass all over the place. Doris, breathless and red-faced after her walk over from her home in Stepney, said, 'Looks like a bleedin' snow scene out there.'

And it did. In fact, if you looked at the pub on the corner from the right angle, it almost looked like something you'd see on a Christmas card.

Gordon Evans's funeral was what has come, even in such

a short space of time, to pass for normal. Tired, hand-picked flowers, a coffin scarred by millions of tiny glass shards and Walter, reeking of booze, swaying gently by the graveside. I suppose I should count myself lucky he sets off on the proper foot, the left, when he's bearing, even if he is three sheets to the wind. But it isn't good. Dad would have died of shame had he still been around. After all, when Hancock's started, funerals were probably as elaborate as funerals had ever been – with the exception of the Egyptians, Tutankhamun and all that. When old Francis died in 1913, Dad sent him off in a hearse pulled by four black horses followed by mutes carrying ostrich feather wands and a procession of friends and family in the deepest mourning imaginable. You used to see so many flowers at funerals before the Great War. But, then, during and what seemed like for years afterwards, there were so many dead there weren't enough flowers in the world for all of them.

Having said that, I did perform one big old-fashioned do back in late March. For an old bookies' runner, it was, Sid Nye. The bookie coughed up for the funeral – he could – but Sid had been popular with his many customers in and around the Abbey Arms pub so a lot of people wanted to pay their respects with heavy mourning, flowers and what-have-you. Funny to think how hot it was back then. Hard on the heels of that terrible winter, the diggers had a real problem getting old Sid's grave dug in time. Funny weather. But maybe that's what you get around wars. In Flanders the locals used to say that they'd never seen so much rain and mud, not in living memory.

Thinking about it now, Sid Nye's funeral wasn't just the last big do I've done, it was also the last normal one. Ever since then there've been few flowers and much talk, not of the deceased but of war and how we all think we're going to survive.

Still the widow Evans was grateful for what we did, and their two boys, both in reserved occupations, were generous to my lads. But it was still a frightening and depressing way to send off a loved one. So many trophies of war all around. I could see the shrapnel embedded in some of the trees and memorials, even if the bereaved could not. I could see a foot I remember too – lying all white and lonely on top of a watering can. But no one else saw it so maybe it wasn't really there. Maybe it was just a foot left over from the Somme, still lodged in my mind like a splinter.

Aggie had only been home for five minutes from her shift down at Tate & Lyle's sugar factory when the sirens went off. I'd dropped Walter at his lodgings after the funeral, but Arthur was still with us so yet again he went down with Mum, the girls and this time Doris too.

I went up on the roof. Something made me not go so far on this occasion. Perhaps I was afraid of meeting wild-eyed fighting men again or maybe I just wanted to watch people doing something rather than sitting in a hole in the ground. There's a fire-watching post on the next roof, over the bank. Mr Deeks, the manager, is in charge. 'Good evening, Mr Hancock,' he said to me, as he watched me lie down on the flat bit of roof over Aggie's bedroom.

'G-Good evening, Mr, er, D-Deeks,' I replied.

I saw him smile briefly before he and his lads went on about their business. He must have thought I was mad, lying down on a roof in a raid – no tin hat, no gas-mask, nothing. He must have thought I had some sort of death-wish. Depending on the day, sometimes he's on the money there.

As the throbbing drone of the bombers came ever closer, I shut my eyes. I've always thought that if I'm going to die, I don't want to have to watch myself do it. Sometimes people ask me whether or not I'm afraid of death and my answer always surprises them. I am. Just because it's familiar to me, just because sometimes I even want it, doesn't mean I can't fear it. How can you not fear something you know nothing about?

But this time closing my eyes had a bad effect. I kept seeing that bloke I'd met the night before, the one who said he'd been stabbed. I hadn't thought about him much since, but now here he was in colour and detail like a frightening villain in a creepy picture. Just his face, twisted in anger, playing over and over in my mind until I couldn't bear it any more and had to open my eyes. Even then, I think now, I was starting to feel guilty about him.

What I saw, the blackness of the night pierced by the searchlights picking out the even blacker ranks of bombers, was really a lot more frightening than anything in my head. But I preferred it because it was real. When I was in the trenches, just waiting as we could do for months sometimes before actually fighting, one of the worst things was not being able to see the enemy. You know they're there – you can hear them, feel the fear coming from them, even smell them at times – but you can't see them and gradually you build hideous pictures in your mind of things more monster than human. When you go over the top you're half mad with fear, which, maybe, was the whole point of all that. After all, what sane person would climb over a mountain of mud, then throw himself willingly at thousands of men armed with guns?

The noise was so loud it felt as if it was in your body. Explosion – like the sound of silk ripping across the sky – the crackling of the fires, Mr Deeks's lads shouting at each other. 'Where the bloody hell are our guns?' one asked. But no one could answer, because no one knows. There's only 'taking it', which we do every night and sometimes in the daytime too. The East End taking it for the whole country, mopping up pain like a sponge. Christ, it's only been a matter of weeks all this, but sometimes I think that at the end there'll be nothing left – only flatness, the whole place gone back to the marshes it grew out of all those centuries ago. I've conducted funerals for people made flat by falling buildings. I've done funerals for a leg, an arm and what's left of a head thrown into a coffin and given a name – Alf, Edie, Ruth, Sammy. Some poor old dear crying over what's left of probably three different people. But for her it is Ruth or Sammy, and that person is dead as sure as eggs is eggs. Some people, see, they vaporise: there isn't anything left, not a thing.

I lay listening to and watching that hell for I don't know how long. But some time I must have gone to sleep because the next thing I really remember is the daylight shining on to all the glass shards that were covering my body. As I sat up, I heard someone laugh and I looked down into the street where I could see Alfie Rosen, Doris's husband. With his cap stuck casual like on the back of his head and his ever-present fag on the go, the only way you'd ever think he was a bus conductor and not a wide-boy was because of the ticket machine hung round his neck.

'She down your Anderson, Mr H?' he said, anxious through his laughter about his big, buxom Doris.

'Yes,' I said. 'Stay there, Alfie, I'll come and let you in.'

As I walked back down through the flat and into the shop, I wondered as I always did at how we'd survived another night. Mum and Nan, I knew, would put it all down to the grace of God and the Blessed Virgin. Like Aggie, I just felt we'd been lucky, got away with it again.

I unlocked the front door and looked into Alfie's smiling, grimy face. Like his father, Herschel, Alfie Rosen is one of those red-haired Jews with very pale, almost colourless, skin. But then as I moved aside to let him in, another person turned up – big Fred Bryant, constable at the local nick. 'Hello, Mr Hancock,' he said, as he respectfully removed his helmet. 'Can I come in for a mo?'

I said yes, let him in and my life changed.

The police brought the body round about an hour later in a mortuary van. Fred said the morgue couldn't take any more – not that the morgue was the morgue any more. That couldn't cope so other places had had to be pressed into service for the reception of the dead. Poplar swimming-baths was now used as the morgue, a nice big area with tiles you could wash down easily.

But, that day, it was full too.

'I don't know who he is,' Fred said, as two of his blokes and the mortuary-van man placed the body in one of my coffins, 'but he's all in one piece and Dr Cockburn's done him a certificate, so I thought that if he could rest here for a bit someone might come along and claim him.'

'I can't keep him long, Fred,' I said. 'At least, not open. I can't risk maggots everywhere.'

Maggots breed quickly in a corpse that isn't preserved in any way. Unpreserved and open in the coffin this happens even more rapidly so you have to be careful to make sure you close up as soon as you can. Maggots underneath the lino is not a pleasant experience, especially if people, like my family and me, have to live in the property.

'Nah.' Fred's heavily jowled face broke into a smile. 'If no one claims him you can make arrangements in a bit. But he's quite a good-looking fella – hard, you know – and I can't believe no one'll miss him. Take a gander.'

Fred pulled away the cloth they'd used to cover his face and there he was, no more at rest in death than he had been when I'd seen him that night after the bare-knuckle fight. His eyes still stared at me with the same hatred I'd seen then. Like with the poor buggers who'd tried to desert from the trenches, nobody had taken the care to close the eyes after death. But that's what you get if you're nameless, like this bloke, and shamed like the poor bastards my comrades and I were terrified into executing.

Made me jump at first, and the rest if Fred Bryant was any judge.

'Christ, Mr H, you ain't 'arf gone pale,' he said. 'Look like you've seen a ghost.'

'You could say that,' I said, as I closed the man's eyes and covered his angry features once again. Then I told Fred about my strange encounter with this man and his apparently barmy belief that he'd been stabbed.

'He ain't been stabbed,' Fred said dismissively. 'Got a bit of blood on him, but who ain't these days?' He laughed. 'No, it's blast what killed him, Mr H. Look at the shock on his face. I've seen it before. Blast takes all the wind out of their bodies, stops their hearts dead, it does. Heart failure's what the doc's put on his certificate so there's no arguing with that. Bloody blast!'

Fred was probably right. I'd seen a few who'd died from blast myself and they were generally as he'd described. Of course there were stories about blast that had to be ridiculous – like the one about the bloke whose clothes had been ripped off his body, or the other bloke who, apparently, had been blown up his own chimney. But deaths like this were not and still aren't uncommon so I left the body out in the back room and took Fred through into the shop. By this time, Doris had been reunited with her Alfie so I had to clear my throat as I went into the office – they had been really worried about each other and were enjoying a good kiss.

'Mind getting me and Fred a cuppa, Doris?' I said.

'Can I make my Alfie one too?' she said.

'Course you can.'

When she'd gone, that left the three of us. Fred offered round the fags, a bit reluctantly to Alfie, I noticed. Alfie was born and bred, like Doris, in Spitalfields, but his parents had come from Germany originally. Poor Jews they were, who came to England to get a better life. But Alfie's old dad was put in an internment camp as soon as war broke out. Six months and him nearly eighty and a Jew. It's well known Hitler doesn't like Jews, so why Herschel Rosen was interned is beyond me. But Fred, maybe because he is a policeman and is paid, especially in these times, to be suspicious wasn't happy in 'German' Alfie's company.

'I'll give him a bit of a clean-up in a while,' I said, more than anything else to break the silence.

'Who?'

'The deceased,' I said, tipping my head back in the direction we'd just come from.

'Oh.'

He'd lost interest, too busy looking at Alfie sucking at a Woodbine. When Doris came back with the tea, the mood got a bit better. Tea can always do that, tea and the fact that Fred has always liked Doris. Only a couple of days before he'd said to our Nan, 'I like that Doris Mankiewicz, as was, she's a good, straight girl.' If he'd added 'for a Jew', I wouldn't have been surprised, but Nan never reported any more than what was said. Both Doris and Alfie are in their thirties. He's on the buses on account of his age and not being fit enough for the forces. There's some sort of heart problem. Not that it was, according to Doris, that much of a problem until his dad was sent away.

'We've got Florrie Starr at ten, Mr H,' Doris said, as she sat down and rolled herself a fag. 'Do you want my Alfie to stick around?'

'Yes, please.'

Florrie Starr had lived with her daughter in a flat in Plaistow, Inniskilling Road. A wife and mother who took in a bit of washing, Florrie had been perfectly ordinary in every way – except her size. She was what Dad would have called a 'whopper'. Florrie had to have been over twenty stone. And with only Arthur and Walter, with me conducting, we needed all the help we could get.

Fred left soon after that. I had to organise a suit for Alfie and get the other two lads in order and then we were off. I didn't have time to think much about the man out the back until well after Florrie'd been interred. In fact, I waited until I was on my own that night before I unwrapped him and this time had a good proper look. This man had, after all, if briefly, entered one of my waking nightmares. And although I don't believe in ghosts, shades or any rubbish like that, I felt I owed this fellow madman a bit more than just closing his eyes.

26

Chapter Three

There was more blood, just below his chest, than I'd remembered. He had put his hand there, it was true, but I couldn't see any cuts even when I washed him. All there was was a small red hole, like a pimple, just under his breastbone. I looked at it closely but it meant nothing to me so I carried on washing, my ears straining for the sirens like they always do now.

After a while, when nothing happened, Aggie came down with a cup of tea. If it'd been Nan, I would've covered the body, but there was no need around my younger sister. Not squeamish in any way, Aggie. Strange that Nan is, given what she's been brought up around, but there it is and that's that.

'He's a dark, vicious-lookin' thing,' she said, as she passed the cup and saucer to me.

'I think he might've been a fighter,' I said, as I rinsed the carbolic off my hands, then dried them on a cloth.

Aggie got in closer to have a better look. Fascinated, she always was, even as a kid. I once heard Dad say that if she hadn't been a girl he'd have passed the business over to Aggie instead of me. I wasn't meant to hear that, of course, but I don't feel anything about it because I can see what he meant. Not that it's death itself that interests Aggie. No, it's the human body. She always liked nature at school and I think sometimes that maybe if things had been different she might have found herself a position in that line. But the same as everyone now, she works for the war effort. In her case in a factory, filling tins with golden syrup and suchlike and laughing with other girls whose very breath would turn the air as blue as their works' overalls.

'Doris said that Fred Bryant brought him in,' Aggie said, wrinkling her nose in disgust at mention of the policeman's name. Nobody likes Fred that much. He's an idiot a lot of the time, with his opinions about everyone and the way he gossips. But, like coppers the world over, he has to be tolerated.

'Yes. Fred reckons the blast killed him,' I said, and then I recounted my own story about the deceased and his possible route into my parlour. I suppose I must have needed to tell someone I felt might have some sympathy with me and what I'd done.

'I mean, he can't really have been stabbed,' I said, 'but it bothered me so I've been looking at him while I've been washing and…'

'What about this?' Aggie said, pointing to the red pimple under his breastbone.

'I don't know. Not a stab wound, that's for sure.'

'Could be.'

I looked across at her, frowning. 'Ag, it's a spot or something.'

Aggie leaned back on the bench behind her and lit a cigarette. In the yellow light from the one bare gas mantle she looked older and paler than when her makeup was just freshly done. But two kids and a husband who chose to hop off with his best mate's missus will do that for you.

'Not if whoever stabbed him used a pin or something like that,' she said.

'A pin?'

'A long one, like a hatpin,' Aggie said. 'One of them big ones like Mum has on her mourning hat. Stick one of them into a bloke, you'd kill him.'

'No.'

She got up and came back over to the body. 'Look, it's around where his heart is, Frank,' she said. 'Stick something in the heart and you've had it. Ask Dr O'Grady if you don't believe me.'

'I don't not believe you,' I said. 'It's just that it's such a strange idea. I mean, who would do something like that?'

She shrugged. 'A woman. You said he said "she" stabbed him, didn't you?'

'Yes. But with a hatpin?'

'Why not? If he was attacking her, she'd use whatever come to hand, wouldn't she? Maybe he'd just been down one of them certain houses in Rathbone Street and forgot to pay his dues.'

'In a raid?'

Aggie shrugged again. 'Hitler don't stop what goes on down there,' she said, and her voice broke into a coarse laugh. 'And them as don't pay get what's coming to 'em. Maybe one of the girls spiked him.'

'With a hatpin?'

'I've heard it said, yes.' Aggie puffed heavily on her cigarette and looked me hard in the eyes. 'I've never heard of no one killed. But some blokes, some of the rougher 'erberts at work, well, they say they've been spiked in the leg. Not all of them girls down there have blokes looking out for them. I'd've thought you'd've known that, Frank.'

And then, before I could even draw breath to protest, she left. Not that I would have protested. For our own various reasons, both Aggie and I know Rathbone Street – or, rather, certain houses and 'ladies' in it. Some of the blokes at Tate & Lyle are regulars down there. Getting what they need, then going back to the factory and talking about it in loud voices in front of the women. Working men, relieving their frustrations with street women, well, it's just what they do, isn't it? Stops the wives complaining about getting in the family way all the time if nothing else. But what if a man hasn't got a wife? And what if that man's skin is the colour of tea and his job is about burying the dead?

I only go down there to see Hannah. I don't go often and we talk as much as anything. She's bright, Hannah. Things just turned out bad for her, a bit like they did for Aggie. Difference being, of course, that Hannah doesn't have family. Now she has to put up with all sorts, including me, and the way her situation sometimes makes me go on. 'There's no point talking,' she always says. 'I have to see men as well as you and you have to pretend you don't come here.' Which I do, although Aggie knows. I don't know how because we've never spoken about it, but she knows.

I covered the body over then and turned out the light. Maybe I would ask Dr O'Grady just to take a look at that thing below his breastbone, just to see whether what Aggie had said was possible. Or maybe I'd go and see Hannah, ask her whether what Aggie had said could be true. I'd have to be careful, of course, down there. Canning Town, where Rathbone Street is, can be a rough place even in the daytime. Not that I stick out. Lascars, black men and all sorts get down there. Men off the ships, torpedo-happy and far from home. Although not all of them are simply passing through. Down Victoria Dock Road there's what I suppose you might call a community of Lascars. That poor, squalid little area is only a minute or two from Rathbone Street. Me, I'm just another dark bloke, invisible really, visiting a woman who sees a lot of blokes like me. Not that all of the women will happily entertain my colour even if, as Hannah's told me, I'm taken for a Jew more often than not.

When I went to bed that night I thought about how I might get out to see Hannah. It's not often possible and I only ever do it when I can get an hour away from the shop with no questions asked.

Although the sirens did go off eventually that night, the raid, when it came, didn't affect us that much and so, although I did go outside, I got off to sleep. Out in the yard, leaning against the stable, I thought about Hannah and what she might be able to tell me with regard to my corpse. Better, really, would be to go round the corner to Dr O'Grady and get him to come and have a look. But as well as wanting to know about my unknown man I was also keen, I knew, to see Hannah. Same age as me, lonely and hurting inside, Hannah is the nearest thing to a wife I'm ever going to have. At that moment, just before I dropped off among the smell of horse dung, I tried to imagine myself curled up in her arms, my brown skin next to the hair she dyes yellow to attract other blokes like me to her door. Blokes that might have included my strange, dark, raving man. After all, hadn't he called the 'she' who had supposedly stabbed him a whore? And if, as Aggie said, spiking was a recognised practice among the girls who didn't have pimps, like Hannah . . . I suppose I should have been horrified by this thought, that someone I knew might have killed another human being. But at that moment, I was just jealous – of him and what he might have enjoyed of Hannah. Made me ashamed when I thought about it later.

Fred Bryant arrived early the next morning. Aggie, who can't stand the way he moons over Doris and hates the way he is with Alfie Rosen, as well as having no time for his gossip, came into the kitchen and said, 'That copper of yours is downstairs, Frank. Got two women with him.'

I went down to the shop where I saw Fred with a woman of about thirty and another one of probably sixty-something. The younger one, who was naturally blonde, was quite pretty in a tired sort of a way. She was wearing a worn-looking short jacket and skirt, and had the biggest dark eyes I've ever seen in a fair person. The woman with her wore on her toothless mug an expression of bitterness bordering on hate. As soon as I saw her, I knew she and I were destined to fall out.

'This is Mrs Dooley,' Fred said, as he tipped his head in the direction of the younger woman. 'Come to have a look at the bloke I brought in yesterday.' He lowered his voice conspiratorially. 'Thinks it could possibly be her husband.'

'And my son,' the older woman put in. With her arms crossed over her large bosom and her thin mouth turned down into a scowl, the older Mrs Dooley wasn't going to be ignored by anyone.

'Right.'

I took Fred and the two women out the back and pulled away the sheet. With his eyes closed now and because I'd washed him the previous night he didn't look or smell that bad. I glanced down like everyone else. It was quite by chance that I looked up suddenly and caught the younger Mrs Dooley's eye. Blank, she was – or seemed to be – no emotion, nothing. If it hadn't been for the slight trembling of the old woman's chin, I would have thought my bloke was unknown to both of them. But the old girl was obviously holding back something, even if it wasn't to be tears. Grief is a funny, unpredictable thing.

Then the younger woman, her voice cracking with suppressed emotion, spoke: 'Yes, it's him. That's Kevin.'

'Your husband?'

'Yeah.'

The old woman, her mouth twitching with the effort of concealing her feelings, shot the younger Mrs Dooley a vicious glance.

'Thank you for looking after him, Mr Hancock,' the younger woman said, with a soft smile. 'Me and the kids,' she looked across at the old woman, still with that smile on her face, 'and Vi, his mum, are very grateful to you.'

'Don't think that gives you the right to do his funeral!' The old woman jabbed a finger in my face. 'We'll have Cox's undertakers, like we always do!'

'I told the ladies that Mr Dooley died of the blast,' Fred said, as if he hadn't heard Vi Dooley.

'Yes.' I could, I suppose, have said at the time I had doubts, but I didn't. After all, I had no real evidence that Kevin had been stabbed. His words, even though they had affected me greatly, didn't necessarily contain any truth. And besides, the police doctor, Dr Cockburn, must have seen that small red pimple on Kevin's torso. He must have seen and dismissed it for a good reason. Why upset these women with an unsavoury story that might well be false? Why make trouble by disagreeing with a copper? Not that I was comfortable with this, even then. Doctors can be wrong, especially when they're as busy as they are these days.

'He was a good son, my Kevin,' the old woman said, as she looked down over her bosom at him. 'Not that she ever knew it,' she added, as she flicked her head towards her daughter-in-law. 'Always asking for what she couldn't have. Should've been grateful you should, where you come from!'

The younger Mrs Dooley, in a demonstration of great dignity, turned to me and said, 'Do you know Mr Albert Cox of Cox and Son, Mr Hancock?'

'Yes, Mrs Dooley, I do.'

'Then would you mind, please, asking Mr Cox to come and collect my husband's body and bring him home to us? That Cox's do it is important to my mother-in-law.'

Which meant that the Dooleys were probably a docks family – Canning Town or Custom House, very heavily bombed manors. But I stopped myself asking whether they still had a parlour to place poor old Kevin in and just said I'd telephone Albert Cox to make the arrangements.

Then I started to show them out. Just before we got to the door of the shop, however, something not at all pleasant happened. The old woman, obviously nursing a grudge of some sort against her daughter-in-law, turned and pushed her jowly face into hers. 'And don't think you're staying on!' she hissed. 'You and that basket of yours can sling your hooks!'

It was obvious to me that she was one of those women who considered themselves poor but decent. Under no circumstances would the word 'bastard' pass her lips.

Then Vi Dooley turned her attentions to Fred Bryant. 'Took her in with another man's kid, my Kevin did, and what thanks did he get? Got rid of his last nipper, that one!'

'Mrs Dooley!'

'I fell!' the younger woman cried, her eyes now filled with tears. 'It was an accident!'

'My eye!'

'It was!' She looked pleadingly at Fred. 'I've got ten kids, Constable, and it's hard. It was in May. The baby, as was, was crawling to the stairs. I ran after him and slipped.'

'You believe that you'll believe anything! Just look at her! Calm as you like! I bet she's glad my son's dead! I reckon she's relieved she won't have to have no more kids she'll have to kill!' the old woman said, as she let herself out of my shop, then stood, fuming, on the pavement outside.

Grief can, of course, as I'm always saying, take people in lots of ways and this wasn't the first time I'd seen anger. But it was the first time I'd seen such anger since the bombing raids started. Most people, for good or ill, take it out on the Germans these days. Hitler usually gets a right going over at wakes all over London. But it's usually the Germans doing the killing now. In the case of Kevin Dooley, though, that was not, I'd begun to feel, a certainty – not that either of the women knew that. Or, at least, I imagined they didn't.

'Your mum-in-law's obviously a bit upset, love,' Fred said, smiling at the young woman in front of him.

'You don't believe her?'

'Look, love, if you say you fell then you fell,' Fred said. 'There is a war on. Things happen.'

When she'd finally left, I asked Fred what he really thought might have happened.

He shrugged. 'I dunno. Nothing to do with me. Up to me ear'oles in dead and wounded every night. I need a woman complaining about her daughter-in-law getting rid of a baby like a hole in the head.'

Which just about summed up what he felt about Kevin Dooley's possible stabbing too. What Fred doesn't see he doesn't worry about, and he isn't alone. There's no time to look for trouble where it doesn't obviously exist. But I couldn't help wondering. Whether at that point it was just to do with what I know is my mad jealousy over Hannah or not, I wasn't then sure. I felt I needed to know if she had been with such a person, done this thing to him, even. Perhaps because he had a name now, Kevin was taking on a personality. That didn't help much with getting at what might have happened to him, of course. Our deserters in the first lot had had names, but that didn't mean those in charge hadn't lied to their families about their deaths. They'd all been 'killed in action' not shot by Ken White or Francis Hancock. Morale had to be maintained and to hell with the truth, or so those above us, those real lunatics, in the army and the Government had felt. Decent men killed for being afraid. The truth willingly sacrificed for something called 'the war'. Life is difficult now and the last thing this city and this manor need is a murder. Bad for morale. Once Fred had gone I 'forgot' to telephone Albert Cox and went over to see Hannah.

Chapter Four

I'm not keen on markets. Too many people. Just as being underground or enclosed can make me go barmy, so can lots of jabbering people. It's the noise, I suppose – voices coming at you from all over, muffling and distorting the words and sentences, making ordinary people sound mad. Not that Rathbone Street is anything like it once was. There's nothing much to look at, not much to buy now. Well, not on the stalls anyway.

I know that the Duchess draws the line at knocked-off goods, but I'm no Snow White myself. And with the tea ration down to two ounces, butter down to four since June and clothes under price control, I felt I had at least to keep my eyes peeled. But there was nothing doing. Just a lot of empty tins with 'Not for Sale' written on them and a couple of rough-looking 'erberts flogging knives and forks. No more than twelve either of them, running wild like so many of the kiddies round here. I did think for a minute that I might ask them where they'd got their cutlery, but then I thought better of it. I hate looters as much as the

38

next man, but when I look at some of these kids' faces I just can't bring myself to speak to them. A lot of the Canning Town children were half starved before the war. Now some of them look like they've spent a year in the trenches. Cheekbones like seagulls' wings.

When I arrived Hannah had only just got up. Because the raid the night before had been so small, her business had been brisk. She was tired and, with her hair all over the place and no makeup on, she didn't look her best and I could tell that she knew it too.

'It's all right, love,' I said, as I took my hat off at the door. 'I only want to talk.'

'Thank God.'

She moved aside and I went in. Hannah, like a lot of the local girls, lives in one room. Because it's damp, it's cold most of the year round. Even when she makes a fire, it doesn't do a lot. She hasn't got much. There's a bed, an old range, a couple of cupboards for her clothes, a table and a chair but not a lot besides. Hannah doesn't have bits and bobs or photographs, at least not where anyone can see them. I went and sat down while she turned the gas up. Even at midday her room doesn't get a lot of light.

'Want a cuppa?'

I said that would be lovely so Hannah went down to the scullery to fill her kettle and put it on the range to boil. While she was busy with all that, I rolled up a fag for myself.

'What do you want to talk about, Mr H?'

She obviously wanted to get this over with so she could

go back to bed. Jealousy reared up inside me. What she'd done and with how many men isn't something that I like to think about. Not that I can do anything about it. Hannah, like all of us, has to live.

'You ever heard of a bloke called Kevin Dooley?' I said. 'About six foot, black hair, long nose.'

Hannah shrugged.

'Looks a bit like a fighter,' I said. 'Bit mean and that.'

'Bit mean and a fighter could be almost anyone as comes down here,' Hannah replied bleakly. 'Why?'

I sighed. It wasn't easy doing this, mainly because I wasn't sure what I wanted Hannah to say. However, if I was to get any way to finding out if my own and Aggie's thoughts about Kevin's injuries had any truth in them, I had to ask her.

'Hannah, love, tell me honestly, do you ever hurt, really hurt, blokes who cut up rough with you?'

Hannah, now pouring the hot water on to the leaves she tipped into the teapot, said, 'What do you mean?'

'Hit out, maybe jab at them with something.'

'This Dooley bloke get hurt down here, did he?' Hannah said.

'Well, I don't really know . . .'

'So why you asking?'

I sighed again. 'Look,' I said, 'this bloke may have come down here three nights ago and—'

'How do you know this, Mr H?'

I was in two minds as to whether to tell her Kevin was dead. But then I decided I had to – if she knew him or his family she'd find out anyway – so I gave her the official line on it and added on my own strange experience with the man afterwards.

Hannah, frowning, said, 'So if this bloke died of the blast, I don't see what your problem is.'

'He said he'd been stabbed,' I said. 'And there's a mark on his chest that could have been made by something long and thin and sharp.'

'So? Raving, weren't he?' She shrugged. 'And, anyway, even if he were stabbed I don't get how that could mean he come down here.'

'No . . .' I looked down at the floor to avoid her eyes. 'It's said,' I started, 'that some of the girls down here sort of . . . they have been known to stick hatpins and other sharp things into blokes who cut up—'

I was interrupted by Hannah's deep, throaty laugh. 'Christ, H, there's one girl done that a couple of times down here, but she's long gone now. Blimey, even her, Barmy Betty we used to call her, only ever spiked rough types in the leg.'

'Oh . . .'

'Years and years ago some girl did kill a fella with a spike but that weren't round here. Christ, H, I don't know where you get some of your information from. People with pretty funny ideas, I should think.'

I'd never thought of Aggie as one to harbour 'funny ideas', but then the spiking notion hadn't actually come from her. It had originated from the tough-talking, hard-drinking blokes she spent her shifts with down at Tate's. There were, after all, always stories about places like Rathbone Street as well I knew.

'Anyway,' Hannah continued, 'most girls down here got fellas to protect them these days. Only the old girls work alone now.' She suddenly looked damp-eyed. 'Me, Bella and Rita. Not even desperate pimps touch us old girls now. Lucky we've got Dot, eh?'

'Yes, love,' I said, with a smile. 'Yes, it is.'

Boyfriends, these usually oily little toe-rags like to call themselves, but they're pimps really, lurking around the back alleys at night, beating up their girls' customers for more money when they can, smirking up against walls when the market's on. In Hannah's house there's only her landlady, Mrs Harris, who's getting on a bit now to be chucking drunks out of her place. Not that she doesn't try. There's two girls besides Hannah in Dot Harris's house, none of them with pimps, so the old girl has had to be tough to carry on all these years. It's said she used to be on the game herself when she was younger so she must have learned a thing or two in her time. It's also said that Dot's good to go to if a girl gets herself into trouble. Dot knows just what to do in that situation.

Hannah poured out the tea into a chipped cup, then put it down on the table in front of me. She sat on the bed, watching, as I lit my fag, which I passed across to her. She must have been quite something when she was younger, Hannah. She's got very thick brown hair – bleached with peroxide at just below the roots of course – and her features are strong, probably because she's got her own teeth. I like her eyes, big and very deep blue, turned down at the far corners a bit like some Chinamen's do. I like women who look as if they're having a go at fighting life. There's dignity about Hannah. Seeing me looking at her, she smiled. 'I don't mind if you want . . .' she said. 'I'm not too tired for you.'

Our conversation about Kevin, spiking and death was obviously at an end.

'No, you're all right,' I said. 'Although I could do with a cuddle.'

Hannah put her fag down and lay back on her bed. I went and lay beside her and she wrapped her arms round me. 'You're a good man, Francis Hancock,' she said.

'You're not so bad yourself.'

And then we both laughed. We laugh whenever we can. It wouldn't do to get too serious. Things are as they are. I'm as I am and she does what she has to. And, besides, even if things were different, she's still a Jew so we could never be more than we already are to each other.

I tried to see the Canning Town undertaker, Albert Cox, on my way back from Rathbone Street, but he was out. His wife said he was working. I told her to ask him to ring me if the telephones were working or come over and see me when he got back. Whatever had or hadn't happened to Kevin Dooley, and I was still far from certain at that time, I'd have to get him moved or I'd have his dragon of a mum on my back.

Walking back towards Plaistow along the Barking Road, I found myself thinking about Dooley's wife. Like Hannah, young Mrs Dooley had had great big eyes. Dark, though, black eyes and blonde hair. Hannah, as she is naturally, in reverse. If Kevin had been going to Rathbone

girls with her at home, he must have wanted his head
tested. But, then, who could know what was going on
behind closed street doors? Maybe the old girl had
poisoned her son's mind against his wife. Maybe the
younger woman had chucked herself down the stairs on
purpose when she found out she was in the family way
again. It's not unheard-of, not in big families like that, and
especially not now. Feeding the nippers you've got gives
most women a headache. Poor young Mrs Dooley, if she'd
done it, she had to have been desperate. But possibly not
as desperate as she was now. I wondered if her mother-in-
law had made good her threat and chucked her out
already. If the old girl was paying for the funeral she
probably had. I lit a fag and began to consider whether I
shouldn't just forget about what might have happened to
Kevin and think about more straightforward things, like
replacing some of the wood the horses had kicked out
during the last raid.

'Mr 'ancock?'

No grief in her voice, just stroppiness.

'Yes, Mrs Dooley.' I raised my hat to her.

'My son ain't at Cox's, is he?' Vi Dooley folded her arms
under her bosom and clicked her false gnashers in
irritation.

'No, Mrs Dooley,' I said. 'I'm sorry. Mr Cox has been
busy . . .'

'I've chucked her out, you know,' she said, 'that tart!'

'Mrs Dooley!'

'Oh, you can think what you like, Mr 'ancock!' she said.
'But she was a wrong 'un. Told him, my son, I did. Orphan

she was, then she gets herself married to some old bloke, that's the basket's father, and he dies. Tipped her cap at Kevin she did and that was him under her thumb! I don't want to see her mug or that basket's round here again!'

'But there's nine other kiddies . . .'

'What are my Kevin's, yes,' she said. 'Me and mine'll look after them much better than she ever could. Bring them up proper we will. Her and her girl can go on the streets where they belong.'

'I think that your daughter-in-law has a right to come to her husband's funeral,' I said.

'Oh, do you?' Vi Dooley's downturned mouth sucked on its teeth as she looked at me with great distaste. 'What? Even if she's a fallen woman?' As she leaned in towards me I could see that she had on a stained apron underneath her coat. 'That one was on the game for years as a nipper,' she whispered. 'Up West, afore she married the old geezer. Don't s'pose that girl's even 'is!'

I didn't know how to carry on, to be honest. It was all said with such spite.

'Anyway, you get our Kevin over to Cox's,' she said, 'so we can get on. I've got a wake to organise and it ain't easy with all his little 'uns, his wage gone and a war on.'

And with that she stomped off into Murkoff's. No doubt soothing her soul with mint humbugs and Five Boys chocolate bars – provided they had them, of course. She had the look of a person who ate her way out of misery.

I went back to the shop with a heavy heart. In three months' time it would be Christmas. Still a way off, but there was so much talk about how London could 'take it' these days. I wondered how we'd all shape up with half the borough flat to the ground and all the food so 'rotten', as Aggie would say. Just keeping decent-looking was a problem for me. Climbing over tons of bricks and mortar every time you leave the shop plays havoc with your boots and, war or no war, an undertaker needs to be smart. The families expect it. And yet how much worse to be poor young Mrs Dooley! Out on her ear with a little 'un to look after, separated from her other kids with autumn upon us and soon to be winter. An orphan, she probably didn't have family, leastways not close. Even though I knew I couldn't do anything I wondered where she was and hoped that she was all right.

But then what if she had spiked her own husband? I didn't know what Kevin Dooley had been like as a person. But if he'd been anything like his mother he must've been difficult to live with. Maybe he'd been violent to her and then maybe she'd hit out at him in the way she'd learned to do – or, rather, heard tell of if Hannah was to be believed – when she was on the game, if indeed that was true. That fiery night Kevin had never said who 'she', his 'whore', was, only that she'd stabbed him.

'Frank!'

I'd walked in and half-way up the stairs without even noticing. Nan, above me on the landing, burning candle in her hand, looked like something out of that Bela Lugosi picture.

'Nan!' I put a hand on my chest. 'Give me a turn!'

'Where have you been?' she said. Her face, lit from

beneath by the candle, looked even darker and more lined than it usually does.

'I went down to Canning Town, to Albert Cox,' I said. It was partly true. 'Why? What's the matter?'

'Mum's been took bad.' Nan leaned forward and lowered her voice: 'Dr O'Grady's in with her.'

'Oh.'

The Duchess always has pain, but from time to time it gets very bad. Then she can't eat or sleep. All she does is push her rosary beads through her crippled fingers, every 'Hail Mary' a dart of pain. There isn't anything anyone can do, including Dr O'Grady.

'I've given her quinine,' he said, when he finally came out into the parlour. 'The stairs are a problem, Frank.'

'I know.' Every time there's a raid she has to get down them to the shelter. Sometimes hours in there, cramped up, the damp earth all round, and then out again, up the stairs back into her cold bedroom. I wish she'd have a fire in there sometimes, like she used to, but she's too worried now, like everyone else, about the coal running out.

Nan asked Dr O'Grady whether he wanted a cup of tea. He said he'd like that and so, while I paid him for his visit, she went off to make it.

'So how are things, then, Frank?' Dr O'Grady asked, as he lit up his pipe. I can't remember a time when he wasn't our doctor. Always straight round when Dad was taken bad with what he called his Indian fever. Malaria – horrible disease – but Dad, God bless him, always said it was a small price to pay for meeting the Duchess, the love of his life. It was the malaria that eventually killed the old man.

'Can't complain, Doctor,' I said. 'At least, no more nor less than anyone else. A fellow rarely gets bored in my line of work.'

Dr O'Grady laughed. Although he's old now, he's never lost his sense of humour. You need that in his business just like you need it in mine. Sometimes it's the only way to get through the day. Not that I was too full of it myself on this occasion. The Duchess was bad, Nan was showing the strain of it and my head was still full of Kevin Dooley and what, for me, was building up into something of a mystery.

Once Nan had been with the tea and gone, I asked him about what I had downstairs. Maybe as Aggie had suggested, when she'd first seen Kevin's body, the doctor was the best person to ask about it. Dr O'Grady readily agreed to 'give him a look'.

'He's starting to get a little bit ripe, if you don't mind my saying so, Frank,' the doctor said, as he lifted the lid of the shell and, wrinkling his nose a little, looked inside.

'Yes. Sorry, Doctor.'

In the normal course of events, when somebody dies I'll go out to the house with a shell, a flimsy wooden coffin, and measure up the deceased for a proper box. On the day of the funeral my lads will slip the shell into the coffin and seal up. But Kevin Dooley was, as I explained now to the doctor, strictly Cox's so I'd just put him in a shell for transportation.

'So what is it you want me to look at, Frank?' the doctor said.

I pulled the deceased's clothes aside and showed him the small raised pimple just below the ribs. 'Do you think this could be a stab wound, Doctor?' I said. 'From something long and thin, like a pin or whatever.'

Dr O'Grady looked down at the body for some time before he turned his gaze, squinting, to me. 'By a pin, Frank, what do you—'

'I don't know,' I said. 'Maybe a ladies' hatpin or . . .'

'Oh, well, now, there was a case many, many years ago,' Dr O'Grady said. He rubbed his chin thoughtfully as he continued, 'Not round here, but in London somewhere. Woman, prostitute, I think, stabbed a man with a hatpin, killed him.'

This sounded like the crime Hannah had spoken about. Obviously quite a famous case. Not that it had had any effect on me. But, then, maybe if it had happened in the last lot or near it, the whole thing had simply passed me by.

'What happened?'

Dr O'Grady shook his head. 'I can't remember. Murder or manslaughter? No, it's gone. I don't know. I've a feeling the woman hanged but . . .'

'So what do you think, Doctor? About this bloke and . . .'

'I think he might possibly have been stabbed by something like a hatpin, yes,' he said, 'but I'd have to do a post-mortem examination to be sure, and as a family doctor I'm no expert.' He looked up at me, frowning. 'Frank, besides this mark, do you have any reason to suppose that this man might have been stabbed?'

I told him about the night of the bare-knuckle fight and of my strange and frightening encounter with an apparently wounded Kevin Dooley. I also told him what Aggie had said about the girls down Rathbone and how they might sometimes protect themselves.

'Well, I, personally, have never come across any of these so-called victims,' Dr O'Grady said. But then he added, with a smile, 'However, that doesn't mean they don't exist. Most men around here, Frank, as I'm sure you'll agree, come to me only when all earthly hope is lost. A little stabbing, unless it involves a vital organ, is something of an occupational hazard.'

'Yes.' We both looked down at the corpse for a moment. 'So, Doctor, what do you think I should do?'

'Well, I wouldn't do anything alone, Frank,' he said. 'Maybe speak to Albert Cox when he comes to collect him. But as for a post-mortem . . .' He shrugged. 'I don't know. Without his family's involvement you'd be hard pressed to get a coroner to take it on and I don't suppose the police would be very interested, not if their doctor has already ascertained the cause of death. I assume he was seen by Marcus Cockburn?'

'Yes,' I said. 'Why?' There'd been something in Dr O'Grady's tone that suggested to me he didn't entirely like or trust Dr Cockburn. But I'd heard more than a few stories involving the police doctor and heavy drinking sessions.

Dr O'Grady, however, didn't take that particular bait and went back to the subject of Kevin: 'Some people don't hold it together as well as others during raids,' he said. 'He could have been raving when he talked about being stabbed.'

He could've been. Yes.

Dr O'Grady replaced the lid of the shell and took out his pipe again. 'But I can see that you're worried, Frank,' he said, 'and maybe with good reason. Perhaps this poor chap has been done to death by some woman he was seeing. But unless you or Albert Cox want to take him up to the London then I can't see how you can go any further with it. And, anyway, even if you do go to the hospital with him, you won't find anyone who will take any interest. He's dead.'

He was right, of course. Not even the London Hospital was taking anything other than the most seriously ill now and even then people only stayed there for as long as they couldn't be moved. It wasn't safe. Not that any of this helped me at all with Kevin Dooley, who might or might not have been murdered.

Albert Cox turned up at near on six. He's a lot shorter and fairer than I am, but we're of an age, Albert and I, so we have an understanding between us as well as professional respect. Cox's undertakers haven't been going for as long as our firm. But they know what they're doing and they're a decent lot of lads.

'I'll take him round to the old girl's in the morning,' Albert said, after we'd loaded Kevin Dooley's remains into the back of his hearse. 'With any luck the place'll take a direct hit and I won't have to bother with Kevin or his bleedin' mother.'

I pointed out that this was hardly fair on Kevin's children, which Albert did agree to, but he was unrepentant with regard to the man and his mother. 'Go to any pub in Canning Town, ask for Dooley and you'll see what I mean,' Albert said. 'Been slung out of every one.'

'What for?'

Albert coughed, then lit up a fag. The mist was thick from the river that evening. 'Scrapping,' he said. 'Kevin Dooley was a scrapper. Man, woman or child – he didn't care. Give one of my lads a black eye couple of years back in the Chandelier. The mother's no better and his brothers are animals.'

In view of what Albert's opinions seemed to be about the Dooleys it didn't seem worth launching into my story about Kevin and his stab wound. He wouldn't, I felt, have had a great deal of interest in what might or might not have occurred on that mad, bomb-soaked night down in East Ham. Maybe I would just leave it alone, like Dr O'Grady had said. But I did tell Albert about the man's wife.

'Poor girl,' he said, shaking his head. 'Sometimes I'd see her, she could hardly open her eyes for the swelling.'

'He beat her up?'

'Well, somebody must've,' Albert said. 'Always in the family way, always with a black eye, that one. It was either Kevin or his mother, probably Kevin. I think the old girl got her fun making a dog's life for poor young Velma.'

Velma, it turned out, was the one Vi Dooley had called the 'basket', the one who was from the younger woman's previous marriage. She was, Albert reckoned, about fifteen. Not only had Velma had to clean up after her step-father and his mother, she'd had a lot to do with her nine half-brothers and -sisters too.

According to Albert, having a lot of kiddies was important to Kevin. 'Used to boast about what a man he was in any pub that'd have him,' he said, as he locked up the back of the hearse and climbed into the cab. 'Bleedin' idiot.'

'Albert, you don't think anyone could've killed Dooley, do you?' I blurted, unable to keep it from him any longer.

'What do you mean? If he hadn't died from the blast?' Albert replied. 'I can't think of many who'd want him to carry on living, to be honest – apart from his mother and brothers, of course.' He laughed. 'Why, Frank?'

I had to tell him and so, with the exception of Hannah's comments, I told Albert about what I'd witnessed at East Ham, who'd said what and what I might have found on the body. But strangely to me, I must admit, he just shrugged, his eyes blank with what looked like disregard. 'So someone might have knocked him off? Probably with good reason.'

'But, Albert,' I said, 'if he's been murdered, whatever he was like in life, then . . .'

'Marcus Cockburn said he died from the blast.'

'Yes, but . . .'

Albert peered up at me hard. 'Leave it, Frank,' he said. 'Do as you're told and just get on with your life.'

It was almost word for word what one of our old sergeant majors had said to me when I'd questioned why a certain young man, a supposed coward, was to be executed by, among others, me. My next words to poor old Albert were therefore bitter and furious. 'What? Like we did in the first lot, Albert?' I said. 'When we were asked to shoot little kids who were a bit frightened? Their families never ever told the truth about their sons? Living a lie? It matters how people die, it matters that those who killed them suffer – like I do, like all of us suffer who went out there into the mud and the blood and killed people.'

Albert put his hand wearily to his forehead and said, 'I know. Look, Frank, I'm sorry.'

'Yes . . .'

'But, quite honestly, from what you've told me there's nothing we can do,' he said. 'Cockburn's made his decision. All the rest, what you've said, is just people's stories and opinions. The toff doctor has spoken so the working class have to shut up.' He sighed and then he smiled. 'Anyway, I'd better get him over to my shop before Jerry turns up.'

I felt my whole body turn to stone. I couldn't remember when I'd had an unbroken night's sleep. Suddenly, coming on top of my anger and frustration, the thought of another raid made me panic. 'You think he will? In this mist?'

'Just because Hitler couldn't get many of them out of their pits last night don't mean he won't shift himself to put on a good show tonight,' Albert said. And then, wearily, he added, 'Who knows what Jerry's thinking, eh, Frank? Certainly not the bleedin' Government. Bastards!'

It was more of a twitch than an act of conscious movement that made me look first over my shoulder and then back at Albert once again.

'Be careful!' I said. 'We don't know who might be listening!'

'Couldn't care less,' Albert said defiantly. 'I don't think it's treason to call those who can't seem to protect us or even care a bunch of bastards. Do you?'

'No, but—'

'They can put me in the nick if they like,' Albert said. 'What you said about the deserters in the first lot was right, Frank. And I tell you, it's still them and us today. War or no war, the rich against the poor. I mean, all them poor Jews they interned – Harry Rabin, poor old Davy Klarfeld. Yeah, right bleedin' Nazis they are!' And then with one finger up at my face to emphasise his point, Albert said, 'This is what all wars are, Frank, and that's a class war just like the last lot!'

I'd hated the stupid upper-class officers in the first lot just as much as Albert hates the Government. But for some reason I've never been able to find it within me to feel quite so political about it. For me justice, for want of another word, is more personal, as in my concern over Kevin Dooley and what might have happened to him. Also, I know it's because I'm afraid of what people might think: I'm scared, like a lot of people, of being branded a Communist. After all, we might be at war with the Nazis, but that doesn't mean Churchill and the rest of them are going to let the country go like Russia.

When I did eventually speak I just said, 'Yes,' in that vague way people are used to getting from me sometimes.

But then Albert fired up his engine and I waved him on his way, my hand making vague patterns in the dim, blacked-out mist. As the car disappeared through the gate, Albert called, 'Here, Frank, let me have a look at Dooley myself and I'll speak to you tomorrow.' I felt he was humouring me, but I thanked him anyway. After all, he didn't have to do anything about it.

Although it was chilly, I didn't want to go inside immediately so I stood out for a bit, looking up at the grey, mist-streaked sky above. If the Luftwaffe came tonight I knew I'd have to carry the Duchess down to the shelter before I set off on my usual terrified travels. Somehow I'd have to keep my nerve for just enough time to make her safe. Then the picture show in my head could do what it liked. Faces half eaten by rats, the scream that Georgie Pepper let out as he sank into the mud, the scream that's always just about to start again . . .

You have to be careful what you say these days but, like Albert Cox, if quietly, most people wonder what's going on. Every night without exception we've been pounded. Those who've been bombed out just wander more often than not – a lot of them looking not unlike me. The dead out and about, looking for something to feed to their kids. I've even heard that some have gone up into Epping Forest, sleeping out on the ground like gypsies. I know they can get help from the assistance people, with money and billets and what-have-you, but I don't think the authorities understand that it takes so much time. People have to get over the shock of losing everything for a start-off. More often than not they're hurt, sometimes in their minds where it doesn't show. I can see it in their faces: it's like looking in a mirror sometimes.

I went inside soon afterwards and told Doris that she could go home. Now that Albert had picked up Kevin Dooley there wasn't anything left to do except shut up shop and wait for the sirens. No one really wanted to believe that anything untoward could have happened to Kevin so I felt disquieted and quite alone as I started to lock up. It all felt, even through doubts that I had myself, very wrong. I was just about to go up the stairs to the flat when I heard the knocking on the front door.

Chapter Five

Her Christian name was Pearl. She said I should use it rather than keep calling her Mrs Dooley. She and the girl, Velma, who was a skinny creature anyway, looked as if they hadn't eaten that day.

'I'm so sorry, Mr Hancock,' she said, as I took them both up to the kitchen, 'but I didn't know where else to go.'

'It's all right.'

'You were so kind this morning when I come for my Kevin and . . .' She started to cry. 'No one else has had so much as a good word . . .'

Velma put her arm round her mother's shoulders as they followed me into the kitchen. Nan was washing a couple of spuds at the sink when we arrived.

'Who're they?' she said, when she saw the pale, distressed blonde and her hollow-eyed daughter.

I told her Pearl was a customer. 'In a bit of a state,' I said. 'Put the kettle on, will you, Nan?'

She did, if grudgingly. Some people happily share short

rations, but not Nan, and as soon as the tea was made she went off up to the Duchess without another word.

'I'm sorry,' Pearl said, as she watched her go. 'I never wanted to make trouble for you. Your wife . . .'

'She's my sister,' I said, with a smile. 'You just drink your tea.' And then I watched as she and her daughter both drank it down, scalding, almost in one gulp.

'Mother-in-law chucked us out,' Pearl said, once she'd finished. 'Soon as I got back from here.' I noticed that with some tea inside her the colour of her face had improved.

Her daughter scowled. 'Old cow!' she said. 'I hate her!'

'Velma!'

'Well, it's true, I do hate her. She's took everything!'

'The later it got the more scared I was,' Pearl said. 'I know that me and Velma could go to one of them public shelters, but I can't really think straight at the moment, Mr Hancock, and so—'

'The old cow took our coupons,' Velma said bitterly. 'Said she needed them to feed all the kiddies.'

'Your brothers and sisters?'

'Yes. All Mum's money too.'

'Such as it was,' Pearl put in.

'So neither of you has eaten?'

'No.'

I cut them some bread and spread some Marmite on it and, unlike most women I know, Pearl didn't even try to protest. They must have been ravenous, both of them.

'Don't you have any family you could go to?' I said to Pearl, once she'd finished her food. I knew she was an orphan, or so her mother-in-law had told me, but there had to be someone she knew. 'Friends, maybe?'

'No one I know would dare take us in,' she replied. 'Kevin's family, well, they're . . . they bully people, if you know what I mean. If Vi Dooley takes against you, you're finished round our way. She never liked me. I got on with Kev's brothers all right but that's all finished now. They do what Vi tells them to do. They don't have friends, me included, I suppose. The Dooleys only have each other and them as are scared of them.'

I wondered why such an apparently decent woman had married into such a family. But maybe she had loved Kevin, for all his faults. Some women do like the brutal type after all. Or maybe when her first husband died she was left destitute and took the first offer she got from a man.

'I'm an orphan, see,' she went on. 'Mum and Dad been dead for years.'

'So, no brothers or sisters?'

'I've sisters but not that I've seen for a long time,' she said.

I knew she wasn't trying to make me take her in, she didn't seem the type – and, anyway, I could hardly do that with the flat already busting at the seams. But at the same time I couldn't put her and the girl out on such a chilly night with no real place to go.

'You know, I do want to get all me kids back,' she said. 'They're *my* kids, not Kevin's mum's, whatever she might like to think.'

Her coat had been threadbare, probably, before the

start of the war. Long and shapeless, it was covered with smudges of dirt, and what had once been a thick fur collar hung in wet and filthy strings down her back. Like her daughter, Pearl Dooley had bare legs, which were still blue with cold even though she was now inside. My sister Aggie, her of the lily-white skin, always dyes her legs with gravy browning when she hasn't got any stockings. She even puts seams down the back with an eyebrow pencil, but if Pearl Dooley was in the habit of doing such things, she certainly hadn't that day. Neither she nor Velma had anything in the way of luggage – only Pearl's handbag.

'Is there really no one you can go to, no one who will take the children in?' I began. 'Not an aunt or—'

'Look, if you just want us to go!'

'No, no.' I tried to sound, as much as I could, reassuring. But she'd really flared at me and deep down I hadn't taken kindly to it. I wasn't averse to either her or her girl, in fact I was genuinely sorry for them, but that didn't mean I wanted to take on two more hungry mouths.

Pearl, seeming ashamed now of her outburst, put her head down and said, 'I'm sorry, Mr Hancock, it's just that . . . The only family I've got any notion of is my sister Ruby.'

'Where does she live?'

'Last I heard, which has to be more than five years back, she was lodging in Spitalfields.'

'Do you know where?'

She shrugged. 'Not really. We've not stayed close. All I do know is she was staying, housekeeping like, for a bloke running a paper-and-string shop.' She leaned forward so that only I could hear her whisper, 'An old Jew.'

'I see.'

'Gawd knows whether she's still there or not.'

The sirens have what I think is maybe a unique effect on me. I don't shake like some. I don't run about or get hysterical. I just lose control of my speech. I stutter, stammer, drive myself and everyone around me mad. And during a raid it stays like that.

Momentarily paralysed by my own lack of speech I just looked at Pearl and Velma with a stupid grin on my face. It was only when Nan came down from upstairs and Arthur called up from the yard that I started to move.

'Mr H!' I heard Arthur call. 'Raid!'

'Y-y-y—'

'Frank, you've got to go up and get Mum!' Nan said. 'She's stiff like a bloody tree. You'll have to carry her.'

'Mr H!'

'Keep your hair on, Arthur, for Gawd's sake!' Nan yelled down the stairs. 'Frank, will you go and get Mum?'

'R-Right.'

As I ran up the stairs I heard my sister say to Pearl, 'You'd better come down our Anderson with us, Missus.'

There isn't much of the Duchess. She's tall, like me, but she's not much more than a bag of bones. She wasn't even awake when I picked her up. But by the time we'd got outside, her slung over my back like a sack of coal, she'd come to enough to tell me to secure the horses as best I could. Poor buggers, I'd not got round to repairing their stable since the last raid. If I didn't do something, and quick, they'd be out.

'Francis, please, please stay,' she said, as I laid her down on the little cot at the back of the Anderson.

'Duchess, the h-horses,' I said.

'If the horses get out, they get out, poor beasts,' she said. And then, her eyes wide with terror, she said, 'Where is Doris?'

'Gone home,' Nan replied, and then, turning to Pearl Dooley and Velma, she said, 'This lady and her girl are customers, Mum.'

'Oh.' The Duchess smiled. As I made my way back out of the shelter I saw her extend her hand to Velma, who shrank back into her mother's arms. The Duchess is both dark and old-fashioned looking enough to be beyond the girl's memory. Obviously like Nan, whom I'd caught her eyeing with suspicion earlier on, the Duchess was a foreigner and, to a kid like Velma, probably quite threatening. After all, who's to know who is the enemy, eh? Some of them round here know so little: they couldn't tell a German from a Russian, a Jew or even an Indian if their lives depended on it. As soon as everyone was in who should be, I closed the shelter door and went into the stable.

My horses, both black, as undertaker's horses should be, are called Rama and Sita. The Duchess named them, so she says, after the old Hindu gods. I bought them from a gyppo over in Beckton. They're geldings, which means their coats are not top-notch, but they've nice quiet natures, except of course when they've got thousands of tons of high explosives falling about all around them. There was nothing to hear yet, beyond people getting down into their shelters, but the 'boys' were already agitated.

'You should've made time to repair this stable,' Ken said, as he walked in casual, as he always is with me, from the yard. 'You'll have to spend the whole raid in here with them now.'

'Y-yes, I know.'

My old oppo, Ken White. We joined up together in 1914, like a pair of bloody idiots. He lost his health and I lost my mind. But we survived – sort of. Horrified, like me, that the Empire is involved in another war, Ken's taken to coming up from his billet at odd times for a chat. His wife died some years ago and he can't work like he did, not with all the shrapnel inside his body, all the scars he got on the Somme. Quite often he'd be passing at night and sometimes he'd even come out running with me, still does. After all Ken, like me, knows what that's about. Ken never goes down any shelter either.

I rolled a fag for myself, stuck it in my face and then took hold of the boys' bridles. Ken took himself off to the back of the stable where we store the hay and sat down, out of the horses' line of sight. And then it began. The first explosion, deafening, rocked the ground beneath our feet. Rama tried to rear but somehow I managed to hold him. I could feel Sita's body shivering beside me. Different, quieter personality. It's always Rama causes damage to the stable.

Being in there, trapped if you like with the horses,

would have been unbearable without Ken. Even at the height of the raid, when all I could see through the cracks in the door was red and yellow flashes of flame, there was always Ken with his great selection of the old songs, 'Nellie Dean' and his 'Tipperary', which still leaves a bitter taste even now, but it keeps me alert even if it's only to curse at him. There's something very dark about those old Great War songs, especially when they're sung by a man with only half a face.

In the morning I had to carry the Duchess back up to her room. If anything, she was even stiffer than she'd been the day before. In some areas it doesn't matter what you do to try to make an Anderson watertight, it just carries on taking in water. Like a trench.

Once again 'Hancock and Sons' had survived the latest attack from the air, so the Duchess and Nan said a quick little prayer to the Virgin Mary for that. The rest of us, including Pearl Dooley and Velma, started the business of picking up things that the blast had knocked on the floor, and when Aggie got back from Tate's, the cleaning started. She's a dab hand with the mop and brush, our Aggie, as was Pearl Dooley, who also mucked in. When Ag asked her to use our Hoover, though, Pearl looked at it like it was something off another planet. 'I've never seen nothing like this before,' she said, when Aggie demonstrated it for her. 'It's marvellous that, isn't it? What a lovely place you do have here.' Laughable really, given the state of our shop. But also a good indication that whatever bullying the Dooleys might do and whatever bunce that might bring them, it was probably the pub rather than the home that got the benefit.

The Duchess, in her many hours cooped up with them, had told Pearl that she and Velma could stay with us for as long as they liked. She's a very generous heart, my old mum. But I knew this wouldn't go down well with either Nan or even the more generous Aggie, so when Doris eventually made it in, just before one, I took her to one side. We had no work booked for that day so after I'd telephoned Albert Cox and learned that Kevin Dooley's body was to be held at his shop until the funeral, I had a word with her about taking Pearl and Velma down to Spitalfields to look for this sister, Ruby.

'I don't know of no shikseh staying with no paper-and-string man,' Doris said, when I told her the information Pearl had given me. 'Mind you, don't mean it ain't true. There's quite a lot in that line of work.'

She told me the name of one paper-and-string man she knew and said that talking to him might be a start.

'Be better if you had a bit more Yiddish,' Doris said, shaking her head at the thought of it. 'There's a lot down our way don't do so well with English, Mr H, especially the old ones. They might not tell you anything even if they know.'

I did think for a bit that I might take Doris with us. But then I had a better idea. 'What the roads like, Doris?' I said, as I ushered what were not an enthusiastic Pearl and Velma out of the door.

'Bloody awful,' she replied. 'You'd do better walking today, Mr H. Mind you, go round Plaistow, round the back. I'd give Canning Town a miss, took it bad last night they did down there.'

I knew that, I'd heard it myself, and from Albert Cox who was still, even after looking at the body, unconvinced that Kevin had been stabbed. In the night I'd even started to pray at one point for Hannah. To hell with the safety of Plaistow! And so, without another word to Doris, I set off with Pearl and Velma for Rathbone Street.

The strain of enduring the previous night's heavy raids was evident on Hannah's face. But at least she was alive which was a big relief to me.

Doris was right: Canning Town was a state. Bricks and rubble, some of it still smoking, everywhere. Firemen and wardens trying to move some of it out of the way, blokes standing staring up at houses that looked as if the slightest puff of wind would have them over. People's belongings in the street . . . Tin baths, mattresses, mangles, fire irons, some old girl with a kiddies' tricycle across her knees, gently stroking the handlebars with rough, swollen hands. Ordinary things take on importance when half your house has collapsed and you don't know where you and your kids are going to sleep. For Hannah the most important things, she says, are her hats. She has about five, some with feathers, one made of some sort of shiny, stiff material, pleated into a kind of a fan shape. I like that one: it suits her. But this day she was tired so all we got was her plain black beret, which, nevertheless, looks very stylish.

'I've seen that woman about in the market,' Hannah

whispered to me, as we passed in front of Canning Town railway station.

'What? Pearl Dooley?'

'Yes. I'm sure she knows me, knows what I do,' Hannah said. 'She something to do with that bloke Dooley you was telling me about the other day?'

I'd not gone into much detail when I'd introduced the two women. Pearl wouldn't go inside Hannah's place for some reason and my girl, for her part, was just someone who was going to help us find Pearl's sister.

'She's his widow,' I said.

'Oh, well, maybe that's why she's like that,' Hannah said. 'I mean, if I've seen her she must've seen me and if she knows somehow what I do . . . A lot of the "decent" women, especially them with husbands, hate us. See the way she's looking at me!'

Pearl Dooley did, it was true, give Hannah the odd 'old-fashioned' look. 'Have you asked her whether her old man went out with tarts?' Hannah whispered.

'No, of course not!' I whispered back. 'I've told her you're a friend. I said we need someone as speaks Yiddish so that's what we've got. A friend who speaks Yiddish.'

'Woman who lives down Rathbone on her own in one room. Yeah. Funny bleedin' friends you've got, Francis Hancock!' Hannah said.

It made me smile. She wasn't wrong there. We carried on walking.

My dad, who'd known London well, always used to say that Spitalfields was a magical place. As a nipper I could never see it. Full of sweat shops, kids with dark eyes like my own, except bigger, hungrier and more suspicious. It always seemed dirtier and more closed in on itself than our manor. But Dad had a different take, which I suppose was helped by the fact that he could speak a bit of Yiddish. Where he learned it, I don't know, but he was good with languages. I remember him speaking to the Duchess in Hindi when I was a kid. Having said that, it wasn't only the language as helped him. In our profession people talk to you about big things, about life and death and what those words might really mean.

Dad's sister Eva worked up on Fashion Street years ago and sometimes he'd go over there to meet her. Somehow one day he got talking to a rabbi who then became a friend. Like Dad, he's dead now. But when Dad was alive he used to tell me about this old bloke, stories that thrilled and made you shiver at the same time too. 'You know the old Jews have ways of breathing life into stones,' Dad would say. 'Magic. They use it to protect their people. Christ knows, they need something, poor sods. There's a story they tell about an old magical rabbi, somewhere like Warsaw I think it was, walked clean through the walls of his synagogue. Poles or whoever they were were out to kill him. But he just walked through this wall. Never seen again. It's said, the Jews say, that he isn't neither alive nor dead but something in between.'

When Dad told me this, I was a nipper and I didn't understand what he meant. But maybe now I do. It was, after all, a sort of magic that meant I survived the Great War. I can't account for it any other way. Not that survival is quite the right word for what I've got now. Like that old rabbi out in Poland I'm something in between the state of living and that of death. I know that place the old Jew told my dad about because that's where I spend most of my time. Just occasionally, with Hannah usually, I come alive.

'So, what's your sister's name, then, love?' Hannah was asking Pearl, when I eventually came back to the world around St Anne's Church in Limehouse.

'Ruby,' Pearl said.

'Ruby what?'

'Er . . .' She turned her head to look down what I think is one of the most strangely named streets in the whole East End, Three Colt Street, down beside St Anne's graveyard.

'What?' Hannah was frowning. 'Don't you know your own name or—'

'She could be married now,' Pearl said, as she turned back to Hannah. 'I don't know.'

'Yes, but if she isn't married,' Hannah continued, 'she'll have your old name, won't she? So what was that?'

Pearl turned her face away again and said, 'Reynolds,' as if she were ashamed of it in some way.

Hannah, who had noticed this too, gave me a look before she said, 'Right-o. As you like.'

'I do,' Pearl said, and we all lapsed into silence.

After Limehouse we had to push up north into Stepney on account of a group of coppers blocking the road. There was an unexploded bomb somewhere down in Ratcliff and they were waiting for a team of sappers to arrive. A lot of these bombs the Jerries drop are faulty. When it first started happening, right from the start of the bombing, people would run for their lives. But now they just saunter off, moaning. Somehow, sometimes, the inconvenience of it all has got greater than their fear.

We reached Brick Lane at just before six. It was already getting foggy and dark and all my old dislike of the place came flooding back into my mind. In the blackout I knew those hungry, suspicious eyes would take on an even more sinister look. Hannah wasn't happy about speaking to Doris's paper-and-string man, not for any other reason, or so she said, than she'd never heard of him. So we all followed her into a house that looked as though it was about to collapse into the ground. Not because it had been bombed, it was just so old and worn and dirty.

Chapter Six

Hannah didn't tell me who the old couple were. I knew her parents were long dead and her only brother died in the first lot. Maybe this old man with his black skull-cap and long grey sidelocks was an uncle. Maybe the woman with eyes like a corpse, much of her face hidden behind a headscarf, was his wife. But Hannah never said. We went in, she talked – for what seemed like hours – they answered, in short, hard Yiddish sentences, and then we left. I got the feeling afterwards that there was little or no love lost between these people and my girl.

'They don't know nothing,' Hannah said tightly, as we picked our way along the street, every so often one or other of us falling off the kerb and into the road. At one point poor Velma turned her ankle on a box someone had left outside a darkened shop. It had contained Fry's Chocolate Sandwich bars – once. But the girl looked inside it, just to make certain.

On the corner of Brick Lane and Fournier Street,

Hannah stopped and turned back towards us. 'You wait here,' she said. 'I'm going to see if I can talk to someone.'

'Who?'

'I used to talk to an old bloke done paper and string when I was a kid. But he won't take kindly to strangers.'

And then she walked off down Fournier Street, quickly disappearing into the blackout. Long after I'd lost sight of her I could hear her heels clicking on the pavement. When that noise finally faded there was nothing save for some faint, strange music coming from somewhere nearby. I looked down at Pearl and Velma as they huddled together in front of a door with a big knocker in the shape of a lion's head. I knew we were all thinking alike. Now it was dark the raid could come at any time and, far from home, God alone knew where we'd be able to find shelter. Velma especially looked all done in so the thought of walking all the way back to Plaistow with her in tow wasn't one that I wanted to consider. I knew the Duchess had said they could both stay, but the reality of that was going to be short rations and giving over to them the bed Aggie's kids had shared in her room. I just hoped we could find this sister of Pearl's, and soon. Quite why that thought, if it did, led on to my realising I didn't know what Kevin Dooley had been doing the night he died, I don't know. But I asked his widow, who said, 'He was down the pub.'

'Which one?' I asked. I was curious to know whether it had been one of the East Ham boozers.

But Pearl didn't know. 'Me and Velma was out that night too,' she said.

'Oh. Where?'

I didn't see her face, but I knew she had to have been doing something she shouldn't because she turned it away from me. 'Oh, well, er, we was with friends,' Pearl said. 'For the evening, like.'

'Ah.' I smiled, and she bit her lip. I thought about asking her who these friends were but I decided against it. Maybe I'd heard wrong or something but I seemed to recall that the Dooleys, including Pearl, didn't really have any friends. Only family and 'victims' was the impression I'd got from Pearl. But, then, maybe that night she'd gone somewhere she didn't want anyone to know about. Maybe she'd gone off to another bloke. Given what little, admittedly, I knew about Kevin, I couldn't have blamed her if she had.

A few minutes later I got my tobacco and papers out and rolled myself a fag. We hadn't seen any ARP warden since we entered the district, but I jumped into the doorway just in case someone told me to 'Put that light out!' when I sparked up. It was getting colder all the time and when it began to rain, drizzle, really, Velma put her head on her mother's shoulder and sobbed. Pearl, embarrassed, forced a smile at me. 'Come on, love,' she said to her daughter. 'It'll be all right, you'll see.'

I find it difficult to judge a person's age, especially now that everyone's so tired, but I now revised my estimate of Pearl Dooley's age up a bit. She was, I thought, probably in her middle thirties. She was very thin for a woman with so many nippers. She had false teeth too, which added to the gaunt set of her face. Very like some of the young women I get through, sadly, professionally. Still lovely, poor things, but in the terrible, ghostly way of having too many kids, doing too much work and maybe in her case having secrets. It was a problem, I was finding, for me to take her story about being out with 'friends' seriously. I was almost hypnotised looking at her when Hannah appeared at my side. 'Come on,' she said. 'We've got to go and see a woman called Bessie Stern, lives at number five Princelet Street.'

'Who's Bessie Stern?' I said.

'She's a matchmaker and a right gossip,' Hannah replied. 'She lives next door to Shlomo Kaplan, the man the shikseh Ruby used to live with.'

'She's moved on?' Pearl asked.

'In a way,' Hannah said, and she headed off towards Princelet Street, which was the very next turning.

Bessie Stern was a fat old woman who wore a very matted, very bad red wig. At first she was deeply suspicious, almost hostile. Even with Hannah talking Yiddish, the old girl – from her tone and the way she stood at her street door like an angry wrestler – wasn't having any of it, whatever it was. Strangely it was only when Pearl was brought into it that her attitude changed. Suddenly we were in.

A tiny parlour with a scullery at the back was lit by a single gas mantle that hissed and spluttered as we entered. Over on the range, which had obviously been blackleaded to within an inch of its life, a pot of something was steaming and smelling of cabbage. Out in the scullery I could see a string with washing hanging down from it: a pair of great big stays, bloomers and a cardigan.

'Sit! Sit!' the old woman said, as she ushered us on to a row of hard chairs behind a large wooden table. As Hannah rattled away in Yiddish again, Bessie Stern settled herself in a busted-up armchair next to the range.

Once she'd finished listening to what Hannah had to say, she turned to Pearl and said, 'You know Ruby kept the house for Shlomo Kaplan and he let her live without paying rent. He was a good man. I miss him. Do you want tea? What about the girl?'

'Do you mean he's dead?' Pearl asked.

'Oh, yes, love. Two and a half, three weeks ago. During one of the earliest raids here.'

'So where's Ruby?' Pearl enquired.

The old woman shrugged. 'Who knows? One day she's there with Shlomo Kaplan, doing his housework, ironing his shirts, and the next day he's dead and she's gone! Do you want me to put the kettle on, dear? It really is no trouble.'

'No . . .'

I looked at Pearl, whose face was quite white now.

'How did he die, Mrs Stern?' I asked.

'Head bashed in,' she said darkly. 'Blood up the parlour walls! Saw it with me own eyes. Terrible!'

'The coppers think he was murdered,' Hannah said.

'Yes, although why I don't know,' Bessie Stern said, as she looked at Hannah with, I felt, distaste. 'Nothing stolen and he wasn't a poor man, Shlomo Kaplan, oh, no! There's a gramophone in there and everything! Then some said that maybe it was Ruby, but I put them straight on that, the police. She was down in Katz's shelter with me and Etta Nathan when it happened – there was a raid on!'

'Ruby can't've done it,' Pearl said. 'Not Ruby. It's impossible!'

'But then, soon as the police come, she goes,' Bessie Stern continued. 'So what're they to think, is what they say.'

'His house wasn't damaged in the raid?' I asked.

'Yes, a bit. I'm thinking when I go in there that maybe one of the gas pipes hit him on the head. One of them was down across the table. But the police say no, so what do I know? The police say he was murdered. God willing, whoever done it will get caught.'

'It wasn't my sister!' Pearl was up on her feet now, tears in her eyes.

'I've never thought it was, darling,' the old woman said.

'But you're thinking that because she's gone—'

'I don't know why she ran off any more than you do,' Bessie said. 'When the siren went, I took off to get Ruby. I never saw Shlomo, I admit that. He would never come down the shelter, too stubborn. "No German going to make me leave my home," he always said.' She laughed. 'More like no German going to make him leave the money he kept all over the house. But whoever killed him didn't take his money. I'm sure Ruby didn't do no wrong, but it's not me she needs to convince. It's the police. That she's gone they think is very suspicious. She was the last person to see Shlomo alive. They want to talk to her.'

I found myself looking at Pearl Dooley as the old woman spoke. Sweating, in spite of the cold, her eyes were wide with what looked like terror and, as she raised one hand to wipe her brow dry, I saw that she was shaking. Hannah saw it too and gave me a look of recognition.

'Ruby, see,' Bessie continued, 'didn't take nothing with her. We found Shlomo together, her, me and Etta's brother who it was went for the police. But then Ruby just says she's going out for a while and she's gone. The police asked all of us a lot of questions.'

'About Ruby?'

'Yes. They asked where she come from, was she married, what her name was. I said I didn't know how she come to be with Shlomo, because I don't. She wasn't never married or so far as I knew. All I could tell them was that her name was Ruby House. They asked me that several times and I kept on telling them, Ruby House.' She leaned forward to get closer to Pearl, and said, 'You know, love, your old name before you was married. I'm sure they didn't believe me, but I said, "It's the truth," and so . . .'

I looked again at Pearl, who had averted her eyes. Either she'd made up the name Reynolds for her sister or Ruby had lied. I know people have reasons for doing this, especially in our part of the world, but at that moment it was setting off all sorts of alarm bells in my head and I decided to have it out with Pearl as soon as we left Bessie Stern's place.

'If you want to know more,' Bessie said, 'you should go and see the police – if you can find them. Please God they will find the monster as killed poor Shlomo, but what's one poor dead Jew among a city full of dead and dying people?' She raised her eyes to the ceiling and shook her head. 'Thanks to the Luftwaffe we could all be dead by morning! God willing it won't be so, but . . .'

As we left it was with Bessie's offer for us, or more specifically Pearl, to stay and, if necessary, use the shelter she used, ringing in our ears. 'If a raid starts, where will you go, Missus, you and the girl?' she said to Pearl. 'In the blackout you could kill yourselves looking for somewhere before the Germans even get across the Channel! Stay and take tea, talk a while.' But Pearl wanted to go so we left.

She was a good sort, Bessie Stern. She even offered, in view of the fact that I'm a man of 'business', to find me 'someone nice'. I wanted to ask Hannah what she'd told her. Not, obviously, that we were together. In fact, I got the distinct feeling that Bessie would've thought less of me if she'd known that. I had no reason to suppose she knew what Hannah did for a living, but she had seemed to dislike her. Maybe my girl had said I was Jewish to ease our passage through the mysteries of Spitalfields and that was why Bessie had seemed so keen on me. But neither Hannah, Velma nor I had much of a chance to talk about any of this as we raced up the road to keep up with Pearl. Once out of Bessie's she'd gone off like a silent rocket. I at least was frightened we might lose track of her, that she'd disappear, like her sister, like the old rabbi who had melted through a wall.

If you don't know where the nearest public shelter might be or you're a long way off from one, church crypts are always a decent bet. We'd just gone past St Anne's,

Limehouse, when the sirens went so I doubled back with the two women and the girl and took them down there. I asked Hannah to stay with Pearl and Velma, which she said she would. The vicar, who was in charge of settling everyone in, was a bit taken aback when I left.

'My wife is making tea,' he said, as I headed off through the crowds and up the stairs.

It's often said that London is a collection of villages, each with its own distinctive character. This is true and yet not true too. Take Limehouse. There's a belief some have that it's a place full of Chinamen taking opium. Allow your sons and daughters to come down Limehouse and they'll be dope fiends within days, probably on the game too. There is, of course, a bit of truth in this, but not much. In Limehouse, like everywhere else in the East, there's good and bad of every race and religion you can name. The only constant things are the great big churches and the poverty. St Anne's, Limehouse, just like Christ Church, Spitalfields, was built by the architect Nicholas Hawksmoor. Both white and sporting tall spires, they look more like churches for the smart set up Chelsea way than for the poor ragamuffins around these parts. It does indeed make you wonder why such magnificent buildings were put in places like this. But no one in the old days had imagined something like this nightmare.

I didn't stray far. Maybe it was because St Anne's is surrounded by a graveyard, maybe it made me feel at home. When the bombers came over I was leaning against a pyramid they've got there. It's a big white thing. Not a monument as far as anybody knows, I've heard it said that

Hawksmoor built it for reasons known only to him. There is something mysterious about it, probably because its shape sort of connects it to Egypt. But for whatever reason it seemed like the right place for me to be at the time. As the ground shook, the sky lit up like daylight and I strained to hear the sound of the ack-ack, I turned my mind back to recent events at Bessie Stern's place.

Of course I could understand Pearl being so vehement about her sister Ruby's innocence. I'd feel exactly the same if someone accused either of my sisters of murder. But there'd been more than that. There was the name for a start, Reynolds or House, and the police's seeming belief that there was something wrong with the name Bessie Stern had given them. Why they thought that I couldn't imagine, unless of course Ruby was known to them. Two things came to mind then: first, that Bessie hadn't seen Shlomo Kaplan alive before that fateful raid, and second, if Pearl was out the night Kevin died, where had she been and why had she, as far as I could tell, lied about it? Unbidden, Kevin Dooley's violent face, lit by the yellow and red glow of fire after fire, tumbled into my head. 'I've been fucking stabbed!' he'd said. 'She fucking stabbed me!' And I'd done nothing to help him . . .

I don't know why I looked up then. When a bomb goes in the river there isn't much noise, but a sort of a feeling like an earthquake when it detonates under the water. But the next I knew I was looking at what appeared to be a wall of water screaming up into the sky. Lit by burning wharves and fires on top of what had once been houses, this thing was like a tidal wave big enough, to me, to take over the whole world. Knowing it would do no good I braced myself nevertheless, eyes closed, against the side of the pyramid. I would, I knew, be smashed to pieces by this mountain of water. But after a bit when nothing happened, I opened my eyes and the only things I could see in the sky were the outlines of German bombers. I must've gone mad for a bit again back there. It was almost a relief and I laughed.

'What the fuck are you up to, mate?'

He was about fifty and he had ARP written on his tin hat.

'I-I-I, er . . .'

'I don't know how you bleeders get out!' Then, pulling me by one arm, he said, 'Come on, get you inside.' He must have meant the crypt.

Of course, I resisted.

He wasn't a bad bloke. Quite rightly, he thought I was barmy and who could blame him?

'I-I-I'm n-n-not mad!' I stuttered.

'Yeah, right,' he said, 'and I'm the fucking Duke of York. Come on, Sonny Jim, it's for your own good.'

'No!' I ripped my arm out of his grasp and, pointing at my chest with one hand, I screamed, 'Undertaker! H-Hancock!'

It was all I could get out, over the noise of the bombers, the thud of the explosions, the crackle and spit of a thousand fires.

The warden's creased, toothless face frowned. 'You from . . . You from Plaistow . . .'

'Yes!'

'Ah.'

'Y-y-you . . .'

He moved his head close to mine, his tin hat just touching the edge of my hair. 'You're old Tom Hancock's son, aren't you?' he said. 'I've heard about you.'

There was a lot as could be inferred from what he'd said but principal among all of it was that I wasn't quite the ticket. Only a few years older than me, the warden had probably been in the first lot too. There was indeed a small light of understanding in his eyes. As Albert Cox sometimes says, 'When you're in business round these parts there ain't too many places to hide.' There's no such thing as an invisible undertaker. A mad one, maybe. But that is unusual enough for news of it to travel across all of London's eastern villages.

The warden took one more look at me, then headed off back towards the Commercial Road. Dealing with the dying is one thing – there might just be some sort of hope – but talking to those already dead is pointless.

'I lost them as we was leaving,' Hannah said miserably. 'All these women flying up the stairs with all their kids and blankets and food and whatever, I couldn't keep on them.'

'That's all right, love,' I said, as I put an arm round her shoulders.

'There's something fishy about that Pearl, ain't there?' Hannah said. 'About that name, Reynolds, and . . .'

'Turns out she and, she says, Velma, were out the night

her old man died,' I said, with a yawn. 'She was cagy about where she was.'

Hannah shook her head. 'So sorry I lost them, H.'

But it was as much my fault as Hannah's that we'd managed to lose Pearl and Velma. Once the raid was over, which was just before dawn, I'd fallen asleep. When Hannah, all panicked over Pearl and Velma, had found me and then woken me I'd been dreaming about George Pepper's first communion. He'd done it, in my dream, at age twenty-one in full battle-dress and kit.

I had to be home by ten because we were burying some collection of human pieces the coppers had chosen to call the late Reginald Burman. A bachelor who lived with his sister, Cissie, Reg had left the Anderson behind his house on Plashet Grove to go to the privy during a raid. Neither Reg nor the privy had been there in the morning. So now poor old Cissie was on her own in that house with a shell full of bits that had probably never been anywhere near her brother. But I had to go out and do the honourable thing for her sake and, rather than talk much more to Hannah about the previous night's events, I hurried home.

Before she even asked me where I'd been half the previous day and all night, Nan said, 'Water's off.'

'Christ!'

'Francis!'

I looked at Nan and smiled sheepishly. 'Sorry, Nan,' I said. 'It's just that I'm filthy.'

'Yes, I can see,' she said.

Nan and the Duchess are always good with water. When we've got it, they put some aside in the kettle and in a barrel out in the yard. But this time the barrel had caught some blast so a small cup for shaving was all I managed to persuade Nan to pour out of the kettle for me. I went through the motions of changing my clothes, but those I took off were only a bit dirtier than those I put on. I thought of Dad and laughed as it occurred to me how disgusted he'd have been with my appearance. Tom Hancock was always immaculate, even when he was dying. It was his belief that to be smart and clean was one of the few real things a person could do to show respect for the dead. More important, he always felt, than the quality of the coffin or the size and elaborateness of the monument.

Once I'd sorted myself out I went down to the shop. Doris, all plump and exotic-looking in a tightly fitted green dress, was sitting having a cup of tea with Fred Bryant. He was out of uniform, but just seeing him made me ask Doris if we could have a moment or two on our own. Fred, true to form, watched Doris go with a little smile of regret. How long was he going to hold a torch for the poor girl?

'Fred,' I said, once Doris had gone and I'd taken one of his fags, 'do you know anything about the murder of an old Jewish bloke up Spitalfields?'

'When?'

'Two, three weeks ago,' I said. 'Paper-and-string merchant.'

'Oh. Oh, yes, yes, I do. Course.'

'What?'

Fred is really too much of a gossip to be a copper. In my

line of work you have to have discretion, so it never goes any further. But I do sometimes wonder who else Fred tells and what.

Fred moved in as close as one bloke would consider doing to another. 'Well, they don't know who done it,' he said, 'but I've heard tell that it's the housekeeper they're looking for.'

Nothing so far that I didn't know already.

'Oh?'

'Yes. What you want to know for, Mr H?'

'I was up those parts yesterday,' I said. 'Heard a few stories, you know.'

'Right.'

I didn't say anything else then. Fred usually, once you've shown that you're interested, carries on without any further help. On this occasion, he was true to form.

'There's a sergeant up Shoreditch I know,' he said. 'No names, no pack drill. But anyway, he says this housekeeper, apparently she's the daughter of that woman hung for murder some years ago.'

'What woman?'

'Something foreign,' Fred said. 'I dunno. But anyway, she was a "woman of the night", if you know what I mean. Up West it was somewhere.'

That all made sense. The horrible Vi Dooley had said Pearl had come from 'up West' and if Ruby's and her mother really had been a murderess it would explain why Pearl hadn't wanted to reveal her real name. Not that either 'Reynolds' or 'House' was foreign in any way that I could see. There was also the connection with prostitution. Vi Dooley had said that Pearl was on the game at one time, but perhaps she was just tarring the daughter with the same brush as the mother. That the police were pursuing Ruby despite, as far as I could tell, no evidence to show she'd killed Shlomo Kaplan, seemed like another example of this. But perhaps they knew something that I didn't. In fact, almost certainly they knew something that I didn't.

'This woman they're looking for,' Fred continued, 'her mother killed her fella.'

'What?'

'Some geezer she was involved with, she killed him,' Fred said.

I felt my skin go very cold. 'How? What did she do?'

'Stabbed him through the heart.' Fred said, and then added darkly, 'With a dirty great hatpin, so they say. Apparently the body was soaked with blood.'

'Fred,' I said, as I put one fag out, then instantly lit another, 'I think we should go and see Albert Cox now.'

The policeman, obviously confused, frowned. 'Why's that, Mr H?'

I told him of what my suspicions had been right from the start on the way down to Canning Town. This time, instead of going on about what Dr Cockburn had and had not said, Fred listened.

When we arrived at Cox's shop, Albert told us that Pearl Dooley had left after viewing her husband's body about half an hour before. She'd come not only to see him but to find out when his funeral was going to take place. It was scheduled for the next day, so I knew we'd have to act fast if we were to have Kevin's body examined again before the ceremony. Fred called his sergeant who, after what we were told was a lot of persuasive talking, eventually managed to get Marcus Cockburn out to Cox's shop that night. As bombs fell all around us Dr Cockburn, reeking of whisky and cigars, nevertheless came to a rather different cause of death for Kevin Dooley than the one he had originally given.

Why I'd treated Kevin as I had – like a nutter, the same way people treat me – on the night he died, I didn't know. But the guilt was terrible then. The world was descending into madness again and, just as I'd done in the first lot, I was simply letting it happen. Which, after all, is more unforgivable? To kill a man on the orders of a so-called superior or to let a man obviously not well or in his right mind run off to meet his own destruction? My mates hadn't let me desert: they'd taken care of this nutter and saved my life. I should have tried to save poor Kevin's.

Chapter Seven

The Dooleys were a huge family. As well as the old mother and all of Kevin's kids there were at least five adults who looked similar to the deceased. Brothers and sisters, I guessed, many with husbands, wives and kids in tow. Although none had come out in yellow, there wasn't a lot of mourning wear to be seen. But it isn't cheap as I'd be the first to admit. What doesn't cost, however, is dignity and although the mother was obviously upset, there was precious little grief beyond that. Dodgy blokes wearing trilbies smoking fags, sometimes laughing, sometimes swearing angrily, blokes young enough I would have imagined to be in the services. No, the only real sorrow I could see was shown by Kevin Dooley's wife.

She came alone, still in her ratty old coat but with a hat she'd got from somewhere on her head. It had a bit of a veil, which she'd pulled down over her face that, with the trees she was standing among, concealed her from all but the most keen observer. That was me. I watched her cry for some time before I went over. I knew I wasn't going to like what I had to do next. But no one had known where she was so it had seemed the best, if not the right, thing to do to all involved.

'Mr Cox and his boys have done your husband proud,' I said, as I watched Albert walk towards the graveside ahead of the coffin. It was one of those dank afternoons where the half-bare trees look like ragged skeletons against the battleship grey of the sky.

As soon as she saw me, Pearl Dooley's tears stopped and something that looked like fear came into her eyes. 'I loved him, you know,' she said, 'my Kevin.'

'But he hit you,' I said. 'You had nipper after nipper for him and he still . . .'

'I loved him!' she said. 'He gave me my life, he did. I know it can't make much sense to anyone else, but he took me in and he protected me. He was a hard man, yes, but . . . Anyway, what's it to do with you?'

In contrast to how humble she'd been with me when she and Velma had first turned up at the shop she was now openly hostile. As far as I could tell, Spitalfields, and what had been discovered there, had changed her.

'Did your mother love her bloke?' I said. 'The one she finished with her hatpin?' I turned to look down at her and found a face bursting with both grief and anger. 'You know I saw your husband on the night that he died, Mrs Dooley,' I said. 'He told me he'd been stabbed.'

She shook her head. 'He died from the blast. The coppers' doctor said so.'

'There was a little hole, just under his breastbone,' I

said. 'It could've been where a long pin stabbed into him, maybe from a lady's hat. Where were you and Velma the night that Kevin died, Pearl?'

Her mouth opened and her eyes, even through the veil I could see, filled with tears.

'No, it's not possible!' she hissed rather than shouted. Father Burton, at the head of the grave, cleared his throat prior to beginning his committal. 'You think I killed him? Just because my mum—'

'You know, some of the Shoreditch coppers reckon that your Ruby could've killed old Mr Kaplan,' I said. 'Bessie Stern didn't see him alive before that raid. Ruby was the last person to see him, as you know. Some people believe murder's in the blood.'

I didn't add that I had doubts about that. Although the way Kevin had met his end was uncomfortably like the way Pearl's mother had killed her fellow, it was more Pearl's whereabouts on the night that Dooley had died that bothered both me and the police, who wanted to speak to her and the rest of Kevin's family. This was now, after all, a murder, which meant that everyone connected in any way to it would be questioned.

'So you think that I . . .' Fearing, I imagined, that someone might hear her, Pearl moved in closer to me and dropped her voice. 'I never killed Kevin and I can prove it!' she said.

'Can you? You weren't too clear when I asked you . . .'

'Yes, I can!' she said. 'Ask your girlfriend's landlady if you don't believe me.'

'What?'

'I never killed Kevin. I wouldn't. Why don't you believe me?'

'It's not that I don't believe you,' I said, 'but your story about where you were that night, with friends, just doesn't ring true. You told me yourself you don't have any friends.'

'If you're thinking of calling the coppers . . .'

'No.'

She stared at me. 'Why not?'

'Because we're already here, love,' a deep voice said behind her.

Fred Bryant's guv'nor, Sergeant Hill, gave the order for the funeral to be stopped. Albert Cox duly went over to Father Burton and had a word in his ear. The Dooleys started hollering and swearing almost immediately.

I looked at the chaos around me with fear. The police were taking a destitute, weeping woman away with them – something I'd had a hand in. If only I'd taken Kevin Dooley seriously that night! If only I'd asked him who 'she' was and why she'd done what she had to him.

Because she'd managed to get Father Burton to perform Kevin's funeral so quickly, Vi Dooley had wanted her son's body to stay over at Cox's. Maybe, in part, she'd thought that Pearl might want to see him too – although I didn't suppose that was much of a consideration for her. But whatever the reason, Kevin being at Albert's shop had allowed Marcus Cockburn to re-examine the body, if reluctantly, in something approaching peace. His new conclusion about the cause of death was a lot different from his first attempt. Kevin Dooley's heart had been punctured by a long, sharp instrument that had caused him to bleed to death inside his own body. Like him or not, Kevin Dooley had suffered a painful death that, with or without evidence from that night to back it up, had to have been murder. No one does that to themselves, however barmy.

Dr Cockburn's first thought had been to stop the funeral. But now that I'd told the coppers everything I knew about Pearl, they were keen to speak to her – if they could find her. None of us knew where she might be so it was decided to let something that looked like a funeral go ahead. It was almost a dead cert she'd turn up, and even though Father Burton wasn't happy about performing a funeral for an empty coffin and was, to make things even worse, without the bereaved family's knowledge, he agreed to do it anyway.

So, now Kevin's wife and family were going to have to answer questions about what they were doing on the night he died. The coppers took them down the station while I followed on with the sergeant and the dead man's wife. I was interested in what Pearl had had to say about Hannah's landlady, Dot Harris, and her involvement in all this. I did begin to ask her about it until Sergeant Hill put me right. 'You have to let us take it from here, Mr Hancock,' he said. 'Thank you very much for your help, sir.' He then raised his helmet and, with one hand round Pearl's thin arm, he led her away towards the cemetery gates.

As she went she turned briefly and gave me a look that might have been of either desperation or hatred. But, then, if she did hate me, I could understand that. After all, I'd laid it all, whatever it turned out to be, open to the air. In effect, I had put her in the back of that police car and on her way to the station for questioning and God alone knew where after that. A woman already scorned by her in-laws, with no mother of her own for comfort. And what of her daughter? If she hadn't come to the funeral with her mother, where was Velma? All I could hope was that Pearl would tell the coppers so they could look after her. But that had to depend upon what, indeed, Pearl and Velma had been doing on the night that Kevin died.

I rode back to the shop with Albert in his motor. Hearses are classed as 'essential' transport so he can, most of the time, get the petrol he needs. Makes me wonder sometimes what I'm still doing with the horses. But as the Duchess always says, some people prefer horses and the dung comes in useful for Walter's allotment – something we all occasionally benefit from.

'I reckon me and old Kevin'll be back at the East London before the week's out,' Albert said. 'Murder or no murder, the coppers ain't got nowhere to keep bodies now. Morgue situation just don't get no better.'

'No.'

'You reckon she done it then, Pearl Dooley?' Albert said.

I was looking out of the window at the time. It had begun to drizzle now. It made the houses out on Grange Road look even more miserable than they usually do. Funny the way places around cemeteries always look like that. Even if the people who live in them are happy types.

'I don't know,' I replied. 'She told me she loved him and I think that maybe she did in her way. And even if she did kill him there has to be more than a chance that she was only protecting herself. Kevin Dooley was not, as you've said, Albert, anyone's angel.'

'Bloody right. Vicious bastard. Mind you, if she did do it the same way as her mum, don't 'arf give you the creeps, don't it?'

Yes, it did. People don't like that sort of thing, in my experience. Murder in the blood. Puts you in mind of madness in the family or disease or any other type of ill the average bloke can come up against. If something is passed on through the blood it means people can't have any control over it. And that is frightening.

I looked out of the window again and wondered where Pearl's sister Ruby might be now. God forgive me, I also wondered whether Shlomo Kaplan had had any other wounds apart from those to his head. After all, as far as I knew, the last person who could've seen him alive before the air raid, apart from Ruby, was Bessie Stern when she went to get her neighbours into the shelter. But Bessie had admitted she hadn't seen him. Could the old man have been dead before the raid started? Could Ruby Reynolds have killed him? If she had, not to take any money and, further, to return to the scene of her crime when the raid was over, seemed stupid to me. And why, later, when the police were called, had she run away? If she were innocent, that had to be just plain daft. All I could think of by way of a reason was her mother's crime and the connections the police might make between it and Ruby. Back again to the idea that killing runs in the blood. But as I know only too well, people, even coppers, like to think that lots of things exist in the blood. Frightening though it is, it's easy to understand. It also helps 'nice' people make the separation between themselves and all the 'bad' people. Rubbish! In my case, when I was a nipper, it was selling carpets. We have a few of the Indian men selling carpets door to door around this manor – Johnny Boys, they're called – the Duchess has one in for tea sometimes, Mr Bhadwaj. Despite my dad and his business, that was what some of the kids at school saw me doing when I grew up. I was brown, so carpet-selling had to be in my blood. It was worse at the grammar school, maybe because more of the kids there had parents who could afford to buy carpets, of any sort, and look down their noses at the Johnny Boys as they did so. Some years later, good, bad, black or white, we all fought and suffered in the Great War. You would've thought that might have killed off ideas about things being in people's blood, wouldn't you?

'Hannah!'

I'd already taken the Duchess down the shelter in anticipation of a raid when Hannah turned up at the shop door. Luckily for me, both Nan and Aggie were down the Anderson too, or I would have had even more explaining to do. And with the tale of Kevin Dooley's strange fate still ringing in their ears, Mum and the girls probably had enough to gossip about as it was.

'You've got a visitor,' Hannah said, as she pushed a red-faced and tear-stained Velma into the shop in front of her.

You never can tell when the siren's going to go, so I took them both up to the kitchen for the time being. If the warning went they'd have to go in with Duchess and the others anyway and God knew how I'd explain it, especially Hannah . . .

'She turned up at Dot's a couple of hours ago,' Hannah said, as she took off her hat and sat down. 'I never knew until I heard Dot raving.'

'Raving?' I put the kettle on the range and lit the gas beneath it. 'About what?'

'I don't know.' Hannah shrugged. 'But she was giving this one here a right going over.'

Velma, her head down, began to cry.

'Dot was all for bunging her out in the street,' Hannah said, 'but she's only a kid so I had to take her.'

'Where?'

'Down the pub first,' Hannah said. 'Dot wouldn't have her in the house. Then she said she wanted to come here, speak to you. It's all I've been able to get out of her so far. All she'll say about her mother is that she's gone.'

I looked at Velma, a little guiltily I must confess, and said, 'What you need's a nice cup of tea, isn't it, love?'

She didn't smile, but her tears seemed to slow down after that.

While I poured the water into the pot, Hannah said, 'Dot had the coppers round about half past three. I expect that was why she—'

'They come about my mum,' Velma said. 'She's down

the police station now, Mum is!' And then she turned to me. 'You know, don't you, Mr Hancock?'

I sat down opposite her and took one of her hands in mine. 'Were you in the cemetery for your step-father's funeral?'

'Outside,' the girl corrected. 'Mum wanted me to go in but I wouldn't, not for that pig.'

'Your step-father?'

'Yes. I hated him and I'm glad he's dead! I couldn't ever work out why Mum loved him, he done such bad things to her. Why have the coppers taken my mum away, Mr Hancock? Does it have anything to do with her mum and her sister Ruby?'

I looked briefly at Hannah, who registered her surprise. 'What do you know about that, Velma?' I said.

'I didn't know nothing until Mum told me about it last night,' the girl said. 'Spent the night down Bethnal Green tube, we did. It was horrible. Me and Mum couldn't sleep. Then she began telling me all about it. Mum said I should know in case my aunt, Ruby, got into the papers.'

'Why does she think that your Aunt Ruby might get into the papers?'

'Well, you was there,' Velma said, 'at that place in Spitalfields. Coppers think she done that old bloke in. Mum says they have to know about my granny too and about what she done, which was murder, so Mum said. Mum says the coppers'll say her sister done it whether she did or not. Mum don't trust coppers.'

'Velma,' I said, 'what do you know about your grandmother?'

And then the sirens went.

I stood up as my speech went. 'C-c-come on,' I said, 'you'll have to c-c-come d-down our shelter.'

'I'll tell you all about it down there,' Velma said.

I looked across at Hannah before I ran down the stairs. She knew I never went inside during a raid, but she followed me anyway.

Out in the yard it was pitch dark and raining. I opened the door to the Anderson and stood to one side. I heard the Duchess greet Velma as an old friend when she went in.

'What are you going to do, Mr H?' Hannah said, as she stood underneath the pouring water from the sky.

'I-I . . .'

'Now you've got the girl talking . . .'

'Er . . .' I looked away from Hannah, into the shelter, my heart pounding at the sight of it. 'V-Velma's g-granny, this is v-very important...'

'Then you'll have to come down, won't you?' Hannah said.

'Francis, are you going to come in this time?' I heard the Duchess say.

'Who's that with you?' Nan asked.

'M-M-M-Miss J-Jacobs,' I said.

'Who's she?'

'Never mind, there's a raid on,' I heard Aggie say. Then she came to the door of the shelter and ushered Hannah in. 'Come on, love, come in. Frank, you coming in here with this lady or not?'

'Er . . .'

'That kid wants to tell you about her granny, Mr H,'

Hannah said, as she walked past me into the shelter. 'So if it's that important . . .'

I swung myself through the door and pulled it closed behind me. Heart hammering, my breath coming short and shallow, I somehow staggered over to one of the bunks at the back of the shelter and sat down.

Hannah's a really bright woman. I often wish I could ask her to marry me. But there's far too many 'if's – if she wasn't Jewish, if I wasn't like I am . . .

She introduced herself to my family as a friend of Pearl and Velma Dooley. It was sort of true, after all. Not that Aggie was fooled – I saw her face and she was obviously amused. But, then, I knew she knew about Hannah – how I don't know. Maybe she'd seen me leave her once, shaking hands on the doorstep of her boarding-house. But whatever Aggie did or didn't know, she didn't let on to the Duchess or Nan. No one spoke about Pearl either – not yet, at least.

By this time, of course, I was speechless. There was nothing to hear then, save ordinary sounds like Nan pouring tea from a Thermos for people and Aggie's pen scratching across paper – writing a letter to her little 'uns. No bombers, not yet. But I knew it wouldn't be long. Germans and bombs, mud and limbs flying up in the air, yards not feet, then crashing down again, on top of houses and factories, children and old women and me. Burying me alive. How many times had I watched blokes sink into the mud of Flanders, folded into a tomb of muck, sinking into burial, alive and screaming. It was freezing down there in our Anderson, but the sweat was dripping off me. The Duchess, I knew, wanted to put out a hand to comfort me, but I also knew she understood what her action might do. Sometimes, when I'm like this, all it takes is a touch to make me scream.

Then, as that familiar drone throbbed through my chest from the hundreds of planes above, just as I thought I would surely have a heart-attack, Hannah, sitting between me and Velma, began to speak. 'You were going to tell us about your grandma, Velma,' she said.

The girl looked around at the Duchess and my sisters, her eyes full of fear.

The Duchess, who has a knack of saying the right thing at the right time, said, 'If you'd rather just speak to Mr Hancock and Miss Jacobs I promise you I won't listen, my dear. I understand you have some trouble at the moment.'

'Won't be able to listen soon,' Aggie put in. 'Be bleedin' deafened in a minute.'

Nan shot her a disgusted look – Nan doesn't like swearing – and then did what the Duchess says she always does, which is sit in a corner with her rosary. In the dark, squatting like that, she looked like one of those photographs you sometimes see of poor people in Delhi or Calcutta.

'Well?' Hannah stroked Velma's dirty wet hair.

'My gran was called Victorine Reynolds,' Velma said. 'Mum said the papers called her the Bloody French Maid – 'cause she was French originally, like.'

I've never taken a great deal of interest in what newspapers print so neither the name nor the nickname rang any bells with me. But there was Reynolds and there was something distinctly foreign-sounding too. Victorine – I'd never heard the like before.

The ground shook, and somewhere to the south there was the sound of first one and then about four explosions. The docks, getting it again. Inside my head something awful gibbered and jabbered like the ravings of the madmen those evil trenches had pushed out into the world.

Velma took a deep breath before she continued. She was a brave little kid, determined not to show her fear. She put me to shame. 'Victorine had this man,' she said, 'Neilson. He wasn't Mum's dad. I don't know who he was. But he was like Kevin.'

'What do you mean, love?' Hannah asked.

'He hit her.'

A thud, somewhat closer now. Aggie, an unlit fag in her mouth, looked up from her letter. 'Feels like over the Greengate way,' she said, measuring the seriousness of the situation by pub name.

Close. Getting closer. Then a massive explosion. My legs twitched, wanting to run. Stan Wheeler had been sitting when a German Mills bomb landed beside him. 'Jesus!' he'd said, just before he disappeared into nothing. 'Jesus!' I could hear it as sure as if he was still beside me. 'Jesus! Jesus! Jesus!'

'Then one night Mum and her sisters were out.' Velma was speaking again and I made myself turn to look at her. 'He went mad, this Neilson, bashing Mum's mum up. She had to stop him so she stabbed him with her hatpin . . .'

Aggie looked up at the word 'hatpin' then went back to her letter.

'Oh, I see,' Hannah said, looking at me as she did so. 'Right, then, weren't you?'

I nodded. So now she knew – that I'd found out the truth about how Kevin Dooley had died and how the method of his death had led everyone's thoughts to Pearl.

'He died,' Velma hadn't been listening to us and was seemingly in almost a trance, 'and my gran went to prison. Mum and her sisters went to an orphanage, or she and Ruby and Amber did. My gran had said they had to keep together, see. They're all named after jewels, my mum and her sisters.' Briefly she smiled. It's amazing how kids can be when they find something they like. The world can be tearing itself apart but kids can still enjoy things like pretty names. 'But the little sister, Opal, she was just a baby at the time so she went somewhere else. Mum don't know. No one told her anything. They hung Victorine in the end and Mum didn't know until it was over. Never said goodbye or nothing. Then Mum and her other sisters split up too. Mum says she's always been afraid that someone'll find out who she is and try to make up stories about her. So when she heard about Ruby she was scared.' Velma looked down at her hands, her eyes heavy with sadness. 'Do you think the police've got my mum 'cause they think she's done a murder? Do they think she murdered Kevin?'

'I don't know, love,' Hannah said gently, as she stroked Velma's hair.

I said nothing. With a raid in full swing, with the dust

from explosions maybe miles away creeping into the shelter, I wouldn't have been able to put a sentence together anyway.

'So why did you come to, er, to my place when your mum had gone?' Hannah said, carefully avoiding owning up to where she lived in front of my family.

'I wanted to see Mr Hancock,' Velma said.

'Why didn't you just come here?'

'Because I saw him go across to the police car when the coppers took her away,' she said. 'I didn't really know what had happened. I come to see you, Miss, because you're his friend. Mum said you was all Jews . . .'

'Jews!' Nan nearly dropped her rosary. 'We ain't no Jews!'

'Oh, but my mum—'

'Well, your mum thought wrong,' Nan said. 'We're Christian us, English. Are you stupid or something?'

Given that all of us, except Aggie, were a damn sight darker than Hannah, Pearl's assumption hadn't been so daft. But no one said anything to Nan about this.

'No, it's only me who's Jewish,' Hannah said to Velma. Then she changed the subject. 'So you must've remembered where I live from when Mr Hancock brought you over. Did you ask my landlady if you could see me?'

'I never got the chance,' Velma replied. 'She went barmy when she see me. She said the coppers had already been round about my mother and she didn't want no more trouble. If you hadn't come down, Miss, I don't know what I'd've done.'

'Do you know what the coppers were asking about your mum, Velma?'

There was a huge explosion, really close this time. As the dust and muck shot into the shelter we all ducked down and closed our eyes. There was that smell too, the one I can't easily describe, but it's the smell you get when bricks burn. It's disgusting.

'Christ!' I heard Aggie yell.

Nan, in contrast, clung to her beads. 'Holy Mary, Mother of God, pray for us now and at the time of our death. Holy Mary . . .'

Up above, the roar of the bombers' engines. Directly overhead. For seconds that could have been minutes, we held our breath. Somehow I stifled the urge to scream, but I felt my face go white and it wasn't until Hannah spoke again that I came back to the world once more.

'Velma?'

The girl shrugged, half a ton of grey dust from her shoulders falling on to the floor as she moved. 'I don't know. Maybe it was about what Mum done the night Kevin died.'

Velma put her head down as if in shame. In spite of the way that I felt and everything that was going on I was interested in this so I moved a bit closer the better to hear.

'What did your mum do that night, Velma?' Hannah asked.

'She went to see Mrs Harris,' Velma said. 'I went with her. Me and Mum saw you that night, Miss,' she smiled, 'but you never saw us so Mum said not to say nothing.'

Aggie, now given up on her letter, looked at me and

frowned. She'd perked up at the mention of Mrs Harris all right.

'Why was your mum at Mrs Harris's, Velma?' Hannah asked.

Again the head went down and this time I had to get still closer to hear what she was mumbling.

'Mum was ill,' she whispered. 'Mum said Mrs Harris can sometimes make people better. And she's cheaper than a doctor, Mum says. She was in her room for a long time. When she come out her face was white and there was . . . blood, on her, like her slip and that . . . She said I wasn't to tell no one about what she done, but because you know Mrs Harris, Miss . . . you and Mr Hancock, you won't tell no one else, will you?'

Chapter Eight

'**W**ho d'you think you are? Sherlock Holmes?'

'If I'm being told the truth Pearl Dooley couldn't have killed her husband,' I said, and then, lowering my voice to a whisper, 'She was having an abortion at the time. At Dot Harris's. Her daughter told me about it last night.'

Talking about such things, even round the back of the police station with no one else about, you have to be careful. Not that the coppers don't know it goes on. They know all right, and who does it. But I sometimes think that a lot of people consider talking about things almost worse than doing them. So much in life is about how things look to others. Like those women who gave out white feathers to blokes they saw out of uniform during the Great War. I got one once, when I was home on leave. Made me cry myself to sleep it did. I should have rammed it down her stupid throat with my bayonet.

'Look,' Fred Bryant glanced quickly over his shoulder and then came and stood very close to me, 'I know all about the so-called abortion.' He mouthed rather than spoke the last, forbidden, word. 'Pearl Dooley come out with that straight away. But Dot Harris says she never done it.'

'Well, she would. But Velma, Pearl's daughter, she can identify Dot.'

'I don't doubt it. So can a lot of people,' Fred said. 'Anyway, Dot don't deny knowing Pearl Dooley. Said she come to her for a you-know-what last year. But told her she was out of that business now. Dot ain't seen her since, and certainly not on the night that Kevin Dooley died.'

'Velma says her mother was in a bad way after the abortion. Someone must have noticed!'

'Vi Dooley says Pearl was out with Velma the night Kevin died and when she come back in she was perfectly all right. All the family were at home with the exception of Kevin, Pearl and Velma, so Vi says. So Pearl could've just as easy been with her husband as she could've been at Dot's.'

'Velma says her mother had blood on her clothes.'

Fred shook his head. 'Well, she's on her own with that.'

'You should get a doctor to examine Pearl,' I said.

'And what would that prove?' Fred replied. 'Doctor can't tell when she had, you know, it done even if he does find something. She could've had it the morning or the night before or even the next day. Can't prove she had it done that night or that Dot Harris done it, not unless someone turns up what saw her at Rathbone Street. But we've had no luck with that so far.'

'So you going to charge her?'

'You said yourself Dooley talked about a woman

stabbing him,' the policeman said, 'and, anyway, you know what his wife's background is. Ain't no such thing as a coincidence, I don't think, and,' Fred lowered his voice, 'Pearl had made threats against her husband, during arguments.' And then as he started walking back to the station he called back, 'Go home, Mr H, there's nothing you can do about it now.'

I relit what was left of my fag and started to walk. Although I knew in my heart that I'd done the right thing with regard to Kevin Dooley, I couldn't help feeling guilty. I couldn't be certain, of course, that Pearl was innocent, but to use an abortion as an alibi seemed strange to me. If it were legal, I could understand it, but it isn't. Why use one crime, of a type almost as serious as murder, to cover up for another? Besides, Pearl must have known Dot Harris would never back her up. Also, Pearl had loved her thug of a husband for some reason. He beat her, gave her kids she couldn't support, some she maybe did want rid of, and yet she, like so many of the poor women around here, still cared. And then there was Velma. Again, it was me who had brought her in to the police. But only because I thought that what she had to say was important. She was in there with them now and, although Fred had told me to go home, I'd decided to wait for her as long as I could. I just hoped the coppers didn't take it into their heads to keep her in too.

Coming up from the Anderson that morning I'd met Ken passing the back gate. Ken's straight as a die so when I told him about what Velma had said about Pearl he gave me his honest opinion.

'Well, you've got to try and help her if you think there's a chance she might be innocent,' he'd said. 'Mind you, with her background, it sounds to me as if the coppers have got her in the nick and hung already.'

I said something about not believing anything about murder being in the blood and Ken replied, 'I dunno, pal. Sometimes I wonder. After all, them as are fighting now are the kids of them in the first lot, ain't they?'

'Some,' I said.

'You'd think that what we saw would've taught them something, wouldn't you? But they keep on sending their kids for King and country. Maybe it is in the blood, mate. Who knows?' He looked down sadly at his boots and said, 'But there's also the truth – important to old soldiers like us, H, even if them in authority, right or wrong, always get to do what they want.'

He was right there. I only had to think about the so-called deserters we'd been ordered to shoot to know that. Men go mad and then they lose their way, wander right off sometimes. There are reasons for desertion, good reasons, but in the eyes of military law they're in the wrong, and no matter what they've been through, those in power demand only one punishment for such a crime: death at the hands of their fellows. Reasons, the truth itself, rarely mattered. Some of the officers used to call it 'making an example' of a bloke. It was incidents like this that had helped to form Albert Cox's rather 'Commie' style of opinions. And I do agree with him in lots of ways. It's simply that, for me, unjust death need not be political. For me it's about truth and justice for the dead.

Looking after them is what my life is all about. Without them I am nothing.

I waited around for a good hour, but then I had to go. As well as all the usual jobs that go with the business, I had to go out with a coffin up to Plashet Grove again. As gently as I could I was going to place it round the shell with a baby called William in it. The mother had been raving mad with grief when she'd come to the shop, which had been while I was out in Spitalfields. Doris had done her best, but I wasn't expecting an easy time either now or at the funeral, which would hopefully take place some time in the next few days. Jerries permitting. We don't charge for babies' funerals, but that doesn't mean we don't hope for decent conditions and all the usual niceties that should go with such a solemn occasion.

Velma, I imagined and hoped, would eventually return to the shop. If, that is, the police didn't think she had been involved in Kevin's death.

As it happened, Velma gave a statement to the police supporting her mother. The coppers then asked her some questions and later on they let her go. But she didn't come back to us. Fred Bryant told me later that some of the Dooleys, Kevin's brothers and a sister-in-law, had been hanging around the station and shouted and swore at her as she left. So Velma just ran.

I asked Fred why he didn't stop her and bring her over to us, but he just said, 'Moved too quick for me, she did.'

'Well, you could've told the Dooleys to leave her alone at least!' I said. 'What were they swearing and shouting at a child for anyway? I know the old woman doesn't like the girl and her mother but . . .'

But Fred just shrugged, as he does when he doesn't know what to say. The truth was, of course, that having got what they wanted out of Velma, the coppers weren't concerned about what happened afterwards. If I hadn't asked them to keep a look-out for her, I don't know if they would have bothered at all. 'There is a war on, you know,' is what they say. But eventually Fred Bryant did say he'd look for her, which, for what it was worth, I think he did.

Where Velma did run to, however, was a mystery to me for some time. But even though it bothered me and it fretted the Duchess something rotten, I accepted that there wasn't much I could do about it for the time being. So I just waited to see what the police decided about Pearl and got on with my work for the next two days. At that point, to be honest, I was feeling too guilty about what I'd done to Pearl and Velma to want to think properly about it. In trying to get at the truth about what happened to Kevin, had I done nothing more than just bring trouble to people who may not deserve it? I didn't know, so I didn't think too much about it until Fred Bryant turned up with something that had once been a woman called Cherry Hazlitt.

'It's best the family don't have her at home, not in that state,' Fred said, as he and a couple of younger coppers put something large and bloodied into the shell I'd prepared for it.

'There's not many undertakers as can have corpses on the premises, which is why I recommended you to the mother,' Fred went on. 'Well, if I can put a bit of business your way . . .'

'Yes, thank you, Fred.'

If he was expecting some sort of backhander from this, he was going to be sorely disappointed. But, then, perhaps what he had in mind was more in the way of a discount on possible future services. After all, we none of us know what will happen to us or our loved ones, these days, and Fred has a very big family.

'We charged that Pearl Dooley,' Fred said, once the younger policemen had gone.

'What with?'

'Murder.'

'Murder?'

'What else? We've only got Pearl's word she was at Dot Harris's place that night and a lot of people, local, like, said Pearl made threats against her husband's life. Not just the Dooleys saying it, see.'

I felt sick. 'Yes, well, people have been known to make threats when other people are beating them senseless,' I said.

'Well, yes, that can happen,' Fred said. 'But whatever the circumstances she made threats to him that were heard by others and, given her background and the fact we don't know where she was . . .'

'But what about Velma?' I said. 'She confirmed her mother's story.'

'Well, of course she did,' Fred replied. 'She's Pearl's daughter. Anyway there was blood in Pearl's room, on her, you know, her underclothes—'

'Yes!' I shouted – agitated by what seemed to me the casualness of this arrest. 'I told you about it. She'd had an abortion, Fred!'

'So she says,' Fred said darkly. 'And that's a crime in itself . . .'

'So why admit to it?' I said. 'If she had killed Kevin and then needed to make something up for an alibi, why choose something illegal?'

'I don't know. Maybe to account for that blood, which could, you know, Mr H, be her husband's.'

'Possibly. But to say she'd had an abortion when she hadn't still doesn't make sense,' I said. 'She could've said that the blood on her clothes was her, you know, her . . . when she has the painters in, like once a month . . . And, anyway, Pearl loved Kevin. He beat and abused her, she shouted at him – you know what those docks couples are like – but she still loved him.'

'How do you know she loved him?'

'Because she told me.'

Fred laughed. 'Gawd help us, Mr H. That don't mean nothing. This woman's mother loved the bloke she done too. Went to the bleedin' gallows begging his forgiveness, she did, so they say.'

'Do they?'

'Oh, yes, very much so.'

But how was I to know without finding out more about Victorine Reynolds and the death of Neilson? It was all news to me.

'Anyway, she's been took over to Holloway now so it's for the judge and jury when she comes to trial,' Fred said.

'So that's that, is it?' I said angrily, at what seemed to me to be Fred's lack of concern.

'Looks like it, Mr H.'

'You don't think you ought to look at other possibilities? You know, just in case someone else might be involved.'

'I don't see the need,' Fred said, with one of his irritatingly self-satisfied smiles.

'Christ!' I shook my head despairingly, and then I said, 'I don't suppose you've found young Velma yet?' We certainly hadn't seen her in or around the shop.

'No, not yet,' Fred said, as he left to go about his business. 'But I'm sure she'll turn up some time.'

'I wish I shared your confidence,' I snapped back at him. But Fred only laughed at my sharpness, which he is far too dull to take seriously.

With a heavy heart and a troubled mind I walked back into the shop where Doris was just finishing off talking to a bereaved relative.

'Poor geezer's lost his old dad,' she said, once the man had gone. 'Sounds like a bit of a tyrant to me, but he loved him, poor bugger. No rhyme or reason to who we choose to love, is there? Here, Mr H . . .'

'Yes . . .' I said it absently, my mind still concerned with Pearl and what might be happening to her now she was inside the grim walls of Holloway Prison – the place where I, with the best of intentions, had put her. The Government, I knew, kept traitors and spies in prisons, these days . . .

'You know you was after some paper-and-string man lived with a shikseh the other day?' Doris said.

'Yes.' Now she had my attention. 'Well?'

'You know some bloke who used to sell paper and string was murdered a couple of weeks back?'

'Yes,' I said. 'Shlomo Kaplan.'

'That's it,' Doris said. 'Old bloke, retired a while back, well before he died. Now his son Gerald does the same business out of somewhere in Bethnal Green. Well, anyway, I heard that he lived with a shikseh – not Gerald, the old bloke.'

'Yes, Doris,' I said. 'We did actually find that out when I went over with Mrs Dooley. But the housekeeper, Mrs Dooley's sister, had gone.'

'So you know the coppers think she done him in, then? The housekeeper?'

'Yes. Although why she would do so is unclear,' I said. 'It would seem that Mr Kaplan was very generous to her.'

Doris frowned. 'Who told you that, Mr H?'

'Well, Mr Kaplan's neighbour, a Mrs Stern . . .'

'Bessie the matchmaker?' Doris laughed. 'Wouldn't say nothing off-colour about Yiddisher people to no goy, that fat old frummer wouldn't! Yiddisher could murder all his neighbours and their kids and she'd swear blind he was a proper mensch. No, Mr H, old Kaplan treated that housekeeper like a dog, take it from me.'

'How do you know?' I said. As far as I had been aware, Doris's knowledge of paper-and-string men had been limited.

'I've asked around,' she said. 'I know you didn't say nothing when you come back from Spitalfields, and I know it's none of my business, but I'll always keep me ear to the ground for you when I can, Mr H.'

I smiled. She's a good girl, our Doris, very loyal. Her Alfie once told me that she's just so grateful for the work. 'She could be doing bloody awful stuff and she knows it,' he'd said. 'Her sister Ida works in munitions, twelve-hour shifts, comes 'ome sometimes with her skin the colour of jaundice.'

Some of the girls work in terrible places. Even our Aggie down at Tate & Lyle's isn't so badly off as some of them. She moans, of course, about the sugar dust getting into her eyes and making her throat dry, but it isn't like munitions. I don't either know or understand what they put into bombs, these days, but if it's anything like the stuff they used in my day, it's evil in every sense of the word.

'Er, there is something else too,' Doris said, interrupting what to her must have looked like me simply gawping into space.

'What's that?' I asked. Doris's face was unusually grave, which gave me cause for concern. 'Well?'

She moved a little closer to me and said, 'You know in Jewish places people talk? Everybody knows everybody . . .'

'Yes.' I frowned. 'Doris?'

She waved a hand in a flustered way across her face. 'Well, I heard you was with a woman, Hannah Jacobs, not been seen down our way for years.'

At this point I didn't know what to think. That Hannah had been recognised didn't surprise me – after all, she had grown up in Spitalfields. But what her old friends and neighbours knew about her life subsequent to that, I didn't know. Although from Doris's nervous tone I didn't imagine it could be anything good.

'She's an acquaintance,' I said lightly. 'Why?'

'Well,' Doris said, 'it's just that if you're going to visit real frummers, like Bessie Stern, Hannah Jacobs ain't the best person to take along with you.'

'Why not?'

'Because of what she done,' Doris said. And then, seeing the complete lack of recognition on my face, she continued, 'Hannah Jacobs's parents are frummers. Hassidics – you know, with the hats and locks and wigs, like Bessie Stern. Their kids don't go to the Jewish Free School, they're all too bloody religious to do what everyone else does. But anyway, years ago Hannah Jacobs, frummers' daughter, ups and says she wants to marry this Christian boy. Well, they're not having none of that so they tell her it's this bloke or them and she chooses the boy. So they chuck her out. Her father puts his face to the wall, says she's dead . . .'

'Says *she's* dead?' As far as I was concerned Hannah's parents were dead, or so she had told me. 'So did she marry . . .' I felt my heart thump as my voice gave up on the question I didn't know I really wanted answered. Hannah had lied to me.

'No,' Doris said, 'his family wouldn't have her at the finish. I don't think they ever would. Probably just using her, if you know what I mean. Never knew what happened to Hannah Jacobs. Not until you turned up with her causing a scandal, Mr H. How do you know—'

'A friend of Hannah, Miss Jacobs, died some years ago and I . . .'

'Oh, you arranged the funeral. I see.'

'Yes.'

Another girl who had lived, briefly, and then died beneath Dot Harris's roof. Another one with a Jewish name and no family beyond the other girls she worked the streets alongside – or, rather, no family that wanted to acknowledge her existence. Why hadn't Hannah told me? Even knowing, as I do, how strict the Hassidic Jews can be, I felt hurt that she hadn't seen fit to tell me about this. I'd always liked to think that I was more than just a customer to Hannah. And maybe I was. After all, she had taken a risk, albeit one I didn't know about at the time, in going with Pearl, Velma and me to Spitalfields. She must have known that people, especially Bessie Stern, would be hostile to her and yet she'd done it anyway. I liked to think it was for me.

'Look, all I'm saying is,' Doris said, 'if you go there again it might be best to take someone other than Hannah Jacobs. All right?'

'Yes . . .' Not that I felt I was really, but I thanked Doris for what she'd said and then, looking at my watch, I realised I needed to get over to East Ham pretty smartish.

One of my dad's old mates had been killed by an incendiary over there and Hancock's were honouring a long-ago-given promise to do right by old Eddie Smith buckshee. However, things didn't start very promisingly, which was made worse by the fact that I was now troubled and upset by what Doris had just told me. I'd always hoped that Hannah and I had honesty between us if nothing else.

I didn't even have to see my driver Walter Bridges: Arthur's terrified face said it all.

'I'm afraid Walter's not very well, Mr H,' the boy said nervously, as I walked into the yard. The hearse was clean, prepared, and the horses were dressed and ready and everything would have been fine had not Walter been lying unconscious on the ground in front of me. The smell coming off him was a mixture of beer and urine. He'd done a right job on himself this time.

'Well, I'll have to drive then, won't I?' I said, through clenched teeth.

'But you're conducting, Mr H, you always—'

'Well, this time I'll not be able to conduct, will I?' I said. 'This time I'll have to bloody well drive!'

I thought about taking Walter home quickly on my way out, then thought better of it and flung him into the stable. Except when a raid is on, most of the time I just get on with things. Life's hard for everyone these days – the food's 'rotten', there isn't always water, everything's filthy, you never know whether you or any of those you love are going to live till morning . . . But you take it and you take it and then something like Hannah's, to me, pointless lies, or someone like bleeding Walter Bridges and his sodding milk stout, comes along and suddenly you go absolutely barmy.

'If I didn't have no choice but to employ someone like Walter Bridges then he'd be out!' I said to Arthur, as we drove slowly down the Barking Road.

'Yes, Mr H.'

Hunched men with hands like my mother's took off their flat caps out of respect as we passed. Old dockers, their bodies wrecked by work and damp, wondering when the hearse would be coming for them. But although I noticed, I wasn't touched by this as I can be. I was far too angry for that.

'I'm not paying him for today,' I said, 'so it's his loss. Won't get a brass farthing from me, Arthur, I tell you!'

'No . . .'

How Arthur and me got through poor old Eddie's funeral with any degree of dignity I will never know. I couldn't conduct, my mind was boiling with anger, and we, just the two of us, looked a shambles. But when we got back to the shop a smartly dressed stranger was waiting to see me and all but took my mind off my other troubles.

Chapter Nine

'**M**r Hancock, my name is Blatt,' the man said. He gave me a card with his name and business address in gold lettering on it. It was somewhere in Knightsbridge. He was, so this card declared, a solicitor. Older than me, by a few years I should imagine, he was also immaculately groomed and obviously wealthy. What Mr Blatt might want with an East End undertaker was, as yet, a mystery.

'How can I help you, Mr Blatt?' I said.

Doris, who had already apparently made this man several cups of tea, went to make another for both of us. As she passed me she said, 'Don't worry, Mr H, I'll use the same leaves as before.'

'Thank you, Doris.'

She left me with this dark, unsmiling man.

'I am Pearl Dooley's solicitor,' Blatt said. 'I understand you've had some involvement with Mrs Dooley, Mr Hancock.'

'I went with her to try to help her find her sister,' I said.

122

'When her husband died, her mother-in-law threw her out. I was sorry for her, and tried to do what I could to put her in contact with her relatives.'

'And did you find this sister?'

'No.'

He looked down at the floor, then up again. 'Mr Hancock, I need to speak to Mrs Dooley's daughter, Velma.'

'Well, she isn't here,' I said. 'I'm worried about her, really. I've asked the police to look for her.'

'The police told me she'd been staying here.'

'She was, yes,' I said, 'but, as I'm sure they must've told you, after she'd given her statement to the police she just took off. I don't know where she's gone.'

'What about family?'

'The Dooleys chucked both her and her mother out,' I said. 'And beyond Mrs Dooley's sister Ruby in Spitalfields, the one we couldn't find, I don't know.'

'No other relatives living locally?'

'I know she's got two other sisters,' I said. 'They've all got names of precious stones, those girls. I think one was called Amber. If you don't mind my asking, Mr Blatt, how come you're working for Mrs Dooley? I mean, it isn't every day that a woman from Canning Town gets herself a Knightsbridge solicitor.'

He smiled, which made him look even more spare and hawk-like than he already was. 'I gather from the police that you are aware of some of the details regarding Pearl Dooley's background,' he said. 'Specifically her mother and who she was.'

'Yes.'

'It was you who, as it were, raised the alarm *vis-à-vis* Kevin Dooley, was it not, Mr Hancock?'

'Well, yes . . .'

'Without at the time, I understand, having any knowledge about the life and career of Pearl's mother, Victorine, and her very similar *modus operandi*.'

Luckily for me I'd got into the grammar school so I knew what he was on about. I'd quite enjoyed my Latin classes.

'No. Although I've learned this and that since.'

'I was Victorine Reynolds's solicitor,' Blatt said. 'With Mr Couch, her barrister, I tried to convince the court that Harold Neilson's death was as much his own doing as Victorine's.'

I frowned. 'What do you mean?'

'That his acts of violence towards her, over a long period of time I should add, drove the poor woman to kill him in defence of herself and her youngest child, Opal.'

Opal. That was the other name.

'But unfortunately we failed and Mr Justice Morgan handed down the death penalty.' He shook his head sadly at the memory of it. 'Poor Victorine, she was so worried about her daughters. Wanted them to stay together, had visions of a family living on after her, as it were. But it didn't work out.'

'Pearl told me they were orphaned,' I said.

Blatt leaned forward and lowered his voice. 'They all have different fathers,' he said. 'God knows who they are or were. Who outside can fathom the shady world of female prostitution, Mr Hancock?'

'Who indeed?' I said, with what I knew was a guilty swallow. 'So, do you know what happened to the girls after their mother was executed?'

Doris came back in with the tea at that point. Only when she'd gone did Blatt, after lighting up a fag, continue.

'Ruby, who's the eldest, Pearl and Amber were sent to an orphanage,' he said. 'Opal, who was only eight at the time, was, I believe, put up for adoption. Victorine killed Harold Neilson, Mr Hancock, but I don't believe that Pearl murdered her husband in the same fashion, do you?'

'I don't know,' I responded honestly. 'It seems unlikely.'

'Murder, or rather murderous tendencies, cannot be inherited like some sort of disease,' he said, with passion in his voice. 'It's just too fantastic.'

'Maybe,' I said, not wanting to give my opinion either way to this unknown man as yet. 'But if she or anyone else, for that matter, is innocent, I know that we have a duty to see the authorities know it. The truth is important, especially in war-time. People are frightened. The truth is all they have to hang on to, you know . . .'

'Absolutely! Absolutely!' I'd gone off a bit and I could tell that he was humouring me. I could see in his eyes he knew I wasn't quite the ticket.

And then he asked me what I knew. He had, of course, spoken to Pearl and the police so he knew about the abortion and Dot Harris's denial of it.

'Do you think that Pearl indeed had an abortion performed on her, Mr Hancock?' he said, after I'd finished.

'I don't know,' I replied. 'How can I? But I think it's a possibility, whatever Dot Harris might say. Otherwise why would Pearl own up to such a thing?'

'Precisely!' Blatt smiled. 'Exactly! The abortionist, this Harris woman, has to be lying!'

'Dot Harris does have something of a reputation,' I said, without thinking.

'Oh, so you know this woman, do you?' Blatt came back immediately. 'How so?'

I felt my face redden but I managed to speak in spite of this and quite quickly, even if I do say so myself. 'Everyone round here knows Dot Harris, Mr Blatt,' I replied. 'As I said, she does have a reputation for helping girls out when they're in trouble.'

'Mmm.' He looked at me with a hard if also rather amused eye. No wonder he had his office in Knightsbridge, I thought. He had to be an astute man, mainly because I felt him looking into my own guilty soul. He could, I felt, sense I'd been in Dot's house – knowing what she was and what she did, going to one of her girls to satisfy my lusts. But, then, even as Mr Blatt had to know, we're not in the habit of giving up our own in this part of the world. Young girls get in trouble and Dot Harris, just like me, has to make a living. However, Mr Blatt's understanding of this didn't seem, perhaps, all that I thought it should be.

'A terrible thing to destroy a child like that,' he said, as his face gradually assumed a grave aspect. Almost faraway now, he said, 'It's such a waste! Like yourself, I imagine,

Mr Hancock, I served in the Great War. Leaves one with such an abhorrence for loss of life!'

But I didn't answer. His comment about the first lot didn't need one. And although I knew he'd use the abortion as a defence for Pearl, it was obvious to me that he didn't approve of such practices. Not in any circumstances. I know what the Church and the law have to say on the matter, but I find it hard to agree with that myself. Maybe I've buried too many girls who should maybe have had abortions. I've also buried more than my share of poor, twisted and deformed infants, who would probably have been better had they not lived at all. If only it could be done properly, by doctors. But it never will be.

Mr Blatt didn't stay long after that and, to be honest, I was quite pleased about it. I preferred to think that Pearl was innocent, but I felt that with Blatt there was a forcing of that position I didn't feel comfortable with. I knew he was her brief and had to be like that, to some extent. But he was a bit much for me, I decided, Mr Blatt.

'Makes you wonder what's going on with those Reynolds women,' I said to Ken, as I swept the yard at the back of the shop. 'Pearl and Kevin, Ruby and Shlomo. Funny Mr Blatt never asked me about that.'

'Perhaps it's because it ain't his case,' Ken said.

'Yes, but it could have some connection to Pearl or, rather, there could be a possibility of that,' I said. 'I mean, it does seem a bit of a coincidence that both those sisters' fellows should die in mysterious circumstances.'

'Well, maybe the women did do them,' Ken said. 'I

mean, H, women do kill, some of them quite pretty women too.'

'Yes, I know,' I said. 'It's Velma I really feel bad about. If I hadn't had all those doubts I did about Kevin and how he died, she'd be with her mum now instead of God knows where and in who knows what danger. I wish I knew where she was.'

'Maybe you do.'

I looked up at him, frowning.

'Bethnal Green tube?' Ken said. 'Ain't that where she said she went that night with her mum?'

'Yes . . .' Although whether she'd go back there on her own, I didn't know. If she was on her own. 'But shouldn't I tell the coppers?'

'What, and frighten the kid rigid? Nah!'

'Yes, but on my own, I . . .'

'It's got to be worth a shot,' Ken said, as he made his way out into the back alley behind the shop. 'She trusts you. Look, someone's coming!'

'Yes, but . . .'

I was about to say, 'Yes, but I can't go down there, not down a tube,' but he'd gone. Looking as he does, his face in the state it is, Ken isn't comfortable around those he doesn't know. There's nothing for these blokes, these heroes of the trenches, whose wounds are so bad people shrink from them in the street. King and Government don't care, that's for sure. If they did they'd do something for the poor buggers – they'd think more than twice about getting into another war too. So Ken just took off as he always does when strangers turn up.

'Just watch yourself, H,' I heard him say, as he walked down the alley. 'Just make sure you can always see your way to the exit.'

Too bloody right, I thought, as I rested the broom against the privy wall. As well as being underground, the tube stations are hazardous, packed with people in all states and conditions. Afraid and starved of daylight, some of them down there can be funny about their 'pitches' on the platform. I've heard stories about women effing and blinding at each other, fights blocking exits, blood on the platforms – everything.

'Francis Hancock?' The voice, although not that deep, was gruff and almost without a doubt unfriendly.

I looked up into the face of its owner and noticed that there were two other faces, one on either side of it. None of them were in any way appealing to me and all of them bore a resemblance to the late Kevin Dooley.

'Yes,' I said, 'who wants to—'

'Never mind who wants to know,' the speaker, who was, I reckoned, about twenty-five, said. 'Just listen and learn, Hancock.'

The one on the speaker's left very obviously punched his right palm with his knuckleduster-crowned fist. I can handle myself in a fight, I know, but I'm also good at recognising when I'm beaten. I stood quite still, waiting to hear and learn.

'We've heard a rumour,' the speaker said, 'that some people think that murdering slag Pearl Dooley didn't kill her husband.'

He looked at me as if he wanted a response, but when

I did open my mouth to speak the creature on his right, a small, weaselly-looking thing, darted forward and put one of his hands round my throat.

'I said to fucking listen!' the speaker said.

Seeing as how I could hardly breathe I didn't have a lot of choice. So, wondering just how indiscreet Fred Bryant had been about my assistance to Pearl, I waited for the man to speak again.

'Now, we know that you've helped the slag, Hancock,' he said, 'so don't bother to try and lie. Not that I'm interested in what happened in the past, you understand. It's the future as bothers me.' He moved his face, which smelled of beer, close to mine. 'If I hear you've been helping her again . . .'

'She's in Holloway,' I gagged. 'It was me helped put her there!'

'Yeah, I know,' he said. 'But you took her in once when my old mum chucked her out. I don't like that. People don't usually cross my family like that. I want you to have nothing more to do with the murdering bitch and I want you to tell me if you so much as sniff her bastard kid.'

This Dooley obviously didn't share his old mum's dislike of swear words.

'Why?'

He went to punch me in the stomach, I even tensed to receive the blow, but then he changed his mind. 'Because the kid'll defend her mother and I don't want that slag to get away with murdering my brother.'

'How do you know Pearl killed your brother?' I said. 'You can't.'

'Because I just fucking know, right?' he yelled. His face was bright purple now, his already coarse features stretched into an ugly mask of hatred. 'Because no one else would've dared touch our Kev! Because she'd had a go at him before, making threats, and because she's a lying, baby-killing tart!'

The weasel-faced one loosened his grip on my throat while what I assumed was his brother collected his thoughts.

'So, what I'm saying, Hancock, is this,' he panted. 'Help that slag again and you'll have to deal with us. Do you understand?'

'Yes.'

'I'm not talking about a bit of a punch-up either,' he said. 'Know what I mean?'

'Yes.' The possibilities were endless. They could break my kneecaps, cut off one of my ears, even shoot me with a gun some older brother or uncle had hidden away after the Great War. A lot of old soldiers still have guns. My old Webley, unused since the first lot, lay in the top drawer of the tallboy in my bedroom at the time. I thought then that perhaps I ought to try to find the ammo at some point.

'So we understand each other, then?' he said, as he attempted to tower over me, without much success.

'Yes,' I said. Isn't it strange the way that so many short men have this bullying side to their nature?

The weasel let me go and then, with what sounded like a growl made through his gritted, broken teeth, the leader led his troops out of the yard and into the alleyway.

I wasn't so much shaken up as angry. I knew that if the

Dooleys cut up rough there wasn't a lot I could do about it, even if I did get my old revolver out. But that they should have come into my yard and threatened me made me furious – and, I have to say, suspicious. I know, God knows I do, how important family is in the East End. I've seen rival families fight almost to the death over this, that or the other. I've seen women launch themselves at other women and their kids in the street and we all know all about nobbling witnesses to a crime. But in this case I did wonder. I couldn't know any more than anyone else whether Pearl was telling the truth about where she was when Kevin died. Even if she'd been to Dot Harris's, the old girl had to lie about what she'd been doing at the time – and, what was more, the police had to know that too. But then the police would also know that they'd have to get the whole affair sorted very quickly. Murder isn't good for morale in a city so wounded as our old London and a quick clear-up has to be favourite. Justice withers and can die in war-time, as I know.

But I wondered. If Pearl didn't kill her husband, then who did? And did it have more to do with her and who she was, her dubious parentage, or was it just down to Kevin and who he'd been? Had he just had relations with, and possibly roughed up, a street woman who then took her revenge? Even though Hannah hadn't heard anything like this on her travels, it didn't mean that such a thing was impossible. After all, there are other places round here besides Rathbone Street for blokes with needs to go. Also, Kevin Dooley hadn't been a popular bloke. A violent drunk, although his mum and Pearl – so she said – had loved him but I wondered about whether anyone else had. After all, just because someone's family it doesn't mean we have to like them. It doesn't mean we can't hate them. Perhaps there was a family member who had had a problem with Kevin. Perhaps this person was who the Dooley boys were protecting when they threatened me. They had, after all, kicked up quite a stink and were very certain about Pearl's guilt. I decided then and there to do something I'd never done before – something that just the thought of made my skin crawl. I did it alone too – without the coppers and without Hannah. I wasn't ready to see her just then.

I'd heard that some people spend all day down tube stations, but I never understood what this meant until I went to Bethnal Green that evening. I walked there, through the rain, past some people crying and others singing. You can see every feeling in this city now. You can see firm chins and stout spirits even in the most awful circumstances and you can see despair that goes far beyond the loss of hope. A woman staring into a rain-filled hole, her eyes dry and numb as if they're blind. Makes you wonder what or who is down that hole. But unless there's just been a raid, you probably don't ask. Whatever it was is dead now.

I have so few clothes these days I have to wear what I wear for work or I'd go naked most of the time. So there I was, all in black, the veil around my hat sodden with rainwater, hanging down the back of my neck, walking through the shattered remains of people's lives and what was left of their property. Like Death himself. I could see the marks of fear in their eyes as I passed. I heard the way many of them went silent as they looked at me. Maybe some thought they were suffering visions, finally gone mad with it all.

Even when I got to the tube station that illusion continued.

I asked the bloke at the ticket office for a platform ticket and he said, 'Someone copped it down there, did they, pal?'

'Not that I know of,' I said, as I raked in my pockets for coppers.

'Oh,' he replied. 'Not here on business, then?'

'I hope not.'

'You know they're all packed in like sardines down there, don't you?' he said.

I felt my face flush with anxiety, but I smiled weakly and walked away without answering.

It's the smell as hits you first. Musty and rank. A mixture of rain-sodden clothes, fag smoke, sweat, urine and something sweet and sickly, like milk. All of it overlaid with the usual smells of the tube: the wood of the carriages, oil, the brilliantine on the men's heads as they get out at the stations. The trains keep on running, the passengers getting off on to platforms that serve as parlours, bedrooms, kitchens and brothels.

A train had just pulled in when I got down on to the platform. I had to press myself against the wall so that shop girls and old clerks, tailors and soldiers home on leave could get to the exit. Stepping gingerly over mums trying to calm excited youngsters, the passengers would pick their way, saying, 'Sorry, love,' 'Excuse me,' or 'Mind out the bleedin' way, Missus,' according to how they felt. As I looked down the eastbound platform, I felt my heart sink. How on earth was I ever going to find Velma among this lot? There were thousands of them, hordes of jabbering people, mostly in brown or grey coats. They looked like a great mat of cockroaches spread out on the floor in front of me. Just to breathe I had to concentrate. I was so scared and could have lost myself to my fear so easily. To prove to myself I could do it, I raised an arm a little bit and then I started to feel better.

As soon as I began to move among the largely seated crowd, the problems I'd experienced earlier with people outside reappeared.

'Fucking hell, you know when Death's in town, don't you?' one bright spark said. 'Bloody smell!'

A lot of people say that all of us, in my line of work, smell of the french polish we use to shine up the coffins but I've never noticed it myself so I just pushed on without comment.

'Here, you've not come for Gracie Rose, have you?'

The woman, who was probably about fifty, had one hand on the bottom of my coat while the other one clutched on to an older woman sitting beside her.

'No . . .'

'Well, her chest was shocking until about an hour ago,' the woman said. 'Then it all went quiet. I could well believe she'd passed on.'

'God love her!' her companion said, shaking her head as she did so.

'I'm actually looking for a living person,' I said. 'A young girl, about fifteen, thin. She's on her own . . .'

'She your daughter?'

'No,' I said, and then I added, 'She's been staying with our family. Her mum's bombed out and—'

'Oh, poor kid,' the fifty-year-old said.

'God love her,' her companion chipped in.

But no, they hadn't seen a girl like that on her own so I went on my way, aware that the two women and, indeed, many other people were watching my progress. If Velma was trying to hide herself away I was going to be easy to avoid. Between being asked whether I'd 'come for Eddie', 'been sent by the Reverend Goody' or being told to 'Tell that bastard Cox he can have his money when our Gordon's been paid', there wasn't much chance I could pass unnoticed. It was only when I moved down one of the small corridors that connects the eastbound to the westbound platform, where most people seemed to be asleep, that I managed to regain anything like a bit of peace. In fact if she hadn't pulled on my coat to catch my attention, I would most certainly have stepped right over Velma. But she did pull my coat, which made me look down and see her dirty, desperate little face. She must, I thought, have finally got tired of all the noise, the smell and probably the hunger too.

The Duchess had knocked up some chapattis that morning, one of which I'd grabbed for later. It was wrapped in greaseproof in my coat pocket. I wondered what the hell Velma would make of it.

'You should keep away from me, Mr Hancock,' Velma

said, as she sat up and I gingerly slotted myself down beside her.

I handed over the chapatti. 'Eat this,' I said. And when she opened it and pulled a face I said, 'It's an Indian pancake. My mum made it.'

I knew that Velma and the Duchess had got on famously. The girl began on the chapatti without further ado and with a ravenousness that was painful to watch. Christ knows when she'd last eaten. I rolled up and then lit a fag.

Once Velma had finished the chapatti she turned to me and said, 'It ain't safe for you to be with me, Mr Hancock.'

'Why's that, Velma?'

She put her head down and hugged her knees to her chest.

'Is it because of the Dooleys?'

She looked up again sharply, her face white with fear. 'They said that my mum was a murderer,' she said. 'They said she was going to hang and that if anyone tried to help her they'd kill them.'

'Who said this?'

'Johnny. Outside the police station.'

A deep, sucking sound heralded the arrival of a train and so, for the moment, Velma and I didn't speak as the rails first hummed and then clattered under its weight. As the people got off, I put out my hand to Velma in case we should become separated. After a moment's hesitation, she took it and we remained joined by our hands until all the passengers had either gone to the exit or joined the throng on the platform.

'Who's Johnny?' I asked Velma, as soon as the train had gone on its way.

'One of Kevin's younger brothers,' she said. 'There's Johnny, Ernie and Dickie, but it's Johnny who's really mad about Kevin and Mum and everything. And Martine. She's in a right state, she is.'

'Is that Kevin's sister?'

'No. She's Johnny's missus. She was really cut up about Kevin. She liked him. When they told her he was dead she cried and cried. Johnny had to slap her to stop it in the end.'

It was said with such innocence that it made me almost ashamed to have the thoughts I was having. But I had them anyway. All the men who'd visited me that afternoon had been younger than Kevin Dooley; the one who'd threatened me was probably Johnny. Johnny whose missus, Martine, was so devastated by the death of her brother-in-law she was reduced to hysteria. What, I wondered, was Johnny really so 'mad' about? And why was he so convinced of Pearl's guilt? Did he, perhaps, know something no one else did? What, I couldn't help thinking, had Johnny been doing on the night of Kevin's death? The family had supposedly all been together. But Johnny's behaviour made me wonder.

'What do Johnny and his brothers do, Velma?' I asked.

'I dunno what Johnny does,' she said, 'but Martine always has nice things. Ernie's in the navy and Dickie's waiting to go in the forces. He's only seventeen.'

You come across people like Johnny Dooley, blokes whose occupation is 'uncertain', in pubs, down back alleys. I even had one come to the shop once. He'd lifted his hat, put a big metal can in front of me and asked me if I wanted to buy any petrol. I took him out the back, showed him Rama and Sita, then threw him into the street.

'Velma, do you know of anyone who has anything against your mum?'

'What do you mean?'

'Anyone who doesn't like her.'

'Only Kevin's mum,' she said. 'Johnny and all the others used to be all right with her until now. She was quite pally with Martine who did used to sometimes try and stop Kevin when he hit Mum. Sometimes he did too – stop, that is. But then all this happened and now they all hate Mum, even Martine . . .'

Up above, over the sound of the voices and the bodies down the tube, the piercing sound of the air-raid sirens wailed into life. For a moment, everything else went silent. People stopped whatever they were doing and looked up as if searching for the source of the warning up above.

'The Jerries are coming,' Velma said.

'Y-y-yes.'

And I was deep underground.

Velma took my hand and said, 'It's all right, Mr Hancock, we're safe down here.'

I tried to smile but knew from her face that I'd failed. Over on the eastbound platform they started singing 'Roll Out The Barrel'.

Chapter Ten

Once the all-clear had sounded I persuaded Velma to come back with me. I told her about the visit I'd had from Johnny and his brothers and what they'd said, but I reckoned that if she stayed in the flat for the time being, she'd be all right. Anyway, the poor kid had to go somewhere and I knew that, if nothing else, the Duchess would take care of her. There was also Mr Blatt to consider. He wanted to speak to Velma so he could use what she said about the night Kevin died to help defend her mother. So, all in all, it was better she was with us, in spite of the risk from the Dooleys, for the time being.

When I got back to the shop, however, I found more than the coffin containing Cherry Hazlitt waiting for me. I decided to bring Velma in through the back door so the first person I saw as I entered the premises was Walter Bridges mucking out the horses. Arthur, who was doing his bit too, quickly made himself scarce. I told Velma to follow the boy in and wait for me in the kitchen.

'I'm ever so sorry about—' Walter began.

'If you ever let me down like that again, you'll have your cards,' I said, without looking at him. I was too tired to want to listen to his apology. 'We've an interment this afternoon at two,' I continued, 'a woman from a family of women, so you'll have to drive and bear, and if I smell so much as a drop of the sauce on you I'll hit you so hard not even your own mother'd recognise you after I've done.'

I went inside without another word to find Fred Bryant waiting to see me.

'You found the kid, then?' he said, as he watched Velma walk up the stairs with Nan. 'Should've called us, Mr H.'

'Yes. Well. Good, isn't it?' I said. I didn't want to dwell on the fact that I'd been more successful than the police. After all, Fred and I knew that.

'You know her mum's solicitor, Mr Blatt, wants to talk to her?' Fred said. 'Building her defence case and that.'

'Yes. I'll let him know,' I replied. 'But I don't want the Dooleys knowing too, Fred. They threatened Velma. She isn't safe with them.'

'They're the nearest thing to family she's got.'

'Fred, she's frightened of them,' I said. 'If you let them know where she is, you could be putting her in danger. You saw for yourself how they called abuse after her when she left the station. She was so scared she wouldn't even come back here and tell me!'

'So, she want to make a complaint or—'

'No,' I said. 'But look, Fred, they not only threatened Velma, they – or, rather, Johnny Dooley – threatened me too.'

'Oh, so do *you* want to make—'

'No, I don't want to make a complaint either,' I said. 'Just keep that family away from here.' I pulled the policeman to one side and lowered my voice. 'Look, Fred, the Dooleys say they were all together on the night that Kevin died, all except Pearl and Velma.'

Fred frowned. 'Now, you know I can't discuss police work with you, Mr H.'

'Johnny Dooley wants Pearl to go down,' I said. 'I don't think he cares too much whether she's guilty or not, but there's something very dodgy about him.' I didn't go into what I'd made of Velma's innocent observations about Kevin and Martine Dooley. After all, they were a child's observations.

'And how do you know Pearl isn't guilty?' Fred replied smartly.

'I don't,' I said. 'I just think that Johnny's a bit . . . over-eager, shall we say?'

'Evidence seems to point in Pearl Dooley's direction at the moment . . .'

'Yes, but . . .'

'Everyone but her has got an alibi,' Fred said. 'Vi and all her lot, including Johnny and his missus, were down their Anderson. Went down as soon as the siren went. Watkins next door saw 'em go.'

'Yes, but hard families like the Dooleys,' I began, 'they can intimidate . . .'

'If other people support their story then that's that,' Fred responded bluntly. 'Only Kevin, Pearl and Velma were out that night. He went out lunch-time and was in and out of pubs or making a general nuisance of himself in the street all day. His wife and her girl went out at about six and came home in the early hours of the next morning. Gawd knows where they'd been.'

'Well, Dot Harris . . .'

'Dot Harris, she says, spent the night alone,' Fred said. 'Like a lot of the old folk, she won't go down no shelter. Them "ladies" she lives with don't even bother to knock for her now. Whatever happened, no one saw Dot, Pearl or her girl all night.'

When the bombing started Hannah told me that Dot wouldn't use the Anderson one of her mate Bella's admirers had put up in the garden. Pearl could have been with Dot or, equally, elsewhere. Unlike Johnny she didn't have an alibi. Also unlike Johnny, she wasn't threatening people. She was just, so far as I could tell, continuing to maintain her innocence.

'Anyway,' Fred said, after a pause, 'we've got Pearl in custody. She ain't going nowhere so we got plenty of time to get all the evidence we need. There's a war on but we'll do it.'

I shook my head gloomily. What Fred had said put me in mind of Ken's comments about the coppers having Pearl tried and hung already.

But then Doris arrived and, briefly, we all talked together about other things until she finally went upstairs to get the company books. We'd had a bit of money from one of our customers and Doris wanted to make a proper record of it. She's very meticulous like that, which is just as well because I'm not. I do the funerals, I'm down there with the dead, as it should be.

Once I was on my own with him again, I said to Fred, 'So, what do you want then, Fred? You must've come over here for some reason.'

'Oh, yes, I did,' the policeman said, as he put his hand into one of his pockets. 'I come to give you this.'

It was a small piece of paper, folded in half.

'It's from your mate Pearl Dooley,' Fred said. 'But it's all right. Guv'nor up Holloway's seen it and my guv'nor down the station. Ain't nothing bad.'

He left out that he and I both knew that Fred had read it too, but I let that pass and just said, 'Well, that's all right, then, isn't it?'

'Yeah.'

Irony is something that is easily lost on Fred Bryant. So I let him witter on until he got bored with waiting for me to open Pearl's letter and left. I occasionally punish his nosiness with just small acts of cruelty like this. As soon as he was out, I read it.

It said the following:

Dear Mr Hancock,
I'm writing to you because although I've got Mr Blatt now I think I can trust you. The coppers let me see Velma for a minute and she told me she told you everything. I know you put me in here but I think it's only because you want what's right. So do I. Because Ruby is in trouble as well as me I wonder if it's anything to do with our mum and what she done. I wonder if someone knew where I went the night Kev died and killed him in a way so it looks like it could have been

me. I don't know who but I'm afraid it might be someone who knows who the Reynolds sisters are and wishes us and those close to us harm. I'm worried now about my sister Amber. I haven't seen my other sister Opal since the coppers took her away when they come to get Mum. She was little and was adopted. Amber come with me and Ruby to the Nazareth Sisters Orphanage in Southend. She left there after me and I left in 1920. I don't know what she did then, but the Sisters might know. Could you please try and find out where she is and tell her what's happening? I know I've got a nerve, but I'm afraid for her.

Regards, Pearl Therese Dooley.

The letter read as if Pearl was afraid that someone, probably someone with a grudge, was setting up her and her sisters as murderers. To me, notwithstanding the way Kevin had died, it all seemed rather far-fetched that someone should do such a thing to innocent women after so many years had passed. But I showed it to Velma who, after asking who Mr Blatt was and what his connection to her mother might be, said, 'Well, if he's her lawyer then really he should look for Amber. You ain't got time to go gallivanting down to Southend, have you, Mr Hancock?'

'You know that Mr Blatt wants to talk to you, Velma,' I said. 'About your mum.'

'Yes, but I don't think she trusts him,' Velma said darkly, as she looked down at the paper again. 'The letter sort of says it, really.' Which, in the sense of what it didn't say, was true. 'She certainly don't trust him like she trusts you.' Then she asked, 'Why do you care so much, Mr Hancock, about Mum and me?'

'I've been puzzling over that one,' Nan said acidly, as she came in and sat down at the kitchen table, a dirty chamois leather fresh from the front parlour windows still in her hands.

It wasn't an easy question to answer – not because I couldn't, more that I was afraid they wouldn't understand.

But I gave it a go anyway. 'Well, first, I don't think it's right to kill people,' I said. 'And when I cleaned your stepfather's body and saw that mark on his chest I knew someone had taken his life. Even if I hadn't met him that night and spoken to him, I think I would've known that something was wrong.'

'How?'

I shrugged. 'I don't know. My old dad used to have a name for it when a body comes in you don't feel right about. He called it the Undertaker's Third Eye.'

'Third eye?'

'It means seeing beyond to what really happened to that person,' Nan said. 'It's a gift that allowed my father to raise the alarm with the police over more than one murdered soul.'

'But all that aside,' I said, 'the point is, I think that if the law or the army or whoever want to kill people for committing crimes then they have to be very sure about who they're condemning. It's murder, to me, to shoot or hang a person who hasn't committed a crime. I don't care if it's a mistake or not. That's no excuse. It doesn't matter if there's a war on or not. You can't just execute people and—'

'Frank!'

Nan had heard a lot of this before, when I'd tried to tell her and the Duchess about what had really happened out there in the mud of Flanders. But she hadn't wanted to listen then any more than she did now. Most people don't, especially when your eyes, those of a grown man, fill with tears.

'Not in front of the kid, Frank!'

I turned away from my sister, towards Velma, and tried a smile. 'So we always look for the truth, is what I'm saying, love.' I wiped my eyes with my fingers and continued, 'So, suppose the good old Essex seaside—'

'But you ain't got time to go to Southend!' Velma said. 'That could take all day.'

'Yes,' I said, 'and I am busy in the next few days. But you could go, couldn't you, Velma? I'm sure you're quite able to ask about your aunt at the convent. Nuns are, after all, good people. They'll help you if they can. You could even take Miss Nancy with you, if she'll go.'

Nan looked up sharply. 'What?'

'How do you fancy a day out in Southend visiting some Nazareth nuns?' I said to my sister. 'I'll pay your train fare and—'

'You know the trains get stopped every five minutes now, don't you, Frank?' Nan said. 'They're packed too. And there's no buffet.'

'Well, take sandwiches and a Thermos,' I said. 'I'll make it up myself for you if you like.'

'Oh, I think I can make a sandwich or two, Frank. That's not the problem. But what about Mum?'

'Well, if you go tomorrow, Aggie'll be off shift and she can look after the Duchess,' I said. 'All you have to do is ask the nuns about Pearl's sister and then . . .'

'Well?'

'If she's still in Southend, go and visit her, if you can. Take your mum's letter,' I said to Velma. 'Show it to her.'

'And if this Amber isn't in Southend, if she's gone somewhere else?' Nan asked.

I sighed. 'Then you come home,' I said. 'Maybe you could buy a pint of whelks for tea.'

'Frank!'

Velma laughed and then, obviously happy about the prospect of a trip out, she left the room. Alone with my sister now, I said, 'It'll also get her away from here and out of the reach of those Dooley brothers for a bit.'

Nan, for whom all this trouble over a dead stranger was just that – trouble – said she'd do it anyway – for me.

Hannah said she was going to have to come and see me whether she went to Cherry Hazlitt's funeral or not. I didn't even know that she was there until we took the mourners back for the wake to old Mrs Hazlitt's house in Jedburgh Road.

'Roof come off last Thursday,' the old woman said, as she pointed one black-gloved hand at the shattered top half of her house. 'I've shut up the bedrooms. I ain't ready to be bombed out yet, not so long as the range works and

I've still got coal. You coming in for a glass of stout, are you, Mr Hancock?'

When I first heard that there were going to be a lot of women at Cherry's funeral, I imagined that they were going to be members of her family. A lot of funerals are only attended by women these days, on account of the call-up. But only the mum and a sister were related to the dead woman. The rest, like Hannah, were friends. Like Hannah too, the friends wore rather more makeup than the average girl and their language, even in the face of death, was 'colourful'.

'That's very kind of you, Mrs Hazlitt.'

'What about your lads? They want to come in for a drop and a ham sandwich?'

I looked at Arthur's face and then at Walter's anxious mug licking its lips in anticipation of a drink.

'No, thank you, Mrs Hazlitt,' I said. 'The lads have to look after the horses.'

I didn't look back at either of them as I went inside the house. I didn't dare.

All those girls were a bit much for me so I made a quick dash out into the yard, beer in one hand, a piece of Gala pie in the other. It was here that I saw Hannah. She was leaning against the Hazlitts' Anderson, smoking a fag and looking up at the shattered windows of one of the houses next door. I hadn't expected to see her so soon and, in view of what I'd so recently learned about her, her presence came as a shock.

'Cherry's brother Archie used to live there,' she said, as she pointed upwards with her fag. 'His wife and baby died from the blast in that house. Lucky he never come back from Dunkirk or he'd've been devastated. Fucking war!'

There were tears at the corners of her eyes, but I ignored them for the time being. I had to say what I needed to say so I just launched in with both feet, so to speak.

'So that pair of old frummers you took us to see in Spitalfields, they your parents, are they?' I asked, brutally, I knew.

Hannah turned to look at me, her face blasted as if by a lightning bolt.

'I know they're still alive, Hannah,' I continued. 'I know you left them for a Christian boy. I know it didn't work out. What I don't know is why you never told me.'

Hannah took a deep drag on her fag, then swallowed hard. 'How did you find out?'

'Just answer my question,' I said. 'Why?'

'What? You mean apart from the fact that you're only a customer?' Hannah said haughtily.

I reached out and pulled her roughly towards me. 'You know that's not true!' I said.

'It might be! For me!' Hannah hurled back violently. But then, as quickly as she'd lost her temper, she dissolved into tears. 'Why do you think I do what I do?' she said, as she sobbed against the buttons of my waistcoat. 'You think I can't do no better than selling my body?'

'Hannah . . .'

'Those people, those ones we met, were my parents long ago. But I shamed them,' Hannah said. 'I let that goy use me, I turned my back on my people and, when it all come to nothing, I went to the one place I could.' She looked up into my eyes. 'The street. They never ask you to leave on the street.'

I put my arms round her now. I bent down to kiss her. 'But you can trust *me*,' I said gently.

Mindful that others could come into the garden and see us at any moment – or, rather, that was how I read it then – Hannah pushed herself away from me. 'My family are Hassidic Jews,' she said. 'Do you know what that means, Mr H?'

'Not really.'

She looked down at the ground to where two of the Hazlitts' bantams pecked mindlessly around her feet. 'My father's a religious teacher,' she said. 'All Hassidic men are scholars. They devote themselves to study of the Torah while the women raise children to wait, as we all do, for the coming of the Messiah. Hassidic women, H, are religious, chaste, they wear wigs to cover their natural hair – vanity, see. And . . . Bessie Stern . . .'

'Yes, I know she's Hassidic,' I said.

'Well, she doesn't like me because of what I done,' Hannah said. 'You must've noticed how she didn't like me.'

'I could see that something wasn't right,' I said. By this time I was beginning to wish I'd never brought the subject up. Poor Hannah looked so sad. 'Look, love,' I said, 'I know it must've been very hard for you to take us to your parents. I'm sorry I got cross, but I just—'

'Bessie Stern the matchmaker come to see me this morning,' Hannah interrupted harshly.

Taken by surprise at the sudden change of subject and tone, I said, 'What? How did she know where to find you?'

'One Yiddisher leads to another. Give a man or a woman a name they understand, they can find that person. Whatever Yiddisher told you about my past will know that,' Hannah said bitterly.

I turned my head away, not wanting to mention the name Doris or even hint at her existence.

'So what did Bessie Stern come to see you about, Hannah?' I said after a pause.

'You,' Hannah said. 'She wanted to contact you.'

'So why didn't she? She knows my name. Knows I've got a shop.'

'Yes, but she don't *know* you, do she?' Hannah said. 'I mean, you ain't from our manor, are you? You're a goy. I may be a tart and one that she hates too, but that's still better than what you are in Bessie's eyes. And, anyway, at her size it was probably as much as she could do to get to Canning Town, much less schlep all the way over to Plaistow.'

I didn't like the harsh way she was speaking now. But partly because I'd caused it myself, I was trying to ignore it. 'So do you know what she wanted, then?' I said. 'With me?'

'She told me to tell you to go to the synagogue at nineteen Princelet Street, near to where she lives, as soon as you can.'

'Why? What for?'

'So you can find out more about Ruby Reynolds,' Hannah said. 'Maybe you'll learn why all the frummers seem to like her so much. She's a goy, like you, I don't understand it.'

I put out a hand to her, but Hannah flinched away. 'Maybe things have changed . . .'

'Yeah, and maybe Hitler's a friend of Churchill. Maybe my parents chucking me out never happened!' Hannah snapped back viciously.

'Hannah.' I reached out towards her again and, once again, she pulled away from me.

'I need to be on me own for a bit now,' she said wearily. 'I've told you what Bessie said, but now I need you to go.'

'Look, Hannah,' I said, 'I'm sorry I was angry. I'm sorry – maybe I presumed too much. But I do feel . . . things for you . . .'

'Yeah, all right. Don't go on. You going to the synagogue or not?'

'Yes. Well, I'll go after I've finished here,' I said. 'I'll make it the first thing I do.'

'Good.'

'Right.'

In the long silence that followed, I finished what was left of my beer, threw the crust of the Gala pie at the bantams and lit a fag. Eventually it was Hannah, still bitter and tearful, who broke the silence.

'She was a good girl, Cherry,' she said sadly. 'If only she'd kept her head down in raids. Silly cow! Even when she was with a customer she had to know what was going on outside all the time. Bit like you, Mr H. Always got to know what's happening and who's doing what. Got to know the truth. Dangerous. Least, it was for Cherry . . .'

My heart in my mouth now, I said, 'Are you trying to tell me something, Hannah?'

She looked away. 'I'm only saying that Spitalfields ain't your manor, Mr H. You don't understand the rules.' She turned back to me again. Her face was drawn with what looked like anxiety. 'Just be careful is what I say, Mr H. Remember that you ain't among your own and some people might not like that. I mean, look at Ruby Reynolds, out of her own place. She's come to grief.'

Dad had always found the Jews of Spitalfields very friendly. But I'm not Tom Hancock. I'm not even the same colour as he'd been, and things have moved on since Dad died. Since Mosley's Black Shirts, views in the East End have become entrenched. Although we're at war with Germany, there's still people about who favour fascism. The Jews tend to be of a socialistic mind, which is something I broadly support myself. But that view has its problems too and a lot of people don't trust those, like Albert Cox, they call the 'Commies'. The 'Commies' in their turn, and those who live among them, are not very open about what they do so any stranger in their area is suspect, as Pearl, Velma and I had found out when Hannah first took us over.

I left Hannah after that and went to speak to Mrs Hazlitt and her other daughter, Joan. I knew my girl needed to be alone for a bit. What I hadn't reckoned on was that she'd leave the wake without saying another word to anyone.

* * *

154

A horse-drawn hearse does tend to draw attention to itself and its occupants. But after we'd finished at the Hazlitts' house, and especially after my difficult conversation with Hannah, I didn't feel that inclined to walk to Spitalfields and getting a bus, or even a tram, is always a problem. Depending on bomb damage you can't be sure where your transport's going to start off or finish.

Young Arthur had some reservations. He thought the sight of the hearse might upset people, but he agreed to drive for me anyway. I said we'd park up on Commercial Street rather than going down into Spitalfields proper. I couldn't see any problem for him to park over by the Ten Bells or even in front of Christ Church. Besides, I had a feeling I should be discreet about going to Princelet Street. I left the boy and set off alone.

Number nineteen Princelet Street has had quite a history. Dad told me that, like a lot of the buildings in Spitalfields, the 'Princelet Synagogue', as he called it, had been built by the Huguenots. Being young at the time, I didn't know a Huguenot from a poke in the eye, but Dad soon told me that they were Protestant French people who'd come to London a long time ago to escape persecution. They really set the tone for the place, as it happened, the Huguenots, and after they went the Irish came and lodged in the building, escaping from the famine back at home. And when the Irish left, in came the Jews, escaping persecution in Russia and Poland and more lately in Germany too. The old Princelet Synagogue is a place well used to people hiding in its many rooms and cupboards.

As I entered the street, I did keep an eye open for the ample figure of Bessie Stern who, I knew, lived at number five. But she wasn't anywhere to be seen.

They're impressive buildings, the old Huguenot places in Spitalfields. At least three storeys high plus a cellar, many also have wooden attics built up on the roofs. In their day they were elegant old places because the Huguenots, although they were refugees from their country, were wealthy. But in common with a lot of the houses, number nineteen, although in constant use as a synagogue, looked a bit run-down from the outside. I'd never been inside before, of course, and didn't know what I might expect. But the picture was somewhat different when I finally crossed the threshold.

The door to number nineteen was shut when I arrived so I knocked. I waited a long time for an answer, but when someone finally opened it it was done slowly and only wide enough for me to be able to see a nose and a pair of very blue eyes.

'Vass?'

I moved closer to the door so that I could keep my voice down. There was, I could just make out, very dim light, probably from gas, inside.

'My name's Hancock,' I said. 'I've been asked to—'

'Wait here.'

Almost a minute of unlocking noises happened before the boy, no more than sixteen at the most, opened the door and let me in. As I entered I saw, even through the yellowing gloom in the corridor, that he had the most startling red hair I had ever seen, and that included Alfie Rosen's shining mop.

'Come with me,' he said and, without turning to look back at me, he disappeared down a dark flight of stairs into what I imagined had to be the basement.

I followed, past a grimy little sink on the wall and past the entrance to the synagogue, which sticks out the back of the house in what I've been told since was once a garden. Unlike the corridor, the synagogue was far from gloomy, being lit by several large, ornate chandeliers. These fittings, which were fashioned in the shape of double-headed eagles, threw a lot of clean and clear light on to the many rows of pews on the ground. Plain like all synagogues, apart from a cupboard where they keep their holy scrolls, it nevertheless had a wonderful stained-glass roof, which I stopped to stare at for probably longer than I should.

'Come on,' I heard the young man say, so I ran down to catch him up, smiling as I went. But he wasn't too amused either by me or my probably unwelcome curiosity.

Down below street level now, on the dark little landing I shared with the boy, I could see three doors. As he pushed open the one directly at the bottom of the stairs, the boy said, 'I've got to go and put the blackout up now. Some of the comrades are meeting here tonight, so you'll have to be quick.'

'I came as soon as I—'

But he'd gone now so I walked into the room and looked around. It was, I reckoned, some sort of social area for the synagogue. In one corner there was a sink with a big tea urn beside it as well as a load of cheap white cups and saucers like the ones I'd seen on my infrequent visits to Church events. Cups and saucers for the masses, be they religious groups or the 'comrades' my young friend had spoken about earlier. Quite a lot of the Jews are Communists these days, except the really religious, the Frummers, like Hannah's people. They don't do much beyond study their books, pray and get rid of their kids if they don't do as they're told. Not that I could afford to think about Hannah and my problems with her now.

Opposite the corner with the sink, across from the chimney-breast, stood a woman probably in her late thirties. Thin, she had long, dark hair, which, on closer inspection was a very dense black wig. She was unknown to me.

'You Mr Hancock the undertaker?' she said. Her voice was rough, smoke-dried.

'Yes,' I said. 'You . . .'

'My name's Ruby Reynolds,' the woman said. 'Bessie tells me you've been helping our Pearl out.'

As soon as she and Bessie Stern had found Shlomo Kaplan's body, Ruby had decided that it would be best to make herself scarce.

'I was frightened. Coppers can't be done with having to look for criminals with this war on,' she said breathlessly. 'And with my background . . . Shlomo and me was in on our own all that day. He never went out because he was tired. So it was only me saw him before he died. I could've killed him. I didn't but I could've. Bessie and this lot here,' she said, as she flicked one hand around the room, 'they believe I never hurt him.'

'Bessie Stern knew about your mother?'

'Yeah. But not Shlomo. I couldn't tell him. This rabbi here, Numan, he's a political type and him and some of the boys in the Party know too. Bessie, although she's not one of them, she knows them all. They let me be here because they don't trust coppers no more than I do.'

I was, I admit, genuinely surprised. The old matchmaker had played the part of someone who knows nothing very well.

'Which is why, I suppose, you're allowed to be here,' I said.

'Yeah.' She had little of the almost delicate beauty of her sister Pearl but, as I had been told, the Reynolds sisters all had different fathers.

'So why have you asked to see me, Miss Reynolds?' I said. 'I'm really no one and—'

'When we first found Shlomo dead, I knew it had nothing to do with me. I knew the coppers'd probably come and ask all of us lots of questions. But then when I got to thinking about who I am . . . I thought they might take me in. As I've said, I've no alibi. I was terrified so I hid. I shouldn't have maybe, but . . . But then when Bessie come and told me about Pearl too, well, I wondered. Two Reynolds girls, two murders . . . I know Gerald, Shlomo's son, don't like me and what I was to his dad . . .'

'What were you to his dad, Ruby?'

She looked down at her hands in her lap and said,

'Once I'd done everything to convert properly, we was going to get married.'

'Which Gerald didn't like?'

'No. Shlomo, like Bessie and a lot of other people around here, was frum. Hassids. They, we, go to the big synagogue up on Brick Lane. Some people, Gerald I know, feel you can't become one, feel you have to be born to it. Also he was worried about what money he was going to get if his dad died and left me a widow. Started spreading all sorts of horrible rumours about me being a money-grabber and a tart and everything, and when that didn't work he started on his own dad. Told the coppers Shlomo beat me up, he did. I know some people round here believed it too! But he never so much as touched me, Mr Hancock. Bessie'll tell you.'

Although, according to Doris, Bessie Stern was a less than reliable source when it came to bad things done by Jewish people, I was inclined to believe her in this instance. In a sense Ruby was Hannah's opposite, an outsider becoming a Hassidic woman. Wearing a wig like the rest of them, not a scrap of makeup on her face. She had to believe it all and be dedicated to her future husband to put up with it. Not daft, I felt sure that Ruby wouldn't do such extreme things for someone who was a brute.

'Harold Neilson, the bloke my mum . . .' She looked down again into the hands. 'He had a sister, Phyllis. She used to come round before it all happened. But I only saw her once – after Neilson died. She looked at us little girls like the devil was in her mind. She'd loved Harold, see.

160

Mum's defence even said she'd loved him more than a sister should.'

'And did she?'

Ruby shrugged. 'I dunno. All I remember of that time is the beatings Mum used to get off Harold.' She looked away again. 'We was all out, Pearl, Amber and me, when Mum – when Harold died.' She looked back again. 'Mr Hancock, I need someone as can find out what's happening here. I get a feeling as if there could be something going on. Me and Pearl, we're being, somehow, pushed into positions what make us both guilty. I don't know who could be doing it, not really.'

'And you thought of me.'

'Bessie said you was helping Pearl.'

'But Pearl has been arrested.'

'Yes, I know. As I said, as soon as Bessie heard about it she come and told me,' she said. It was then that I told Ruby exactly how Pearl's husband had died and watched her face turn white as she listened to the details. 'Well, that makes it even more important someone gets to the truth. Somebody has to know about our past to do something like that. Pearl's no killer. She's the gentlest of all of us.'

Pearl, of course, was thinking along similar lines and I told Ruby so. I also told her about her fears for Amber in particular and how Velma was going to try to find her. 'It does seem quite odd to me that none of you kept in touch,' I said. 'I mean because your younger sister was adopted, perhaps that was a problem, but the rest of you . . . Apparently Pearl told Velma that your mother wanted you all to stay together.'

'Yeah, she did. But we thought it was for the best that we didn't,' Ruby said. 'Considering.'

'Considering what?'

She looked away yet again. 'Well, considering what happened. On your own you're a smaller target, like,' she said. 'If your mum or your dad kills someone then there'll always be people more curious about you than they should be. You never get free of something like that, you know. Murdered people have friends, family, people.'

'People like this Phyllis Neilson?'

Ruby shrugged again. 'Maybe.'

'So are there others, besides this woman?' I asked.

Ruby closed her eyes and shook her head. 'I dunno,' she said.

'Well, are there any other names you can—'

'No.' She opened her eyes again and looked me straight in the face. 'Point is, I don't know who might have it in for us. Might not even be someone who knew Neilson. People get funny about relatives of killers. That's why I'm asking you to help. All I know is that just before that raid started, the one when Shlomo died, Bessie and me saw some woman we couldn't recognise hanging about at the end of the road.'

'Could you see—'

'What? Whether it could be Phyllis Neilson or not? No. She was quite a way off.'

'Did Bessie tell the police about this woman?' I asked.

Ruby smiled. It was a weird, crooked affair. 'Yeah, course,' she said. 'But they reckoned it could've been anyone and they might be right at that. But, like the comrades say, they want it to be me and I know that an' all. It's easy if it's me.'

I know that some of the coppers try to keep to their standards, but it's hard under the circumstances. Every night, sometimes in the day too, women, kids, men, old people – you name it – are dying. As a copper, as anyone apart from Churchill, there's nothing you can do about that. There isn't much you can do about your own fear either or about the looting, the black-market 'erberts, the call-up dodgers, the pimps, the pros or even the bleeding drunk and disorderly mob, not in the depths of the blackout. Murder, of course, is a different kettle of fish. But with bombs dropping God alone knows where, there isn't much hope of gathering a lot in the way of evidence. And if some people are behaving strangely at any particular time, what of it? Most people behave oddly nowadays. All of this only hinders solving a crime and murders particularly need to be solved these days. People are frightened enough of what flies through the air without having to worry about what walks the streets. Ruby's thought about the coppers going for easy marks like her and her sister might be just right.

I didn't say I'd do anything, but I did ask Ruby about where she thought this Phyllis Neilson might be. She said up Paddington way, near to where her mum Victorine and she and her sisters had lived, which had been in a flat on Praed Street. In her forties now, Phyllis Neilson, as Ruby remembered her, had short brown hair and a very large, distinctive nose, broken in the middle like a boxer's. She had been, and possibly still was, a prostitute.

It was getting dark now and as well as knowing that the 'comrades' would soon want the room, I was also aware that I'd left Arthur and the horses for far too long already.

'You know I'm trusting you not to tell the coppers about me?' Ruby said, as I went to take my leave.

'I won't tell them about you,' I said. 'Just let me know if you move on. Although I do think you should chance it and go to the coppers, but . . . Look, I'll try to find this Phyllis Neilson if you like. I don't know if it'll do any good. Mind you, your Jewish friends'll look after you, won't they?'

'Maybe.'

'They must think a lot of you,' I said. 'Is it because you want to convert?'

'Not this lot. They're all Commies. I'm just another cause for them, a victim.' She smiled at me. 'My dad was Jewish, according to Mum. Don't know who he was, but I've always felt this kind of connection . . . Who knows whether it's true? But it's why I came here, to work and . . . I didn't have to become a frummer. But I always wanted to belong properly, do something right in my life for once. I hope Pearl's kid finds Amber and I hope she's gonna be all right.'

'So do I,' I said. 'Was Amber's dad Jewish or . . .'

'Amber's dad was Harold Neilson,' Ruby said. 'It was when Mum had Opal, by some Jewish bloke she said, don't know if he was the same one as fathered me, but after that the trouble started with Harold, the violence and suchlike. Opal, see, was always Mum's favourite, her baby. Had the best clothes, best food – treated her like a princess, Mum did. Harold was always jealous.'

'And Pearl? What of her father?'

'Mum always used to tell her he was some kind of gentleman. Had a title by all accounts, but what do I know? Pearl was born just over a year after me, so I can't remember nothing. Mum didn't say a lot about other boyfriends once she was with Harold. To him there was only hisself and punters. That's why there was so much trouble over Opal. Her dad was more'n a punter. I heard Mum say so. Harold wanted her to get rid of the kid, but she wouldn't. He hit her everywhere it wouldn't show.'

Considering that I didn't really have anything, personally, to do with any of these women, I was paddling in deep water here. Two, at least, children of a murderess had been affected by the killings of other significant men. In the case of Kevin Dooley it was undeniable that he'd been killed in the same way as Victorine Reynolds had murdered Harold Neilson. Not that it meant Pearl had done it. But if she hadn't then someone who maybe knew about Victorine and what she'd done had. For it to be just a coincidence was a bit hard to swallow. Whether or not Kevin's death was connected to the death of Shlomo Kaplan, who'd met his end in quite another way, was open to question. Given that I was also worried about Hannah and where I was with her, I didn't feel especially up to looking in all these various directions, which were now going a long way beyond making sure that Kevin Dooley got justice. Warning Amber, wherever she was, was one thing, but looking for the villains involved, if indeed they existed, was quite another. There was a lot of history that I knew nothing about and, anyway, I'm not and never have been a copper. Frank Hancock does what he can for the dead – the living shouldn't have too much importance – or, at least, that was how it always had been in the past.

'You know, Ruby,' I said, 'your sister Pearl has got this lawyer, a Mr Blatt.'

'Blatt?' Her eyes had narrowed right down into deep pinpoints of suspicion.

'Yes.'

Ruby reached inside her skirt pocket and took out one battered-looking fag, which she lit by striking a match against the wall. 'She ask for Blatt, did she?'

I didn't know what the arrangement might have been and I said so.

'Well, she'd be barmy if she did ask for him,' Ruby said. 'Might as well have put the noose round Mum's neck himself, that bastard!'

It wasn't how Blatt had described events, but I let Ruby go on. After all, in writing to me about Amber, Pearl had shown that, despite what Ruby was saying, she didn't entirely trust Mr Blatt herself. If she had there would have been no need for me.

'Kept on about her being on the game, about how many men she'd had! He said he was trying to impress the jury with how poor and destitute Mum was. But all it done was make them hate her and want her dead. He even told the court that us kids has all different fathers. How do you think that looks to "nice" people from Forest Gate and posh places like that? No,' she growled. 'I don't want to talk to Blatt and, if she's got any sense, Pearl won't either.

I want you to help us, Mr Hancock. I've had people ask around. People say they can trust you.'

'People?'

Ruby smiled at my confusion and said, 'Good people. Them you've helped, Mr Hancock. Them as don't comment on the colour of your skin.'

Of course it had to be Hannah. Through her probably most unwelcome visitor, the frummer Bessie Stern, from Hannah to Ruby, the full story, as she knew it, of Frank Hancock and his amazing, sometimes almost free, funeral service. Had she, I wondered, also told Bessie that I was barmy?

So what could I do? I said I'd continue to help as I could, which seemed to satisfy Ruby to some extent. I also gave her my card so she could either visit or call me if she needed to. She was safe for the moment and I said I wouldn't ask her to leave the synagogue. I have to admit, though, that I didn't entirely believe everything Ruby had told me. She could have killed Shlomo Kaplan and I only had her word that what she'd told me about their relationship and her own past was the truth. Just before I left she pushed a piece of paper into my hand with the address of where she and her mother and sisters had lived up in Paddington: 125 Praed Street. Phyllis Neilson, she told me, had lived just round the corner from there. Maybe some of the neighbours would know where she was now, if indeed she was anywhere. Old prozzies, as Hannah is always quick to tell me, don't tend to live long unless they are very, very clever.

Chapter Eleven

We were half-way down the Commercial Road when the sirens went off. Luckily I was driving or we might've ended up coming to grief. The horses still can't quite get a hold on themselves when the sirens start off and Arthur is still a little bit afraid to pull as hard as he should on the reins.

'What are we gonna do, Mr H?' Arthur said. 'It's miles back to the shop.'

'Don't you have an auntie round here somewhere?' I said.

In a split second Arthur went from being terrified to delighted. Young people can do that. 'Yes!' he said. 'Auntie Flo. She lives up by Barnes Street. She's got an Anderson in her garden. We can go there.'

So we did. Less than five minutes later there we were, outside Auntie Flo's, me taking leave of Arthur to the sound of the Jerry bombers streaming down over the river.

Auntie Flo, who was about fifty years old and about twenty stone in weight, grabbed hold of my sleeve with one swollen hand. 'You get in here, Mr Hancock,' she said. 'Come on! I won't take no for an answer.'

'I can't leave these horses,' I said, as I hung on grimly to Rama and Sita's reins. 'Without the horses, I don't have any business.'

As gently as I could, I took Auntie Flo's hand away from my arm, then swung myself up into the driving seat. Just before the first explosion, which had to be, I reckoned, down near Silvertown Way, I heard her say to Arthur, 'You're right, he is a bleedin' nutcase.'

I knew I'd never be able to get the horses or the hearse back to the shop in one piece until the raid was over. What I needed was somewhere to hole up for a while, somewhere under cover. I needed it soon too. The horses were beginning to bare their teeth and stamp, which is not a good sign. Sometimes I speak softly to them, in the small amount of Hindi the Duchess has taught me, and this does serve to calm them. But the noise was so terrific now that I could hardly hear my own voice above the din of falling bombs and shattering explosions. Christ, that Ruby Reynolds had done a right number on me! The hearse, at least, should've been back in the yard hours before, with both horses locked up in their stable. But instead I was out, yes, but I was pretty much hobbled by the horses and the vehicle.

Turning out of Auntie Flo's road, back on to the Commercial, the railway bridge hit me in the eye like a gift from God Almighty. Jesus, the Limehouse railway bridge, we could get under there! Not like a proper shelter or anything, but at least it would hold for anything but a direct hit. There were also, I could see now, people there too – about ten if I was right. Maybe they'd even help me with the horses if the poor beasts really got frightened. But as I drew closer I could see that none of them was likely to do that. Those that weren't either pregnant or old women were drunk and filthy and probably lived under the bridge in normal times. For these, as I drew the horses and the hearse underneath and close in on the soot-blackened wall, I was a kind of trespasser in their parlour. One spat, another peered, uncomprehending, while the rest just lay about, passed out some time before I'd arrived.

'I 'ope you ain't got no one in there,' an old woman said, as she flicked her head towards the hearse. One of the long since dark lamps that hangs uselessly from high up on the wall clanked metallically against the brickwork in time to the sound of the bombers from above.

'N-n-no,' I said. I even tried a smile to accompany my stutter, take the edge off it, as it were, but from the look on the woman's face, I'd failed miserably.

'You shouldn't look at a hearse from a distance,' a young pregnant girl said.

'What distance?' another girl said. 'A foot, a yard?'

'I dunno,' the first girl said. 'All I know is you shouldn't look at it.'

And they and the old woman turned their backs on me.

What good I thought the railway bridge would do is something I can now look back on with amazement. Even with their blinkers on, the horses could see just about everything I could and that included fires spearing through the darkness, the clouds of dust so thick you could be forgiven for thinking the smog had come in. And then there was the noise. Some raids, like this one, are wall to wall explosions. I don't know how many tons of the stuff we get dropped on us, but it's a lot because those bastards just don't stop. Wave after wave. I know our anti-aircraft guns are somewhere – some over Victoria Park and some over Barking – but you can't hear them, not when you've been half deafened by bombs going off. So, what with the bombings, the crackling from the fires and my having to hold on for dear life to the horses' bridles, it was like Bedlam underneath that bridge. And when one of the drunks started singing I thought I'd go mad. I was itching to run as it was so it wasn't until I felt the fingers tighten round my throat that I paid whatever had crept in behind me any heed.

Whether I made any noise or not, I don't know. All I could remember afterwards was the voice, gruff and deep it was, like someone who'd lived and well near died on the streets for many a long year. And the fingers, hard, long and very serious in their intent, I felt. Fingers that were also smooth and cool and kind of refined.

'Keep away from the Reynolds women,' the dark voice wheezed menacingly. 'I'm taking care of them.'

To be perfectly honest, I didn't even try to turn round even when the fingers let me go and I felt a swish of wind behind me as my attacker made good his escape. Yes, of course I wanted to know who it was and find out in what way he was going to 'take care' of the Reynolds girls. But with a raid in full swing I knew it'd take me five minutes just to start the question, let alone get the answer.

But I had to do something so I shook the drunk nearest to me and finally got out a question about what he might have seen. But he'd seen no one. The women with their backs to me couldn't have seen anything and I knew that the other drunks were unconscious. Whoever the rough-voiced, smooth-fingered person had been, he had known he'd easily get away with threatening me in this company. But how had he known I'd be there?

The thought that he'd followed me, possibly from Princelet Street, made me feel sick. Had he, already, 'taken care' in some way of Ruby Reynolds after I'd left the synagogue? Had he, perhaps, disguised himself as a 'comrade' to get to Ruby? And what was his point in doing this? What was it with these Reynolds women and why did their past, according to some of them, seem to figure so strongly in their present? Could it be that someone with a grudge, like that Phyllis Neilson Ruby had told me about, was using the chaos of the bombing to cover up what were really acts of revenge? If that was the case then she certainly had to have some patience waiting all of these years to do it. One thing that did seem certain, however, was that Ruby and Pearl's fears had some substance. That gruff, menacing voice had frightened the life out of me.

'Telephone's out again,' Nan said, as I staggered in over the scullery step and into the back privy. My poor Rama and Sita had been so terrified by their experiences of the previous night that I'd had a job first separating them from the hearse and then getting them back into their stable. What the poor buggers really needed was a bloody good gallop over the Beckton marshes, but I knew I wasn't up to it. I was exhausted and worried after what had happened under the Limehouse railway bridge and I needed to decide what I was going to do next.

As I walked out of the karzy, there was Nan waiting for me. 'Did you hear what I said, Frank? About the telephone?'

'Yes . . .'

'Well?'

I shrugged. 'If we need it we can ask Mr Deeks in the bank. I'm sure that if his line's working he won't mind us using it for essential—'

''Cause you see, Frank,' Nan butted in, 'your idea about me taking that young Velma down Southend is stupid. The bleedin' Germans are killing us! You know that redhead woman down Balaam Street, the young one with the baby? Mrs Woods. Well, some German in his aeroplane tried to kill her and the baby last night. Come screaming down Balaam Street as she was on her way back from her mum's. Firing his guns at her he was, at her and the baby! God help us, Frank, what sort of a world—' And then, worn out by the great rush of words she'd just spilled out at me, she broke down into tears.

I went over to her and put my arm round her shoulders. Nan, who isn't one normally for any sort of affection, buried her head in the collar of my jacket.

'It's all right,' I said. 'You don't have to go to Southend. I'll – I'll think of something . . .' After all, in view of my experiences in Limehouse I needed now, probably more than before, to locate Amber Reynolds.

'I thought that maybe me and Velma could phone the Nazareth sisters,' Nan said, 'but then when Mother said that the telephone was out . . .' She put one hand over her mouth as she began to sob once again. Nan is proper no-nonsense, carry-on-and-get-the-job-done normally, but even she has her breaking point and it sounded like the story of the young mum and her baby had just about done her in.

'I'll take Velma to the bank,' I said. 'I'm sure Mr Deeks won't mind if we use his telephone. We'll make do. Velma doesn't have to go to Southend. We'll keep her safe here, eh?'

Nevertheless, I had to find Amber with or without Velma's help and then I had somehow to find the time to get back to Princelet Street to see Ruby. Provided, that was, my gruff-voiced geezer hadn't 'taken care' of her already – whatever that meant.

I had to keep working around all of this too, so once I'd settled Nan down and made sure that the Duchess was all right, I took Velma to the bank and asked to use the telephone.

My plan was to get through to one of the nuns in charge, then hand the telephone to Velma. Asking for information about one of their old pupils had to be better coming from a relative. But somewhere along the line, the girl lost her nerve and I found myself talking, on a very crackly line so I had to shout, to a nun called Sister Joseph. I couldn't work out what she was in the orphanage except that she wasn't the Sister Superior or whatever they call the top-dog nun.

I introduced myself, said where I was from and then I said I was looking for a girl who'd once lived at Nazareth House on behalf of her sister who'd also been in the orphanage. I told Sister Joseph the approximate dates of Amber's residence, and she said that although it was quite a while ago now, she'd do what she could to help me.

'We try to keep in touch with children we've helped after they've left,' she said. 'What was the girl's name?'

'Amber Reynolds,' I said. 'Her sisters, Pearl and Ruby, were also with you for a time.'

Even through the crackling on the line, I was aware of the silence blaring away at me from the other end.

'Pearl needs to speak to Amber. She just wants to know that she's all right, which is why we need to find her,' I added. And then, fearing that perhaps Sister Joseph might think I was some nosy reporter digging about for information on the children of a murderess, I said, 'I've got Pearl's daughter Velma here, if you want to talk to her.'

'No. That won't be necessary.'

It was said coldly and with a finality I didn't much like.

'Sister Joseph—'

'Mr Hancock, I don't think we will be able to help you.'

'Yes, but you said—'

'I said that we try to keep in touch with those children we have helped,' she said. 'But sometimes we fail, as in this case.'

'Yes, but you must have some sort of idea—'

'The Reynolds girls were very troubled children, Mr

Hancock. I assume you know about their mother and the "unpleasantness". When they left Nazareth House they went their own separate ways and wished for no further contact with this institution.'

Normally, I thought, places like orphanages had to pass the kiddies on to someone else, an employer or a landlord or someone, when they grew up. But maybe that only applied to 'good' children, kids who didn't have a murderess for a mother. I've been at odds with the Duchess and Nan over the Church for years, about how the priests and what-not only have an interest in people who live the good Catholic life and to hell with murderers, prostitutes, madmen and the like. This conversation I was having with Sister Joseph only served to confirm my beliefs.

'Look, Sister,' I said, 'I need to get in touch with Amber Reynolds. It's important. Her sister Pearl is in trouble and she needs to know that Amber is all right.'

'As I've told you before, Mr Hancock,' she interrupted, 'there's no record of where Amber Reynolds went from here. The girl just upped and disappeared.'

Then she put the telephone down on me and I had to stop myself saying a very bad word in front of Velma.

I was supposed to work that afternoon, but we had a daylight raid so I ran, walked and then, once the raid was over, got on a bus up to Paddington.

Whatever might or might not have happened to Ruby Reynolds, I had promised her I'd have a go at locating that Phyllis Neilson, which was what I turned my mind to now.

If I say I'm going to do a thing then I generally do it. I was also, I have to admit, intrigued now by the Reynoldses' past. I wanted to see where it had all started all those years ago with their mother. I'd far from forgotten about poor old Kevin Dooley: it was just that other mysteries had now joined his demise in my head.

Paddington and that area just north of Hyde Park hasn't taken the bashing we've had – nowhere has had as much punishment as the East End. But they've had their share. The people look worn out, like ours, and there's damage to be seen, here and there though, rather than in great swathes of destruction, but it's there.

Praed Street is where Paddington station is, and was, I should imagine, quite a grand thoroughfare at one time. They built big and impressive back in the Victorian age, and although the handsome four-storey buildings on the south side of the street are now mainly given over to shops, cafés and cheap flats, it's still easy to see how they might once have been considered smart. There's even what I'd call an air of faded gentility about the place – as if it's been something, now isn't, but can't quite understand why. Maybe it's to do with the superior attitude of the girls on the game in these parts – there are lots of them in Paddington and, dressed up like bandboxes, they're pretty obvious. Or maybe it's the mixture of classes round the station. Out in our manor, people are mostly working class. Even Mum's priest comes from a docks family originally. But in Paddington you can see clerks and surgeons, sailors and lords all briefly rubbing shoulders as they head either into or out of our great city. There are also the Italians in

Paddington too – flat-nosed, slick-haired geezers who run boxing gyms, and little old blokes, like Tony of Tony's Café, which was on the ground floor of 125 Praed Street where the Reynolds girls grew up and where Harold Neilson met his bloody end.

Although difficult at first – he would keep trying discreetly to cross himself every time he looked at the veil on my top hat – Tony eventually warmed to me. Maybe it was the five cups of tea I drank in his almost empty café, or maybe it was because I introduced myself as a friend of someone whom Tony called 'Little' Ruby. Then again, perhaps he was just scared. Ever since March when Mussolini joined forces with Hitler, Italian people and their businesses have taken a lot of abuse in London. In some cases they've even been attacked. Someone with no accent, like me, could have been anyone – a copper, a spy, you name it.

'Used to knock Little Ruby about, that beast Neilson,' Tony said, through and around the stub of an old cigar. 'We live in the flat behind the café, Vicky Reynolds and her girls in the one above that, one hundred and twenty-five B.' He shook his head sadly. 'Sometimes my Pia and our boys, we hear what was going on. But I say to them, that's their business. It wasn't for us to interfere.'

'No.'

Tony leaned forward so that his thin brown cheeks nearly touched mine. 'Of course, you know and we knew what Vicky Reynolds was,' he said. 'But that never made no difference and that were no excuse for Harold and what he done.'

178

Suddenly he smiled, revealing just one top row of straight brown teeth. 'So if you a friend of Ruby, Mr Hancock, what you want here and why she don't come to see us herself?'

Tony obviously hadn't heard what had happened in Spitalfields and so, safe in the knowledge that there had obviously been little love lost between himself and Neilson, I told him about Ruby, Shlomo Kaplan and what the police suspected. What I left out was where Ruby was and what exactly I was doing.

The old Italian scoffed at the idea of murder. 'Nah! Not Ruby! She wouldn't hurt nobody. You know her, Mr Hancock.' And then, turning on me quickly, he said, 'Where did you say you know Ruby from?'

I hadn't mentioned exactly where I'd come from so I said I was a neighbour from Spitalfields. I could, after all, easily be Jewish on first sight and this explanation seemed to satisfy Tony. But then, in my experience, people outside the East End, whatever their origins, are never as close as those of us who live in the old Thames-side villages. Maybe we're a bit too close sometimes. Keeping together and close can sometimes lead to ignoring obvious truths, not doing proper justice to those who've died among us – like Kevin Dooley, maybe.

Tony and I chatted and as we did I tried to work out how I might broach the subject of Harold Neilson's sister, Phyllis.

'Oh, they were lovely girls,' Tony said enthusiastically. 'Ruby – that quiet one, Amber, pretty little Pearl—'

'The tiny one was a madam.' I looked up into the big

dark eyes of Tony's heavy-limbed missus. 'Very pretty but a madam.'

'Pia . . .'

'She was spoiled,' Pia's accent was much stronger than Tony's. 'My 'usband 'e remembers nothing,' she said to me. ''Arold was very jealous of that little one.'

'Opal?'

'Yes. Vicky spoiled the child. When she 'ad 'er so all the trouble with 'arold and then that sister of his coming around causing trouble upstairs, that all begun. Opal, she would show off what 'er mum would buy her, send 'arold crazy – his sister Phyllis screaming about Vicky wasting all 'arold's money on the child. Vicky made all the money as far as I could see. But she would laugh, that child, at the man's jealousy.' Pia sighed heavily. 'In the court Vicky said she killed 'arold because he try to 'urt Opal. But that child pushed him, you know.'

'Pia!'

'Neilson and his sister were evil people, God rest their souls,' she crossed herself quickly, 'but that child made you mad. I looked after her – once. You remember, Tony?'

'Well, yes . . .' Tony put his head down in his shoulders and said, 'But Mr Hancock don't need to know nothing about that, Pia. He's a friend of Ruby.'

'Oh. Oh, well, she always a nice girl. Decent.' Pia's big face broke into a smile, and then she left to serve the only other customer they'd had in all the time I'd been there. What, I wondered, had little Opal done that had been so nasty?

However, now that I knew Phyllis Neilson was dead,

and now that it was starting to get dark outside, I could have gone home but I asked Tony for another cuppa instead. A couple of rough-looking lads were hanging about outside, making comments about 'wops'. Tony seemed a decent sort – not all Italians can be like Mussolini after all – and I wasn't comfortable with the idea of leaving him and Pia alone with them lurking.

'Phyllis, she had the TB,' Tony volunteered, as he put my cup down in front of me. 'It was only a question of time. Maybe ten years she's been dead now.'

No danger to Ruby or anyone else from her, then. Whoever the sinister bloke who had told me he was 'taking care' of the Reynolds girls was, it was unlikely he had anything to do with a woman ten years dead. And there wasn't any reason, as far as I could tell, to disbelieve Tony and his wife. They had, after all, been quite explicit about the family who had once lived above them.

''Cause nobody wouldn't live in Vicky's flat for years,' the Italian continued, as he sat down opposite me again and relit his cigar. 'Not that the old landlord cared. Let the place go to ruin. But Mr Hubbard and Mr Green, they're the new owners, they ain't like that. Got some nice people here since they come. People with a bit of class.'

There was a nice middle-aged book-keeper on the top floor and a 'very smart' lady, some relative of the landlords, in the Reynoldses' old flat. As well as making the flats a bit better to attract a 'nicer' class of tenant, the new landlords had also done some repair work on Tony and Pia's flat. But they'd probably bought the properties so cheap they could afford to keep the tenants happy. In some parts of this city landlords are almost giving places away now, something of which Tony also was aware.

'But if we get bombed by the Germans, what Mr Hubbard and Mr Green done won't be worth nothing, will it?' he said, as he led me to the door while his wife pulled down the blackout curtains.

'All we can do is keep our fingers crossed,' I said, as I put my hat back on.

'And pray,' Pia added. 'The Blessed Virgin, she take care of us. Me and Tony, we don't go down no shelter. If it's meant to be it's meant to be.'

'Yes . . .'

'You know our youngest son, Gio – John – he join the Royal Navy. He don't wait to be called up.' Then, placing one hand nervously on my arm, Tony said, 'Mussolini is a bad man, Mr Hancock, a bad Italian. You know we like your people . . . Italians . . . we – we like your people a lot.'

I smiled. Whether Tony meant my people meaning Englishmen or whether he saw me as a Jew from what is recognised everywhere as a Jewish part of London, I don't know. But I accepted his words with good grace and then I went outside. Those loud, 'orrible 'erberts had gone so I stopped briefly in front of the doorway that led to the upstairs flats of number 125 and stared at it for a moment or two. I'd found out what I wanted to know and it was getting still darker and cold.

As I walked along the street I kept an eye open for Tony's tormentors, but they were nowhere to be seen. Probably gone home, away from the 'wops', the evil servants of Mussolini. I know people say he's as bad as

Hitler, but I find it hard to take him seriously when I see him on newsreels. He's such a strutting, vain little man and vanity is so often the subject of ridicule. Although not always. Pia hadn't found much to laugh at in Opal Reynolds's vanity. Ruby had said she was spoiled and Pia had mentioned a certain unpleasantness of behaviour that neither of the old Italians had wanted to pursue. But Victorine Reynolds had killed Neilson while trying to protect this apparently provoking child she'd had by another man. Harold's pride must have been in shreds. Men like him, like Kevin Dooley, they have to control their women and children: it's as essential to them as breathing. Any deviation, provocation, usually ends in violence.

Eager now to get back to the Duchess and the girls in case the Jerries made another appearance, I didn't stop off in Spitalfields to see if Ruby was all right. I'd do that once my family were settled in the Anderson, I thought. I'd already, by going to see Tony, done a lot for Ruby that day.

All the way home on the bus I kept thinking about how little I'd been able to find out about what had led up to Kevin Dooley's death on that night of bombing, violence and fire. I was, it seemed to me, being sucked ever deeper into the world of Kevin's wife and her strange past at the same time as I was being deliberately excluded from Hannah's peculiar origins. I was near to her place now which was why my girl had suddenly popped into my mind. As my bus moved slowly through what remained of Canning Town I imagined Hannah's face and felt sad for what I'd said to her at Cherry Hazlitt's funeral. Maybe I shouldn't have repeated what Doris had said. But I'd felt hurt that Hannah hadn't told me herself, which now seemed both arrogant and stupid.

Chapter Twelve

When I got home I tried to ring Mr Blatt to let him know I had Velma with me now, but the telephones were out again. I thought I also ought to let him know about my strange encounter with the Reynolds 'protector' in Limehouse. He knew the family, after all, and might have some idea about that. He might too, as Ken suggested when he popped round just after I got back from Paddington, know where Opal was and who had adopted her. But in the meantime, I needed to see Ruby, if indeed my gruff-voiced geezer hadn't already 'taken care' of her. I shook when I thought about going back there, so much so, in fact, that the only way I could get myself out of the shop was by promising myself I'd go and see Hannah first.

Because the Duchess, Nan and Velma had sensibly decided to get some sleep down the Anderson while they could, none of them saw me leave the shop at just before nine. Aggie, however, was another matter. Like me, if for different reasons, she goes out even if a raid might be on the cards. Her face a mask of pink powder, red lipstick and some blue stuff round her eyes, with her jaunty hat and cigarette in a holder, she looked not unlike some of the girls I'd seen earlier up in Paddington.

I held the shop door open for her as she left, eyeing her, as she eyed me, with suspicion.

'Where you off to, Frank? No bombs flying about yet. What's the hurry?' she said, puffing smoke into my face as she passed. I knew she wasn't happy about my being involved, even just by taking care of Velma, in Kevin Dooley's past and the questions surrounding his violent death: she felt I wasn't up to it. Both my sisters fear for me in their own ways.

'Out,' I said. 'And you?'

'Out too.'

For a few seconds we stood on the pavement outside the shop, Aggie pinching her fag out with her fingers, lest the wardens see her 'light', while I stood and rolled myself a smoke from my tobacco tin. Neither of us wanted the other to know where we were going. Not that I was going to be up to no good. I wanted to see Hannah, talk to her rather than anything else. But I knew if I mentioned this it wouldn't look like that to others, especially not to Aggie. She's not bad, my sister, but she has had a rough time in the past with her useless husband and everything, so it's natural she might want to have a good time now. How much of a 'good time' she has I don't know or want to know. She sends most of what she earns at Tate's to her kids out in Essex, so there's not much for her to buy a drink or get some fags with. But somehow she does have a drink a couple of times a week and she's always good for a fag. She's a pretty girl, with her white skin and her big dark eyes, even if her bleached-up hair does look a bit hard to my way of thinking. Some blokes like that and they are, I think, the sort of blokes only interested in one thing from women. The sort of blokes Aggie meets and thinks her brother might have something in common with. I wish she'd never found out about me and Hannah.

'Oh, well, "we'll meet again", I suppose,' she said, referring to what has for so many people become a favourite song.

'I hope so,' I said. 'You owe me fags.'

'Funny bugger!'

When we parted, Aggie went right and I went left, towards Canning Town. I watched her go for as long as I could in the blackout and then I began my own journey across the rubble, occasionally pressing myself up against shop doorways crowded with sandbags as cars, their lights dimmed to almost nothing, sometimes mounted the pavement. In spite of, even because of the daylight raid, there were a lot of people about. Families clearing up damage to their homes where they could, boarding up broken windows, putting down sandbags. Some people were coming out of houses with furniture and kitchen things. People who might or might not have been looters – how was I to know? There was a warden and a copper talking on the corner of Star Lane and they weren't doing anything so why should I?

Even if I hadn't known where Rathbone Street was, if I'd heard its reputation I would've known it when I got there. Even as early as this, before the mad pubs of Canning Town – the Bridge House, the Chandelier and the like – chuck out, some girls are out and about in the shop doorways. Not all their 'trade' goes to the pubs after all. Not the Lascars with skin like mine or the blacks from Casablanca who don't take a drink because of their religion. There's work to be had, for which I was mistaken by one poor lass in a darkened doorway. Just quickly she shone one of those torches they all have up at her face and said, 'Evening, love.'

Even by that little light, I could see she was nearer to seventeen than forty-seven.

'No, thanks,' I said.

'Fuck you, then!' she said. Probably nearer fourteen than seventeen by the sound of her, poor kid. Her mouth already a karzy, probably in more ways than one. Several further incidents like this occurred until I eventually found Hannah. She wasn't alone so I had to wait out of sight until she'd finished whatever she was doing. Luckily, once I'd heard her voice, I didn't have to go any nearer and therefore see what he was making her do. But whoever he was he lifted his hat to her when he'd finished and he paid, which is more than a lot of them do.

'What are you doing here, Mr H?' Hannah said coldly, as she hastily rearranged her skirt.

Trying not to look or even imagine in my head, I said, 'Well, love, I'm on my way to Spitalfields to see about that Ruby . . .'

'I hope you're not expecting me to come with you.'

'No.'

'Then what do you want with me?' Hannah said. 'Unless you want a bunk up.'

'No!' In case any over-enthusiastic punter should try to get between us I pulled Hannah into the doorway of a pawn shop. 'I just need to know that we're all right,' I said. 'I know I hurt you about your parents—'

'Forget it,' Hannah replied.

'But I can't,' I said. 'You even went to see them for me, which must have hurt you.'

'I done it for that Pearl, not you!' Hannah snapped. Her eyes darted over my shoulder at the furtive male figures shuffling awkwardly around the edges of the street. 'A woman on her own like that . . .' Hannah continued. 'Look, are you going to Spitalfields or not, Mr H? Or do I have to lose money while I stand about chatting to you?'

'Hannah!'

I could see there were tears in her eyes, although whether they were tears of misery or fury I couldn't tell.

'If I don't make the rent tonight Dot'll have me out on me ear,' she said. 'So, if you don't mind . . .'

'I'll pay your rent!' I said wildly, and completely without thought about how. 'Just go home, I . . .' I couldn't pretend any more. Suddenly the thought of my Hannah with some slobbering, dirty bloke, his guts full of booze, was just too much for me. 'I'll pay your rent, Hannah,' I said. 'I'll look after you. I will!'

Hannah sighed. She looked as if she were physically deflating. 'I can't and won't let you do that, Mr H,' she said. 'You and me, we can't never be more than what we are now . . .'

'Look,' I said, madly, I confess, 'I can become a Jew. Ruby—'

Hannah laughed. 'But I'm not a Jew any more, Mr H, not really. Don't you understand that? That ain't the point. Or, rather, it is the point but not in any way I can see you'll understand.'

'Hannah . . .'

'But if you want me to come out to Spitalfields with you now, you can pay me for my trouble and I'll take the money for that.'

I could hear men shuffling about behind me. I could even hear some brutish creature on the job with another girl further back down towards the Barking Road.

'But you don't want to go there, do you, Hannah?' I said. 'Not again.'

Hannah reached up and put her hands round my neck, gently cradling my head in the cold, soft darkness. 'I'm not a Jew, Mr H, because I don't deserve to be one. I don't deserve to be anything,' she whispered. 'This is all I do deserve after what I've done. I don't deserve you . . .'

'Hannah, I've done things myself,' I began.

But she put one finger on my lips and said, 'Sssh. You're a good, kind man. You care about people, even when they're bastards, even when they're dead.'

Especially when they're dead, I thought, because I know how they get that way. I've made people that way. Pushing German faces down into the depths of the suffocating Flanders mud, aiming my rifle at some poor kid wetting himself with fear and dishonour. Kevin Dooley, too, must have been terrified as he died.

Everyone is – we don't know what, if anything, comes after life, which is why the dying must be comforted by the living. I let Kevin down, me of all people. I let him die violently, disbelieved and alone.

I put my hand into my pocket and took out some cash, which I gave to Hannah. 'Come on,' I said.

We pushed our way out of Rathbone Street. Past drunks having sex with children watched by other drunks waiting for their turn. I thought about the youngster who'd offered it to me and how coarse and brutalised she had already become. There are so many ways to ruin a child – like this, by spoiling as Victorine Reynolds had done to her youngest . . . It's a risk having children.

Hannah and I took the bus over to Stepney. Slow, ghostly things they are now, blacked out, their lights dimmed to virtually nothing. We walked the rest of the way, past the Jewish soup kitchens, the Yiddisher theatres, the many, many synagogues. I told Hannah everything I'd discovered about the Reynolds family so far.

'Gone.' Hannah shrugged as she stepped out of the Princelet Street synagogue. 'Left last night – well, early hours of the morning.'

'But why?' I said. 'That raid lasted till almost dawn. Why would she leave in the middle of that?'

All my fears about Ruby Reynolds were about to be confirmed. In fact, it was worse than I had imagined.

'Maybe the bloke what threatened you come for her,' Hannah said. 'What time did that geezer approach you?'

'Maybe ten or—'

'Ruby Reynolds left here between one and two,' Hannah said. 'Rabbi says some young bloke knocked with a note for her.'

'And they opened the door?'

Hannah threw up her hands casually. 'It's them Commie boys, Mr H. All fired up on their new ideas. Always looking for new comrades. Raids don't mean nothing to them. They come and go from their meetings, changing the world . . .'

'So somebody knocked with a note for Ruby Reynolds.'

'Yes. So she took it, she read it and then—'

'Then she got up and left in the middle of a raid.'

'Yes.'

I leaned against the wall of the old Huguenot house and closed my eyes. Someone somewhere struck up a tune on a ukulele – something strange and foreign-sounding, not a bit like George Formby, thank Christ.

'Did anyone know this bloke with the note?' I said.

'No, but Rabbi Numan told me Ruby said to him the note was from you.'

'From me?'

'That's what she told him,' Hannah said. 'Them Commie boys wouldn't have let her out unless they were sure whoever she was going to was kosher, and they know you. She's a bit of a cause for them, you know, Mr H. She's a fugitive from British injustice. Frummer or no frummer, they'll help anyone on the run from the law.'

'But I didn't send her any note,' I said. 'I spent that night over in Limehouse.'

Ruby, however, must have thought that the note was

from me. That, or she had to have known the bearer of the missive once she got outside. But I had said to her that I would never ask her to leave the synagogue to do anything for me. And she'd done just that.

'I think we should own up and tell the coppers Ruby's missing. I'm scared for her,' I said to Hannah, as a couple of the comrades came out of the synagogue. One of them was the ginger-haired lad who'd let me in to see Ruby.

'You do that and we'll smash your head in,' he said, as he and his mate closed in around me.

'We're looking for her, all right,' the other, far darker young bloke said, 'now we know she ain't with you.'

Hannah said something in Yiddish and the boys backed away a little.

'The bloke who came for her said he was your lad,' the ginger youngster said to me.

'What was he like?' I asked.

'Small, dark, black suit . . .'

An undertaker's lad. Yes. But not mine. Arthur is six foot tall and has hair the same colour as Jean Harlow's was. This other little lad was someone else, if someone else who knew me. I wondered if his voice had been unusually coarse and rasping for his age or whether the voice I'd heard in Limehouse had been that of someone who was using this lad. But the comrades couldn't remember anything about his voice.

But why had whoever had drawn Ruby out done so? How had he or they known where she was? If they'd been coppers they'd have been all over the synagogue by now, them not liking the Commies too much these days, so it obviously wasn't them. Someone bubbling up from Ruby and her sisters' past, someone not Phyllis Neilson?

The two comrades moved off then without further threats to me.

'I promised them I'd keep you away from the coppers,' Hannah said, as we watched them pass into the thickness of the blackout.

'But someone could be holding her, hurting her,' I said.

'I know,' Hannah said. 'But if you cross the Commies they'll hurt you, so put it from your mind, Mr H.'

When I'd first met her, Ruby had been a frightened woman, suspicious of just about everyone except those closest to her. I'd told her I wouldn't ask her to leave that synagogue. She had to have either known my so-called 'boy' very well or something in that note must have had a real effect on her. There was also, personally, something else. Someone, be it the gruff-voiced geezer in Limehouse or not, knew who I was, what I did and about my involvement with Ruby. For what purpose?

But whatever the reason, Ruby was now missing and not even Bessie Stern, whom Hannah and I went to see afterwards, had any idea where she might be.

'She changed her name to House,' the old matchmaker said, as she gave me a cup of tea and took a fag, if rather sniffily, from Hannah. 'I knew who she was. I recognised the name Reynolds, remembered all them poor little orphaned girls. But I told her I'd keep her secret and I was true to that until I asked the Commie rabbi to take care of her and then I told you. She never killed Shlomo, I don't care what anyone says.'

'Why did you contact me?' I said.

Bessie Stern shrugged. 'Because Ruby told me to. She thought that if you was with her sister and her girl you had to be all right. I thought the sister might come back and see me herself at some point, to be honest with you. I'd've told her everything. But she had her own troubles too. Whatever, you had to be better than the police – no one can trust them now. They'll do anything to make their lives easy, the poor bastards. Who can blame them in such times?' She shrugged again. 'And then this lawyer came to help her sister. Ruby said he couldn't be trusted either. What can a person do? Poor Ruby is afraid she'll hang like her mother. She's afraid that someone wants her to hang like her mother. And now this with her sister . . .'

'You've no idea who she might have gone off with last night?' I said.

'No.' She shook her head, tutting as she did so. 'You know, she was well hidden in that synagogue. I don't hold with Commies myself. We,' she looked pointedly at Hannah as she spoke, 'don't have no politics, our kind. Our rabbi don't hold with breaking the law. But I knew that Rabbi Numan and his people would look after her. The Commies all closed in around her, as they do. You know she said her father was Jewish? He told her mother what town he come from back in his own country. It was Riga. A lot of people come from Riga. Course, Ruby never knew him, but coming down here made her feel sort of close, I think, to Yiddisher people . . . And then there was Shlomo . . .'

'Mrs Stern,' I said, 'do you think that his son . . .'

'Gerald never approved,' she said. 'He even put some very bad rumour around about his father. But he'd never have done nothing mad, not nothing that might've got him into trouble.'

'Why's that?'

'Because he's already got the business from his father,' Bessie said. 'And as for the house and all the rest of it, well, the house is Gerald's now too, so it would've only been old Shlomo's cash and none of that had been taken. Maybe he found out about Ruby's past and killed his father . . . No.' Bessie Stern shook her head. 'He wouldn't've needed to kill Shlomo. He was a naturally suspicious old bastard. If anyone had told him about Ruby's mother he would've thrown her into the street. Much as he loved her he would have done so. He could never have brought himself to trust her. Silly old fool, he believed in bad blood, like a lot of the old ones. I only knew about Ruby's past because, as I said, I remembered that Reynolds murder. You know, Ruby looks the spit of her mother.'

'And you trusted her? So you never told no one?' Hannah said. 'Not even when old Mr Kaplan was found dead?'

'Look, darling,' Bessie said, I felt a little savagely, 'you might think I'm nothing but a gossipy old frummer, you with your goyim ways. But I believed Ruby and I trusted her. She fitted here, you know, with our life. She was a good girl, nice girl, worked to study the Torah – know what I mean? – even before old Shlomo ever whispered about marriage. So her mother, rest her soul, killed some horrible man? That wasn't Ruby. She never killed no one. Biggest mistake she did was running off like that, me helping her, may I be forgiven. But she was so scared and we all know how the coppers are! And, anyway, when they come they did have her real name – knew her! How did they know her? I've thought maybe Shlomo's son found out somehow, gave it to them. But, no, that don't make sense. There's no way Gerald could have found that out. No. If anyone told the coppers anything, if anyone has it in for Ruby, it has to be someone else. Ruby, I know you know, she told me, she thought that maybe someone from her mother's time come to do revenge on her.'

'Yes,' I said, 'a woman. You saw her too, Ruby said, just before the air raid when Shlomo died. At the end of the street . . .'

'Yes, yes. I told the coppers about that,' Bessie said. 'Ruby wondered if it was the man her mother murdered, his sister.'

'It can't have been,' I said. 'She's dead.'

'Oh. Poor soul. God love her.'

'But, anyway, the person who come for Ruby at the synagogue was a man,' Hannah said.

'With maybe a note from some woman? This woman we both saw,' Bessie said.

'No,' I said. 'The Commie boys told us Ruby said the note was from me.'

'But it wasn't?'

'No.' I shook my head.

'And yet if it'd been from the woman she suspected – or she thought it was from her – maybe she lied about you writing it to get out of there to her, confront her maybe. But, no, she was scared, she wouldn't've left the synagogue for anyone she didn't trust.'

'Then maybe she is with someone she can trust?' Hannah said.

'But Ruby doesn't trust people,' Bessie said thoughtfully, as she sucked hard on her fag. 'But maybe . . .'

'What?'

Bessie shrugged. 'Maybe trust didn't come into it. Maybe it was someone beyond trust, someone she loved?'

'But Shlomo . . .'

'Oh, I don't mean like a lover,' the old woman said. 'Ruby never had none of them except Shlomo, as far as I know. No, I mean maybe a relative, someone from her past.'

'I don't think so,' I said. 'The comrades up at the synagogue said that the boy who came with the note claimed to come from my shop. Ruby didn't make anything up. She was lured out.'

However, that didn't mean that Bessie didn't have a point. Although the Reynolds girls had split up after their time at the orphanage, Ruby at least had been concerned about Pearl, which was partly why she'd contacted me. People can find each other and information about each other when they need to. It was therefore possible that one or other of the remaining Reynolds girls had found where Ruby was and . . . But no, nobody outside the synagogue had known where Ruby was, except me. No one in the community knew about Ruby's past, except Bessie Stern and the comrades. Not, of course, that you can trust anyone entirely. The ukulele music, which Bessie said was coming from one of their Yiddisher music halls, had started to get on my nerves by then so we left. Those wailing notes, they give me the shivers. I don't know why: being what I am I should understand – Indian music is even stranger, if anything – but I don't.

Then, walking back home from Bessie's, Hannah and I were reminded of the existence of some other, much more violent parties who had an interest in one of the Reynolds girls. I had, I confess, forgotten temporarily about the Dooleys.

'I warned you, you black bastard!'

We were only a spit from Rathbone Street when Johnny and Dickie Dooley jumped us. Whether they'd seen us coming or just happened to be leaving Canning Town station, I was never to find out. But Johnny had me pushed up against the side of the ticket office, my head pressed against a poster exhorting us all to 'Keep mum', as quick as a wink. I like to think that I can handle myself, but I'm not a young man and I'd smoked a lot more fags and pipes in my time than this young thug.

'You're still helping her, aren't you?' Johnny said. 'My slag of a sister-in-law.'

Somewhere to my left, there was a flash of something shiny. Hannah saw it too and said, 'If you hurt him I'll tell the old Bill it was you. I don't fucking care.'

Johnny Dooley turned to face Hannah who, I could now just about see, was being held by his brother. 'Think the coppers'll believe you, you old tart?' And then, turning back to me, he said, 'Fucking hell, Hancock, you ain't 'arf got a cheap taste in women.'

I wanted to say something in Hannah's defence, but he'd moved his hand up to my Adam's apple so, for the moment, speech was impossible.

'Now, I heard that some lawyer the tart's got herself turned up at your shop the other day,' Johnny said. 'I've also heard that the tart's bastard's been seen in this manor. Now, you know that if I find out that bastard's with you, you and all your women ain't going to be too safe.'

''Specially that blonde slag,' Dickie put in. 'What's she? Your—'

'She's my sister,' I finally managed to gasp. My heart was racing now. If these animals were threatening my family . . .

'Funny.' Johnny moved his face so close to mine I could taste his beer-raddled breath. 'She don't look like a wog, that one. She looks like a slapper.'

'Then maybe she'd get on well with your wife!' I said, through gritted teeth. It had only been a short conversation I'd had with Velma about the Dooleys, but Johnny's wife's name had stuck in my mind. 'Your Martine.'

Even in the almost total darkness, I could see a movement where his face was as he curled his lips into a cruel sneer. 'Don't you—'

'Everyone knows,' I said, knowing that 'everyone' was really a very small church, 'how cut up your Martine was when your Kevin died.'

'Yeah, well, she liked him. He was a good brother, a sort.'

'Oh, I heard she liked him a lot,' I said. And then, further gambling on the little that Velma had told me, I added, 'They've been seen, Kevin and Martine. She liked him a whole big lot.'

'What—'

'Enough to make a younger brother jealous. I mean Kevin was a big, powerful man—'

The punch split my lip and, for a moment, I felt it might have broken my jaw too. But Johnny Dooley was a lot shorter than me so by the time his fist had got to my face it had lost quite a bit of its power.

'You fucking—' I heard Hannah start then a slap and then a small, strangled cry that was obviously Hannah's too.

'Tell your brother to leave her alone!' I breathed at Johnny.

'Don't you ever use your dirty wog's mouth to speak about my Mart—'

'Where was your Martine on the night your Kevin died, Johnny? And where were you?' Questions that had been at the back of my mind and wouldn't go away. After all, if the Dooleys were so blameless, what was this about? Surely not just Vi Dooley's dislike of Pearl?

'What?'

'Kevin said it was a woman as attacked him. She have an argument with him, did she, Johnny?' I felt his fist tighten round my collar yet again. 'Or did she kill him because you threatened to kill her if she didn't? Did you watch her do it?'

'What's he on about, Johnny?' I heard his brother, Dickie, say. 'I thought you had words with your missus about her and Kev—'

'Shut up!'

I could have kissed Dickie for more or less confirming what Velma had told me. 'I'd be very careful if I were you, Johnny,' I said.

'Or what?'

'Or maybe the police might be interested to know about Martine and your brother Kevin. They might want to ask you some more questions about what you were doing on the night he died. Jealousy, especially between brothers, is a strong motive for murder.'

'I never hurt my brother!' Johnny Dooley gasped. 'I was with loads of people down our Anderson. The coppers know!'

'Oh, you don't have to convince me,' I said. 'But you might have to convince the police if they should suddenly develop doubts, if you know what I mean.'

'What?'

'Lay off me and leave Velma alone. She's just a kid.'

'A kid with a murderer for a mother and a grandmother,' Johnny said.

So the Dooleys knew. Everyone knew.

'You don't know Pearl killed anyone,' I said. 'Just like I don't know whether you, your wife or Father Christmas killed your brother. We're all in the dark, Johnny, so none of us should threaten people or point any fingers. Leave Velma alone, leave my family alone, and let's all see if we can find out who really killed your brother and let the court decide. You do want to catch the real killer, don't you? Want to be certain?'

I felt his grip on my collar slacken at the same time as his face came even closer to my own. Now I could see him, his little drink-blurred eyes filled with fury, his few crooked teeth set into a snarl that made it look as if he was about to eat my face.

'I loved my brother! He was family.'

'Yes,' I said. 'Beat up his missus, put her in the family way every five minutes and then, just to prove to everyone what a big man he was, had any other bit of skirt lying around too – including your wife.'

I thought he was going to hit me again, but Johnny only grunted his fury this time.

'But Kevin was a human being who has been murdered and whose memory deserves the truth. So let's just leave each other alone and let justice take its course, shall we?' I said. 'That way none of us gets hisself involved in explaining something he doesn't want to.'

Neither Johnny nor his brother did or said anything else after that. They just walked off, from what I could see in the direction of Poplar.

As soon as they'd gone, Hannah came rushing over. 'Are you all right?' she said. 'Christ, H, I thought that bastard broke your jaw!'

I took her in my arms and held her close for a moment while the shock of it left our bodies. Where I'd got the courage to say all that, I didn't know. On just a rumour, really. But Johnny had been shaken. Could it be that he had a guilty conscience? Something had definitely taken place between his wife and Kevin, but whether Johnny had done anything violent to Kevin or Martine because of it was another matter. Johnny and the rest of them had an alibi but, from what I could gather about the Dooleys, they could easily have organised that, using those who feared them. Johnny had been a bit too scared for a fellow with a snow-white soul. And it was probably that and his knowledge about Martine and Kevin, rather than hatred of Pearl, that made him want her to be guilty. After all, if it all came out about Kevin and Martine, that would automatically put Martine and maybe Johnny, too, in the frame and he didn't want that.

'You're bleeding,' Hannah said, as she reached up and touched my chin.

'Are you?' I asked.

'I don't think so,' Hannah said. 'I don't think the bastard hit me hard enough for that.'

'Come on,' I said. 'Come back to the shop and let's get cleaned up.'

'I can't do that,' she said. 'What'll your mum and them think?'

'I actually think I've got very good taste in women,' I said, 'so I'm going to take you home and look after you now, and nuts to what anyone else thinks. And that includes my mother and my sisters!'

She'd been there, for me. Not all actual wives will do that for a bloke, as I was increasingly sure Johnny Dooley would know. But then the sirens went and new priorities took effect. Some people out and about that night looked surprised, but a second raid wasn't any news to me. War doesn't stop to let you take a breather. It's a close pal of Death, who never has taken time off and never will.

Chapter Thirteen

I'd reorganised yesterday afternoon's half past two funeral to half past ten the following morning, if the Jerries allowed. And, fortunately for the family of the late Sidney Whitehouse, Adolf Hitler couldn't be bothered to send his Luftwaffe boys back out that morning. Old Sid, like a lot of people in this manor, had been Catholic so we had the pleasure of Father Burton, who came up for a few words with me afterwards.

'You know it's Kevin Dooley's funeral tomorrow,' he said. 'Thank the good Lord.'

'Been to see the family, Father?' I asked.

Father Burton gave me one of his acid looks. After all that business with Kevin Dooley's 'first' funeral and my involvement with it, the priest wasn't very well disposed towards me. There was something else, too, something I didn't know until he spoke once again.

'You know,' he said, on a sigh, 'I was never very comfortable about that business with Pearl.'

'Yes, I know you—'

'No, not the funeral,' the priest said tetchily. 'Pearl, the woman herself.'

'What do you mean?' I said. It was really quite cold for the time of year and I was aware that very soon the Whitehouses would be wanting to get on home for Sid's wake. There is, after all, only a small amount of time you can spend looking at two bunches of flowers that were probably nicked anyway.

'Whatever other sins she may have committed, Pearl didn't kill Kevin,' Father Burton said.

'Why do you say that, Father?'

'Because of something she told me,' he said. 'You know, out of all the Dooley family, it was only Pearl ever came to mass or confession.'

So she'd told him something, maybe something vital, in confession. I felt myself groan inwardly. Whatever it was, neither I nor anyone else would ever get at it unless Pearl wanted us to. All the more reason to get Velma, who would, surely, be allowed to visit her mother, in to see Pearl in Holloway. Maybe the child could ask her mum about what she'd told the good Father. Although quite how I was going to persuade her to do so, I couldn't imagine. How do you ask someone about their confession? I thought about Blatt's card in the pocket of my other jacket at home and wondered what the situation was with the telephone now.

'You know they say that blood will always out?' Father Burton said, as he made his way with me back towards the Whitehouse family. 'Well, that doesn't work in the case of Pearl Dooley.'

I put my hand on his shoulder to stop him and said, 'What do you mean?'

Father Burton held up a steadying hand. 'I can say no more than that, Francis.'

'Yes, but—'

'No, my son, there are some things we have to work out for ourselves. I've said as much as I can.'

The only thing I could think he might mean was that maybe Pearl wasn't Victorine Reynolds's daughter. It would certainly make sense from a 'bad blood' point of view. And it's well known that girls on the streets, like Victorine, do sometimes take in other women's nippers. It would explain Pearl looking so very different from Ruby, even taking into account their different fathers.

But whether Pearl was Victorine's daughter or not wasn't going to help her or Ruby right now and, in spite of the fact that I probably knew more than most about these women, I realised I needed some help. Ruby was missing, after all, and as for Pearl, well, surely if she had been to Dot Harris and had the abortion, that needed following up. The old girl had, of course, denied that she'd done it, but I wondered how much the coppers had questioned Velma about the time she'd said she'd spent in Dot's place. Maybe, I thought, if Velma could give them some details about the place, that might help to establish whether or not she and her mother had been telling the truth.

'I told the coppers everything I could remember,' Velma said, when I got back to the shop and asked her about it. 'I even told them the colours of the curtains at the street door. But they said I could've got them details any time.'

'But was your mum friends with Mrs Harris?'

'No, not really.'

'So . . .'

'As soon as the coppers realise or even imagine that two women are or have been "working girls", it's just natural they think they know each other,' Hannah said. Although she'd still been sleeping on the parlour settee when I left to see to Sid Whitehouse, I hadn't thought she'd be at home when I got back. But she'd been talking to Velma who, I could see, was becoming rather fond of my lovely girl.

'My mum never done anything like what her mum used to do for work,' Velma said. She gazed at the floor, ashamed, as she spoke. But then she looked up sharply. 'I know Vi Dooley thinks she was bad. I know she thought Mum was never married to my dad, but she was. He was just a lot older than her, that's all. He died and left us with nothing, so Mum always says.'

It was the first time Velma had ever mentioned her father. But he must have died when she was so young, she had no memory of him. Poor kid, her dad dead, her mum in prison and a dead murderess for a grandmother, if Victorine was her grandmother . . .

'You'll never get Dot to own up to helping girls out,' Hannah said. 'Not at her age.'

No. Dot Harris had to be seventy if she was a day and, as everyone in Canning Town knew, she'd already been inside twice for getting rid of unwanted babies. This time, at her age, she probably wouldn't get out again.

Doris knocked on the parlour door then and I told her to come in. She wanted to check on a funeral booking and, as she was explaining it to me, I noticed that she and Hannah smiled at each other. Because it had been Doris who had told me about Hannah's history, I had been nervous about their meeting up some time. But as soon as Doris left, Hannah told me everything was all right. Apparently Doris had come straight out and introduced herself when she first saw and recognised Hannah. My girl, although not recognising Doris, knew her family so it wasn't a big step for her to work out who had told me about her past. But the two of them had got on so I was relieved about that at least.

But now I needed to think about getting in contact with Pearl. I was troubled by what Father Burton had said, as well as the way that Velma's evidence was seemingly being ignored. It is difficult for the law with evidence from kiddies, I know. I turned to Velma and said, 'How'd you like to go and see your mum, love, ask her a couple of things for me?'

She said she'd like that very much, so I went downstairs and tried out the telephone. It was working again so I got hold of my other jacket and took Blatt's card out of the pocket.

He said he'd get back to me as soon as he could, but the telephone went down again just afterwards so we didn't hear anything from Blatt until the following day. Velma, having had her hopes raised, was all right until it started to get dark, but then, when she still didn't know any more, she went down fast. Silent and, after a while, unmoving, she looked more lost than I'd ever seen her. But then, as I know only too well, there's no way of predicting when a person's going to crack. It just comes, that moment when it's all too much, and the only thing those around the person can do is watch, most of the time helplessly.

Aggie was due to work the night shift and left at the same time as Doris. I did have a little twinge of fear as they both took off in the twilight, imagining Johnny Dooley and his brother, out there somewhere, angry and full of vengeance. But then I remembered what had been said at our 'meeting' and how he'd gone away with his tail between his legs – in the end. Still, just the memory of it made my lip throb again. Bastard Dooley!

Once Doris and Aggie had gone, Nan started peeling veg for supper. Velma turned to when she was asked, silently, but she did it anyway, while I went out the back to fill up the coal bucket. As I came back in I heard the hand-bell ring from inside the shop. Of course I hadn't locked up after Doris. I had thought I might do a bit of paperwork down there. I put down the bucket, wiped my hands on the old towel Nan keeps by the back door, then picked up my jacket off the banisters. It was late, but when did Death keep sociable hours? I went back through the crêpe curtains into the shop.

'Are you Mr Hancock?'

'Yes.'

I've always found it difficult to tell how old nuns are, especially when they wear the wimple really close round the face. With no hair to help identify the person, the face just sort of looms out at you, like something completely neutral, neither male nor female.

'Can I help you, Sister?'

She sat down in one of the chairs beside the desk. Normally people ask, but she didn't: she just sat down.

'I won't beat about the bush,' she said, in what seemed to me a most un-nunly fashion. 'I've come from Nazareth orphanage in Southend. I've travelled all day and I need somewhere to stay.'

The voice hadn't the clipped tones of Sister Joseph, and yet who else would come to see me from there, I couldn't imagine. Anyway, that the tight-lipped Sister Joseph should come had never crossed my mind. As far as I'd been concerned, my involvement with the Nazareth orphanage had drawn a blank and was at an end.

'My name's Sister Teresa,' she said, wringing her hands. 'Back in the world I was someone else, which is what I've come to talk to you about.'

I frowned.

'You've been asking my sister, Joseph, about me,' she said. 'Amber Reynolds.'

She didn't get round to telling me much before the sirens went. I'd asked her if she wanted to be introduced to her niece, but she said no and so, when the warning did go, I just took all the women down to the shelter, then went back to Sister Teresa. She never used shelters, so she said. Apparently quite a number of people in Southend feel they are generally a waste of time. But they haven't had what we've had. I agreed to stay with her for as long as it lasted. I would rather have gone out, but I could hardly leave a woman, a nun no less, alone in the house.

I think it only lasted a few hours, that raid, but because I was neither out nor talking it seemed like it went on for ever. Of course, I didn't talk because I couldn't, but the nun didn't know that which made her own silence all the more strange, really. And so in a sense it was as if I was alone, which meant that my brain did what it usually does: gibbered and boiled, throwing pictures of men ripped to ribbons on first the pitch dark and then the red and gold explosion-filled sky. I don't know whether Sister Teresa knew or suspected she was sitting with a madman, but some time later she said, 'I think this is coming to an end now.'

Sometimes raids can be short, like this, just a couple of hours maybe. But judging the length of things can be difficult for me when I'm on leave from my mind, as it were. I assumed that the raid was over when the Duchess and the others came up from the shelter and went back to their beds, but even now I can't be certain when that was. Sitting there with Sister Teresa, I can remember feeling my chair move as if an explosion had happened some-where nearby and the shop was getting the blast. But I don't know. I rolled a fag as if it was over and then, at her request, I rolled one for the nun too. Sister Teresa held her cigarette between her first finger and thumb like a docker. You see such queer things in war, on the battlefield, which we are.

'So what's all this about Pearl?' she said.

I could speak properly now and so I told her about the various theories that were going about, as well as the facts as I knew them so far. I spared her nothing. 'Pearl was worried that something might've happened or be about to happen to you as well,' I said. 'Both Pearl and Ruby seem to think that this, what's happened to them, could be some sort of revenge to do with Harold Neilson.'

'My father,' Sister Teresa said matter-of-factly. 'Horrible man.'

'There was his sister . . .'

'Phyllis? She's dead.'

'Yes, I know,' I said.

'God rest her soul, she died some years ago and is buried in the same Methodist cemetery as her brother. How did you know?'

I told her about Tony and my little foray into Paddington.

'I always liked old Tony,' Sister Teresa said, 'but I'd never go back to Praed Street, not if my life depended on it. It was good of you to do that for Ruby.'

Something trembled in the ground under my feet, probably shock waves from some collapsing building, and I looked up into her deep, black eyes – just like those of Pearl Dooley.

'Was Neilson Pearl's father too?' I asked.

'No. We're all different, Mr Hancock. Ruby's father was a Jew, Pearl's was some smart fella, mine was Neilson, and Opal, well, her dad, so Mum would have it, was some other Jew.'

'Caused trouble between your parents, didn't it?' I said. 'Opal's father and . . .'

'Oh, yes,' she said. 'The bloke Mum was going with at the time was someone she really loved. Whether he was Opal's father or not, I don't know, but she liked to think he was. Mum lived for that little girl. Neilson didn't like the situation about Opal one bit. Hated the uncertainty of not knowing who or what she was.'

'But he stayed,' I said, 'for many years, until . . .'

'He wanted to.' The nun looked away.

'But he was violent.'

'Just because he stayed didn't mean he had to like it. Whatever's happened to Pearl and Ruby has got nothing to do with what happened to Mum. There's no one left . . .'

'So you . . .'

'I'm all right. Just because Pearl's husband died like Neilson doesn't mean that someone's trying to make a point. I mean, I suppose you've considered the possibility my sister might have done it. I imagine to protect herself. She's a gentle girl, or was.'

'Yes,' I said. 'Of course I've wondered whether Pearl could have done it. I started all this off because I wanted to get to the truth about her husband – I still do. But Ruby going through something similar and now disappearing, it doesn't sit right with me.'

'Maybe not.' She sighed.

'I think that Pearl, begging your pardon, Sister, that she had that, you know, that abortion . . .'

'Yes, yes.'

'I'm sorry,' I said. 'Look . . . what about Opal? Is she all right?'

There was a brief pause before she answered. 'Opal was adopted,' she said. 'Me and the others, we all agreed that as soon as we could we'd split up.'

'Why?'

'Because it was for the best,' she said, just as Ruby before her had. 'I don't know where Opal is, Mr Hancock.'

'You could find out.'

'No.'

'Why not?'

'Just trust me. It isn't possible. It's all too long ago, far too late,' she said. There was something flustered about her now. She looked away a lot, down sometimes at the end of the roll-up in her fingers. She hadn't smoked any of it. Just quickly I did think that perhaps she was a fraud, but then I dismissed the idea. She must have had at least some contact with Sister Joseph and she did, undoubtedly, have Pearl Dooley's eyes. But quite why she'd come I still didn't know, so I asked her.

'I don't want anything to do with Pearl or Ruby, but I want them to know that I'm all right,' she said. 'The message I got was that Pearl wanted to know if I was all right. Well, I am, as you can see. Amber Reynolds no longer exists but Sister Teresa still cares about her old family in her own way.' She moved her head across the table towards me. 'Pearl's husband's death has got nothing to do with our mother and neither has whatever has happened to Ruby. That's all over now. All the badness died with Mum.'

Nun she might be, but I got the distinct feeling that Sister Teresa wasn't telling me the whole truth. 'Sister,' I said, 'don't take this wrong, but there's some as seem to think, I've heard, that Pearl wasn't your mother's child. Is that true?'

The nun laughed. 'Who you talking about, Mr Hancock?'

'Her priest, Pearl's. He told me Pearl couldn't have killed her husband because that crime, your mother's, couldn't have been inherited by her – if you believe in such things anyway. He implied your mother and Pearl were not the same blood. She'd spoken, I think, in confession . . .'

'Well, either he got it wrong or my sister lied.'

'Why would she do that?'

Sister Teresa's face was red. 'I don't know! Mum sacrificed for her, for all of us!' And then, as if the word burst out of her of its own accord, she said, 'Bitch!'

The Duchess and Nan, in particular, had looked at Sister Teresa a little funny when she'd first arrived. With her direct manner, not to mention, later on, her smoking and swearing, she was a very odd nun. When I finally left her in the early hours I still had the feeling she might be a fraud. But if she was, she was very thorough. The next morning when Nan went in to get her up out of my bed – this time I had the settee – she saw her head without its wimple and it was as bald as an egg.

Chapter Fourteen

I saw Blatt get out of his car. Thinking about Amber, or Sister Teresa as she was, as well as mentally preparing myself for another raid, I hadn't slept well so I'd been up since before dawn. As had, apparently, Blatt and the bloke driving the car for him. I had to pull my braces up pretty sharpish when I saw the solicitor walk towards the shop door.

'Your telephone's been out so I came as soon as I could,' he said, as I let him in.

'What's the matter, Mr Blatt?'

He looked agitated. 'I can take Velma in tomorrow afternoon between three and four,' he said. 'That's the only time the prison authorities will give me. Can you bring her or shall I take her now and keep her overnight? I can't be late – I've appointments all this morning.'

I turned away to look in my own appointment book. Doris, as usual, had been very efficient. I had that poor little baby, William from Plashet Grove, later on that day, but there was nothing for the following morning or afternoon.

'Well, it looks like I can bring her tomorrow,' I said. 'Do you want to meet up at the prison, Mr Blatt?'

'I think that would be for the best,' he said. 'I mean, all of this is providing any of us are still standing tomorrow morning.'

I smiled.

'You know,' he said, 'when we got to, I don't know, Wapping or somewhere like that, the police stopped us and said we had to take another route because a house had, as they said, "been blown" into our path. My driver, he's a Cockney lad, asked about the occupants and the officer said that the Heavy Rescue team was at work, but it was a big job. There were five families in that house, Mr Hancock, five.'

I wasn't surprised either by the five families or by Blatt's amazement. There have always been boarding-houses, but since the bombing started people have been jammed up against each other like never before this century. Nobody wants to be a refugee, put in temporary billets with strangers, so people take in their friends and family if they get bombed out. But with money, things, I know, are different. In Mr Blatt's world, people don't often get bombed out and if they do they move out to their homes in the country. I don't suppose he even saw too much that was this distressing when he was, as he must've been at least for a bit, in the first lot. Most of the top brass never did. Personally I don't have a problem with how the rich are, provided they do their bit, but I know that others have strong feelings about it and Doris Rosen is one of them.

'Oh,' she said, as she came into the shop and took off her hat. 'Mr Blatt.'

I was surprised to see her in so early and even more surprised that Blatt should comment on it.

'Very keen staff you have, Hancock,' he said, as he looked Doris up and down in the way that a punter might view a horse he's just been given a tip on.

You didn't need to be a genius to see that Doris was less than flattered by his attention. But she kept it to herself for the sake of me and the business.

'Hello, Mr Blatt.'

We all turned to look at her. Doris, in particular, was openly amazed at the sight of a nun walking through the back curtains.

'I'm sorry . . .' Blatt began.

'You knew me, briefly, as Amber Reynolds,' Sister Teresa said. 'You know, when you "defended" my mother?'

'Ah.'

'Yes,' the nun said, almost menacingly, I felt. 'Mr Hancock tells me you're "defending" our Pearl now.'

'Yes.'

She turned to me and said, 'Mr Hancock, could I please take Mr Blatt up to your parlour? I need to have a word, about Pearl.'

I looked at Blatt, who was quite white now. 'As long as that is all right with Mr Blatt, Sister.'

'It's fine.' He smiled, quickly, using only his mouth.

And then, addressing the nun, he said, 'What do I call you?'

'Sister Teresa,' she said, and then, with a swish of her skirts, she turned. 'It's up here.'

He followed her without another word.

Both Doris and I listened to their footsteps, first on the stairs and then over our heads in the parlour.

Doris spoke first. 'The nun's involved in this thing with young Velma and the dead paper-and-string man?'

'She's Velma's aunt,' I said. 'Mr Blatt—'

'Is Mrs Dooley's solicitor. Yes, I know,' Doris said. 'Although where, with respect, a family like hers would get the money to pay a bloke like him, I can't imagine.'

'He is rather top drawer,' I said.

'Yeah, top-drawer Yiddisher he is,' Doris said. 'Loads of gelt. Don't know why he's working for poor goyim, do you, Mr H?'

'No.'

In a way, I could understand why he would want to be involved with Pearl, having defended her mother, if unsuccessfully, in the past. Maybe he wanted to vindicate himself. But how and why had he decided to take Victorine's case? He'd obviously done his reputation absolutely no good with it and there can't have been any money in it for him. And he was, as I had now learned, Jewish – like Ruby's father, like, reputedly, Opal's father too. Had Blatt been Victorine Reynolds's lover all those years ago? No one had ever mentioned him in that context: the Reynolds girls had spoken only of his incompetence. But that didn't mean he hadn't been involved with their mother or even fathered some of her children. Such things aren't supposed to happen, I know, but I'm also aware that they're more common than most people think.

Suddenly I was gripped by an overwhelming urge to do something I'd never done before: listen at a keyhole.

'I'm just, er, going up for a bit,' I said to Doris, as I went up the stairs. 'Get yourself a cuppa, won't you?'

I just caught her wry smile as I raced upstairs on the very tips of my boots.

'I will,' she said. 'Abyssinia, Mr H.'

My old dad always used to moan about the doors in this place. 'Shoddy,' was how he used to describe them, 'all piss and plywood!'

As usual he'd been right and I didn't even have to put my ear to the keyhole to hear what I needed. I just stood outside, trying for no reason whatsoever to look casual. All the family that was up was in the kitchen making breakfast.

'Why are you defending Pearl?' I heard the nun demand. 'How did you find her?'

'I'm defending her because I feel I owe—'

'Too fucking right!'

I heard Blatt laugh. 'Oh, what a perfect nun you are, Sister,' he said. 'Where did you say you pursue your vocation?'

'Nazareth House in Southend – where you put us, remember?' she said. 'We all do what we must to survive and to make penance. This undertaker seems to think that Pearl and Ruby have some idea about being victimised by someone. Does Pearl really think that's happening?'

'Her husband died in exactly the same way as Neilson, yes,' Blatt said. 'But I can't think of anyone still living who might wish to harm you now. Can you?'

'No, but—'

'Provided I can make it stick, Pearl does have an alibi for the night her husband died.'

'That doesn't answer why someone might be—'

'Why would anyone at this distance in time bother?' Blatt said. 'Phyllis Neilson died years ago—'

'Yes, I know!'

'You haven't had any problems yourself?'

'No!' I heard her move very quickly across the lino and, instinctively, I retreated a little from the door. 'But look,' she continued, 'I think you should at least warn Opal. She, at least, needs to know. Maybe the undertaker's right.'

'Opal is with the same family.'

'I don't want to know where she is, just that she's safe. Ruby's missing too, you know. There could be something going on. Someone could have found something out.'

'You agree with Mr Hancock?'

'I don't know, really.' I heard her sniff, loudly. 'What does he know anyway? What does anyone, apart from . . . But I bet Pearl's worried about Opal. I know she's worried about me. It's because of her Mr Hancock came looking for me.'

'What do you mean?'

'She sent him a note,' she said. 'Sent it through the

prison governor, not you. She didn't want you to be involved.'

'But—'

'Pearl, just like Ruby and me, know what you are, Blatt,' the good Sister spat. 'Now, you'd better get looking to see who might be coming out of the woodwork. My father had more than just a sister to call his family and this bombing means that people can get away with anything – including murder. There's a lot of people out there who have scores to settle with you, as well as us, so you're in the firing line . . .'

'You expect a lot of me, Amber,' Blatt replied smoothly. 'Getting your sister off, solving a mystery that is probably not a mystery . . .'

'Pearl was having an abortion when her husband died and Ruby, well, she loved that old Jew.'

'A common failing in your family.'

'Oh, drop dead, will you, Blatt? Look, do you think that Pearl and Ruby killed their fellows? Honestly?'

'I don't know,' Blatt said. 'After what you all saw at such tender ages . . .' I heard him begin to laugh.

'Fuck you, Blatt! Fuck—'

'Why don't you come back to the office with me and we'll talk about these things?'

'I'd rather die,' I heard her say. 'I'm not going anywhere with someone like you.'

'Francis?'

The Duchess's voice is always gentle, but sometimes disapproving.

'Duchess?'

'I do hope that you are not listening at that door, Francis.' She lowered her voice as she spoke, lest those inside should hear us. 'The Sister and the gentleman came up here for a private conversation.'

'Yes, Duchess.'

'Then . . .'

I moved away, after her, down the corridor and back towards the kitchen. At that point I don't know whether I was more confused or less. Blatt's involvement with the Reynoldses was obviously at a deeper level than the usual solicitor/client relationship. But how deep it went, I couldn't tell. The main thing among all the talk of Neilson's possible relatives, and who might or might not have done what, that had a lot of meaning for me was that Blatt knew where Opal was. It wasn't a case of him being able to find out, nor was it a case of him 'believing' she'd been adopted, as he had told me. No, he knew. Sister Teresa knew it and so, I imagined, did Pearl. It would explain why she hadn't asked me to find Opal. In fact, in her note she'd sort of glossed over Opal's existence. Did this mean perhaps that Blatt had already contacted the girl? There was something about people 'knowing' something unspecified too. What was that, and why had the nun spoken about Blatt being 'in the firing line' as well as her and her sisters?

Had the nun not left without even a thank-you I might have asked her.

As I've said before, Father Burton and I don't often see eye to eye. But we do agree when it comes to the subject of children's deaths. What do you tell the parents? Father Burton will talk about God and all that business, of course, because that's his job. But how to comfort the parents? He doesn't know any more than I do and, even after all these years, I know nothing.

William Clatworthy had been only six months old when slates falling off his mother's roof had ended his life. Mrs Clatworthy had to be no more than twenty, poor woman. Her old man, she said, was in the navy.

'How can I tell him about little Billy?' she said to me. 'He'll go barmy! He just won't be able to take it, I know.'

And then she wept. I had no words. What can you say to someone who loses a child? I'm sorry? What good's sorry? Kids die, we all know, especially round here, especially in the big poor families. They die because of malnutrition, diseases we can't control, because some poor women are in labour for so long both the mother and the baby end up dying, and now they die because of the Jerries. But whatever the reason, kids dying before their parents is an unnatural thing. Our kids, if we have them, are supposed to outlive us. That's the way it should be.

There was to be no wake for William Clatworthy so once he was buried I headed back to the cemetery gates. I'd been aware of another service going on over the other side of the cemetery, and I thought I recognised some of Albert Cox's boys, but I didn't pay it, or them, much attention. At the gates, however, there was Albert's hearse, alongside mine, all its doors wide open to the elements.

'Frank!'

If I hadn't known Albert as well as I do, I would've thought that perhaps he was happy. But his voice was slurred and I could see the hip-flask in his hand, as could his boy, Paddy, who gave me a quick raise of his eyebrows as he passed.

'Hello, Albert,' I said. 'How's it going?'

Albert, who had been slumped down low in the passenger seat, pulled himself upright and smiled. 'I'm going to the pub,' he said. 'Do you want to come?'

I'm not the sort of bloke as goes to pubs a great deal. In fact, a lot of the behaviour that goes on in pubs gives me the pip. I'm usually too busy these days, anyway. But on this occasion I needed a drink and I knew it. Even for me I was all over the place. Poor little Velma aside, I didn't know what to make of the Reynoldses, Blatt and all their doings. I'd started out wanting to get at the truth about Kevin Dooley, doing what I felt I should, really, but now I seemed to be somewhere quite different. Now I was caught up with people's secrets, which is always a dangerous place to be.

'Yes, I'll come,' I said to Albert. 'Just let me send my lads on their way.'

I told Walter and Arthur to drive the hearse back to the shop and then I got in beside Albert.

'Bleedin' Dooleys,' he said, as he passed his flask to me. 'I hope those bastards take a direct hit!'

Vi Dooley, Kevin's mother, hadn't wanted Albert to do her son's funeral.

'How do I know you're gonna bury my boy and not

fetch up with a coffinload of nothing like you did last time?' she'd said, when he'd gone round to talk to her. Both Albert and the police had explained it to her several times, but it took the skill of Albert's father to get the old girl to go ahead with Cox and Son. Harry Cox had always been a sweet talker – my dad had known him for years. Harry's local was the Boleyn on the corner of the Barking Road and Green Street. Albert often went there too, which was why we turned up in the saloon bar at just about lunchtime.

Harry, already three sheets to the wind, bought the first round.

'Here you go, boys,' he said, as he placed the pints in front of us. 'Get that down you.'

Albert lifted his glass up into the smoke-soaked light and said, 'To Kevin Dooley. Thank Christ that bastard's finally in his grave.'

They laughed, I couldn't, and then Harry said to Albert, 'Bad do, was it, boy?'

'I could've done without Vi keep on telling everyone what I'd put her through the first time,' Albert said. 'Never said a bad word about it to Father Burton. All "Father this, Father that, thank you very much for such a lovely sermon, Father." Christ! And then Martine. Jesus, the state of her!'

'What? Johnny's wife?' I said. 'What about her?'

'Well, she's quite a looker, Martine. Or she was. Now she's just like that poor little Pearl always was. Black eyes, her nose all out of kilter by the look of it. That bastard husband of hers, I reckon.'

'I heard there were some "stories" about Martine,' I said.

Harry laughed. 'There's always stories about pretty women, son.'

'Johnny knew she weren't no saint when he married her,' Albert said. 'We all knew it. But I've never seen her like that before. I reckon he must've caught her with another geezer. Right smashed up, but she kept looking across at Johnny as if she wanted him to smile at her or something. Just like Kevin, him, has to be *the* man, no one so much as looking at his missus. What is it with these blokes who knock their women about?'

What indeed? Well, in this case there was, I suspected, just a little of me involved too. Johnny had obviously been aware of what his wife might have been doing with Kevin for a long time before I came on the scene. But somehow, maybe, he'd lived with it. Even after Kevin died he'd carried on as normal, as far as I knew, with his wife. But I'd opened my mouth outside Canning Town station and this was, possibly, the result. But did it mean any more than it seemed to? Did it mean that Johnny, Martine or both of them had had a hand in Kevin's death? It didn't seem that likely to me, but perhaps after what I'd put in his mind, Johnny had felt the need to make sure Martine knew who was boss, as Albert had said. Or maybe she'd threatened to tell someone everything she knew about Kevin and her involvement with him – someone apart from her family and her priest, that is.

I was thinking about these things, coming to no conclusions, of course, when I heard an old dry voice say, 'Morgue's son and the Coxes like a load of black crows.'

I turned quickly and there, half hidden by deep layers of smoke and dust, one thin yellow hand curled round a pint of stout, was the old bloke from St Mary Magdalene's churchyard. The leather-faced geezer from the bare-knuckle fight. He'd left me only minutes before I'd seen Kevin Dooley in his illuminated death throes. He could, possibly, *surely*, have seen something?

Excited now, I didn't take my eyes off him once as I went up to the booze-stained bar to buy a round for Albert, Harry and myself. I didn't want to lose him. Now I had him in my sights I had to hang on to him. Maybe I should have mentioned the fight to the coppers, but I hadn't. Kevin had been stabbed by a woman, so it didn't seem relevant. But now, suddenly, coming upon the old geezer, the only face I could've recognised from that graveyard, I began to wonder what he knew. There had been no witnesses to any sort of attack on Kevin Dooley, according to the police. But in our manor you always wonder. Who, usually, talks to the coppers?

I had to wait until he was on his own, which took some time, what with his bit of business with his bookie's runner and another bloke I think he might've bought some hooky meat off. When I did finally speak to him I had to, first off, spend a lot of time getting him to admit he'd been in the graveyard that night. Bare knuckle is, after all, illegal and 'Gimpy' Charlie, as the old boy was called, knew that as well as anyone.

'Now, look, Charlie,' I said, as I placed a bottle of barley wine in front of him, 'you were there and so was I. You helped me . . .'

'Everyone knows you go off your nut in raids, Mr H,' Charlie responded slyly. 'How'd'ya know where you was?'

'Because even I know a fight when I see one, and,' I lowered my voice, moved in closer to the old chap, 'I know the coppers are always interested in who goes to watch these things.'

'You ain't no grass, Mr H!'

Appealing to an East-Ender's sense of community is always a good one, but I wasn't in the mood. 'You don't know what I am, Charlie,' I said, 'because, as you've said yourself, I'm barmy so who knows what I might do?'

'Yus, but—'

'Charlie, all I want to know is what you saw that night,' I said. 'Not at the fight, I don't care about that; on your way home, did you see anything?'

'Explosions. Brick-dust. A lot of black on account of the blackout—'

'Yes! Yes!' I'd really got his goat now. 'But look,' I glanced from left to right, then moved in close to his head once again. 'A bloke called Kevin Dooley, a scrapper from Canning Town, died that night and—'

'I don't know nothing about that, Mr H. Never heard of that geezer.'

'Are you sure, Charlie?'

'Oh, yes.'

'Because it's been all round the manor.'

'Oh, I don't never listen to gossip, Mr H,' Charlie

said. 'There's them as say women can do these things, but I say you shouldn't be too hasty about such things meself.'

My memory isn't what it was. Of course I knew 'Gimpy' once I had a chance to take a good look at him. He had one leg, hence his nickname, and the story was that he'd lost the other at Mafeking in the Boer War. Or, rather, that was what Charlie always wanted people to believe. 'Gimpy Charlie's whole family are dodgy,' my dad had said, when he'd first heard this. 'Gimpy lost that leg dynamiting a bookie's safe up Dalston!'

'You've always been a rotten liar, Gimpy,' I said, as I rolled up a fag for me and one for him. 'You didn't fool my dad and you're not fooling me.'

'Mr H!'

'If you don't listen to gossip, then how do you know that there's a woman suspected of Kevin's murder?'

'Well, Mr—'

'Look, I met Kevin Dooley a few minutes after he'd been stabbed, just after I left you. You live up on the Barking Road and must've seen something, Gimpy, even if it was only me talking to him. Now, if you did see Kevin Dooley or anyone you think might've been him, you'd better get on and tell me,' I said. 'I'll buy you another barley wine and you can have one fag for now and one to put behind your ear.'

Gimpy thought about this for a few seconds before he said, 'I kept quiet because no one don't need to hear that sort of thing about those what've passed on.'

'What do you mean, Gimpy?'

'I mean if, like, you had a brother and after he was dead it turned out he was an iron, would you want to know?'

'Was Kevin Dooley an iron, then?' I said.

Gimpy nearly got inside my jacket trying to get close enough so no one else could hear. 'Yus,' he said. 'Saw him, you know, with this geezer on the night he died. Disgusting it was!'

Chapter Fifteen

I ron hoof – poof. I had a bit of bother believing it of Kevin Dooley, yet Gimpy Charlie said he'd seen it happen. Just behind St Mary's graveyard, he said, which meant that Kevin must've run from there, or at least walked quickly to get up to the Barking Road at the same time as me. The other man, whom Charlie couldn't really get a good look at, had seemed young. But then, as the old bloke had said, it was difficult to see him, what with the blackout and him being on his knees in front of Kevin.

Had this young man stabbed Kevin Dooley because, maybe, he hadn't paid him for what he'd done? Irons, unless they're very well connected and especially if they're married, generally have to pay for their jollies. As soon as I could string a sentence together again, I'd have to telephone Blatt and let him know. Too pie-eyed to go to the coppers right then, I'd come home in what Nan calls a 'right state' and gone to my bedroom. Not to sleep – the room was spinning round far too quickly for that even if my mind was quite slow.

Of course, this latest bit of information didn't solve anything so much as add further complications. If Kevin Dooley was an iron, then what was he doing having something with Martine – if indeed he had been? And where had Martine, and maybe Johnny too, been that night? I, at least, still didn't feel sure. If Martine had been out, had she seen Kevin maybe, been disgusted by what he was doing with another man and killed him? Kevin did, after all, say that 'she' had stabbed him, which seemed to rule out his iron chum. Maybe 'she' was Pearl after all. How did I know that Dot Harris had really done that abortion on her? I didn't. Pearl and Velma could be lying very well, and with some knowledge regarding Dot, about the whole thing. Then again there was what I'd overheard Sister Teresa say to Blatt about people who 'knew' something about, I had to presume, Pearl and Ruby's predicaments. I'd have to go and talk to Mr Blatt, be straight with him and tell him what I'd overheard if I wanted to go any further with all this. But before I did that, I'd have to do something else first and that was speak, if I could, to Sister Teresa.

Between sobering up, talking to Fred Bryant down the police station, and not being able to get through on the telephone, I only managed to speak to Sister Teresa at near on ten o'clock.

When she came on the line she said, 'Do you have any idea how late it is?'

'Do you have any idea how it feels sitting here with the telephone not knowing if the Luftwaffe are going to cut your call short?' I said. Yes, I knew that nuns went to bed early: I'd had it chapter and verse from my mother before I called.

'So what do you want?' she said.

I didn't go into detail, but I did tell her there was a possibility someone else, a man, could have been involved in Kevin Dooley's murder. 'So if you think your father may still have some angry relatives or mates out there . . .'

'Were you listening in on my conversation this morning, Mr Hancock?'

'Yes,' I responded calmly. I could hear that she was outraged so I got it all over with quickly. 'So I know Mr Blatt knows where your sister Opal is,' I said. 'I also know that he lied about that to me. I don't know why he did that, except that your family seem to have more secrets than most, Sister Teresa, and not for any reason I can easily fathom.'

'Our mother—'

'Yes, your mother killed somebody a long time ago,' I said. 'But that's not you, and I don't know why you and your sisters seem to be so worried about people having some sort of grudge against you. And what is it people might know or find out?'

'You—'

'I'm not trying to accuse anyone here,' I said. 'I just think that those who kill people should be punished.'

'I don't know where Opal is!'

'Yes, I know that,' I said. 'But what about these enemies and what—'

'My dad, Neilson, he did once speak about another kid he had a long time ago—'

The line went dead before she could say any more. I was tempted to throw the bloody telephone down the stairs I was that frustrated with it. But that Bakelite stuff breaks easily and, besides, what would getting into a paddy about it do? Talking to the nun had been a waste of time, but what of it? Talking to Fred Bryant hadn't been a walk in the park either. I couldn't tell him who'd told me about Kevin Dooley's 'thing' for blokes so Fred said he couldn't go any further with it.

'But you must know some of the local pansy boys. You're a copper,' I'd said. 'Ask around them.'

But all Fred would say was that he'd mention what I'd said to Sergeant Hill. I think he's afraid of irons myself.

'Any case the Dooleys won't like that iron business one bit if they find out,' Fred had said, as I'd left.

I thought, Tough.

As the sirens started up for another night's entertainment, I passed Velma in the hall on her way down to the shelter. She looked at me and smiled. 'Seeing me mum tomorrow, eh, Mr Hancock?'

Even with the raid about to start, she was so excited.

'Y-yes, I-love,' I said.

No one slept that night. No one. Not my family, not me – out and about on my run once again. Not the firemen I saw lift a burning girder off a little girl who'd been pinned underneath it. Her legs had melted. I started to shake apart when I heard her scream, 'I'm going to die! I'm going to die!' And, yes, she was, I knew that. But one of

237

the firemen, I don't know how he bore it, said, 'No, you ain't, love. We'll soon have you out of here and back to your mum.' I heard the death rattle in her throat only seconds after that. Then her eyes closed and she was gone. Me, screaming inside and useless, I went over to the firemen and said, 'I am an undertaker.' They ignored me. They behaved as if I was, for all the world, really back on the Somme, my hell instead of this new hell that they lived inside.

'What are you doing, Frank?' Aggie wheezed, as she watched Velma and me step out of the shop on to what was left of the pavement. You get days when, for some reason, all the brick-dust just gets right down on your chest. Aggie's poor pipes sounded like a couple of busted-up old bellows.

'We're going to see my mum's lawyer,' Velma said brightly. I'd found a couple of tennis balls that had once belonged to my nephew and Velma was enjoying herself juggling with them.

'I didn't think that was until this afternoon,' my sister said doubtfully, as she took out and lit up a fag. 'Mum said—'

'I have a few things I need to speak to Mr Blatt about first,' I said, in a way that I thought sounded reasonable.

'You know you're not right, don't you, Frank?' Aggie rasped.

'Why don't you go and play ball up against that wall for a minute?' I said to Velma, pointing to the bit of blank brick down the side of the pub.

The kid went with a smile and no questions.

I turned to Aggie. 'What do you mean?' I said, knowing full well exactly what she meant.

'Wish I'd never put it into your head Kevin Dooley could've been stabbed,' Aggie said. 'If I'd never spoke maybe you would've just thought he was barmy and left it alone.'

'But then we'd never have known he was murdered,' I said. 'A killer would be out there with no policemen on his trail.'

'Oh, what, you mean police like Fred Bryant, do you?' Aggie sneered. 'There's a lot of Jerries causing a bit of death and destruction here and there if you haven't noticed, Frank. Some oik from Canning Town gets what's coming to him, possibly from his poor old missus. No one cares!'

'I do.'

My sister pursed her heavily painted lips.

I moved in closer towards her. 'I've killed people, Aggie,' I said. 'I didn't know them, they didn't know me, but if I could find their relatives, show them who I am, then I think it might help them. It's important to know the truth about the dead.'

'Frank, you killed people in battle.'

'It's no different!' I said, as I felt tears of frustration form in my eyes. Why couldn't Aggie understand this? 'Kevin Dooley came to me for help. I let him down and he died! Who killed him, the truth, it's important for him!'

'But he was a right—'

'It doesn't matter what he was like,' I said.

'Oh, so if that poor cow Pearl did, beyond doubt, do him in, then you'll grass her up with her kid under our roof, will you?'

'Yes,' I said. 'If she's guilty I will.'

'All for the memory of a bloke who got drunk and beat up women?'

'He was a human being!' I said.

'Yes, but what are you getting out of all this, Frank?'

I didn't answer her. I knew I could never make her understand. She can be very clinical. But, then, she's never killed anyone. She can't understand what it's like to know you'll never put right what you did – ever. The guilt that robs you of any notion of peace of mind.

'You don't understand,' I said softly.

'No.' Aggie stopped for a moment to catch her breath and then said, 'But what I do know is, no one saw nothing so anything could've happened that night. Not that that bothers me at all. It's you I'm worried about. All this "investigating", it's taking you over. Stop it – you can't do no good. Look even more like a bleedin' ghost than you do usually.'

She was right, of course. I would've had to be blind not to see how sick I was starting to look. Because I'm dark I've always had to shave more than most so I'd been treated to my wan face at least twice a day. Not that it had registered. The other side of it is that when I get really sick, my eyes get very bright and there's a sort of a wild urgency to everything that makes me forget about how I look or how I might be feeling. I thought about all of these things as I swung along with Velma, on foot and then on

240

whatever buses or trams that were running, to Mr Blatt's Knightsbridge office. But I knew I couldn't change either myself or what the Kevin Dooley affair was doing to me. I had to see it through, whatever the outcome.

The West End, though scarred by bombing, like Paddington, is still recognisable. Blokes with a few readies still take their girls dancing up the Astoria on Tottenham Court Road, and the Corner Houses are as full as they've ever been. But when we got to Piccadilly Circus it was sad to see poor old Eros boarded up and everything around that area looking run-down, dismal and piled up with sandbags. Apparently up on Oxford Street there has been some bomb damage, the National Bank having caught it only a few weeks back, as, I heard, had John Lewis's. But round Blatt's office, down Hans Crescent, opposite Harrods, things – if you can forget the tape on the windows and the sandbags – look almost normal. Not much there to provide a target for the Jerries, I suppose. No docks or warehouses or anything that might help to break us down if it were hit, like St Paul's Cathedral or Buckingham Palace. Just a big department store, a lot of women wearing high heels and furs, and Mr Blatt in his wood-panelled office, not looking very pleased at all.

'You've got no right to ask me anything, Hancock,' he said, after I told him I knew that he knew where Opal Reynolds lived. 'How dare you listen in to a private conversation? Who do you think you are?'

I'd left Velma out in the reception area because what was being said wasn't suitable for a child. But in view of all the shouting I imagined she could hear it anyway. I lowered my voice in an attempt to lessen the volume.

'I'm someone who's looking after Pearl Dooley's daughter,' I said. 'I'm also—'

'You're an undertaker, Hancock!' Blatt shouted. 'Not a policeman! Good God, if it wasn't for you none of this would have happened anyway!'

'If it wasn't—'

'It was you, wasn't it, who insisted that the awful Dooley had been murdered?'

'Yes,' I said. 'And I was right.' Coming on top of Aggie's little rant Blatt was giving me the 'ump now and I made sure he knew it. 'Why? Would you rather a man had been murdered and no one know?'

'Well, of course not.' Blatt ran a hand through his heavily brilliantined hair. 'But Pearl Reynolds, who I know is an innocent woman, wouldn't now be in Holloway if you'd left it alone.'

'No, she'd be on the street with Velma, cut off from the rest of her kids . . .'

'Yes, but she'd be free,' he said, and then he threw himself down into the chair behind his desk. 'And I wouldn't be involved.'

'Yes, but you are, aren't you, Blatt?' I said tightly. 'You've been involved since long before Kevin Dooley . . .'

'What do you mean?'

I looked at him as his eyes darted back and forth across his desk, as if searching for something. Eventually he lit up a fag, without offering one to me, his fingers shaking as they wrapped themselves round the Passing Cloud. Blatt was a worried man.

'I thought you're defending Pearl because you want to,' I said.

'Because of her mother I feel obliged,' he answered.

I didn't say anything about what Sister Teresa and Ruby had told me regarding Blatt's seeming incompetence. But then, surely, if he had done a less than perfect job for Victorine, maybe he felt more than obliged to try to help her daughter. Not that any of that explained why he'd felt the need to keep Opal's whereabouts secret.

'So is Opal—'

'She has nothing to do with Kevin Dooley or you! Opal Reynolds is completely safe, as I told her sister,' Blatt said. 'I don't know why some people seem fixated on the idea of a conspiracy against these women. All right, I know the authorities are probably prejudiced on account of Victorine and all that, but as for "others" out to "get" these women . . .'

'And I don't know about that either,' I said. 'But what you can't get away from, Mr Blatt, is that Ruby Reynolds left what was a very safe place for her, with someone unknown, who used my name to get at her, and has now disappeared. I know Sister Teresa has fears. I heard—'

'Amber Reynolds has probably spent too long brooding on the past,' Blatt said, 'sequestered away in that convent.'

'Yes, but, Mr Blatt, there must be some basis for all this. I heard you and her talk about someone "knowing" something.'

'Amber and the rest of them are all hysterical over an old crime they didn't commit,' Blatt said, as he ground out his fag in the ashtray and lit another. 'They're all as mad as hatters, always have been. I, to some extent, humour them. Not that their insanity is in itself surprising, given their background. But you have to remember, Mr Hancock, that the Reynolds women, though not with any criminal intent, of course, cannot be relied upon. They see enemies everywhere. Ever since their mother died they have been like this. I, for instance, did my best for their mother yet they all insist that it was entirely my fault that Victorine eventually went to the gallows.'

I wanted to ask him some more about his involvement, possibly of a personal nature, and, in particular, with Victorine Reynolds herself, but I didn't. Beyond knowing where she was, I couldn't prove that Blatt had anything to do with Opal Reynolds, much less that he was her father. So instead I said, 'And yet you think that what Pearl has told you about the night Kevin died can be relied on?'

'Yes.' He smiled, but he didn't say any more than that or give any reasons for his opinion. 'Don't you?'

'I don't know, Mr Blatt,' I said. 'Really I don't.'

I went on to tell him about what Gimpy Charlie had said. I didn't mention the old bloke's name, although I knew I could get him to talk to Blatt easier than he would've done to the police, if need be. The lawyer was nothing short of ecstatic. In fact, I thought at the time that it was almost as if he'd needed this piece of information to get back his own freedom. His change in attitude towards me was nothing short of amazing.

Now he offered me a fag. 'I'll have to speak to this contact of yours myself,' he said. 'Just the fact that someone else was present with Dooley, and involved in an immoral act, throws serious doubt on Pearl's supposed guilt, whether she was having an abortion or not.'

'He didn't actually see this iron bloke attacking Kevin, you know,' I said. 'And Kevin told me, as you know, that it was a woman as stabbed him.'

'Yes, yes, but Dooley had been drunk all day and he must have been out of his mind with shock . . .'

'And I don't know whether this – person,' I said, as I lit up my fag, 'will want to come to court.'

'Well, he'll have to,' Blatt said. And then he got up, went over to the door and opened it. 'Miss Atkinson, could you bring me the Reynolds file, please?'

I heard the woman outside say, 'Yes, Mr Blatt,' followed by the sound of metal cabinet drawers opening and shutting.

'I can't thank you enough for this, you know, Hancock,' he said, as the woman came in holding a thick cardboard file. 'Pearl will be delighted.'

That her husband had been an iron? I wasn't so sure about that. But as it happened I didn't get to find that out on this occasion because only Blatt and Velma were allowed into Holloway to see Pearl. I don't know what the arrangements for visiting prisons were before the war, but these days I think they're pretty strict. Nowadays there are all sorts in prisons – traitors, Communists, who I know some see as traitors, and conchies. Conscientious objectors, 'conchies', refuse to fight or have anything to do with the production of weapons. Some of them work in reserved occupations – which is what I am in strictly, as well as being too bloody old to fight – on the ambulances and suchlike. I know a few and I like them, but most people don't. They call them 'cowards' and 'Nazis' and sometimes the poor buggers get beaten up for their opinions. I can understand them only too well. If I were of call-up age, I'd be one of them. I make no bones about that. For a bereaved person there is no suffering worse than grief. For an unwilling killer there is nothing worse than living with the knowledge of what he's done. I try to run away from it. I sometimes think I might kill myself because of it. But it never goes away. In the end I'm always led back to that same old condemned cell in my head. Can actual prison be any worse? In Holloway, it being a women's prison, there weren't likely to be any conchies, but there would be Communists and pacifists and just the thought of them in there, innocent of any actual crime, made me feel bad. I stood outside those grim grey walls while Blatt and Velma went inside and smoked myself to a standstill.

Chapter Sixteen

All the time Blatt and Velma were inside the prison I thought about Martine Dooley and her place in what I knew about Kevin's death so far. On the face of it, her story would seem to undermine Gimpy's tale about Kevin being an iron. But on the other hand, something had to have been going on so I told Blatt about Martine and about my own encounters with Johnny and his brothers when he and Velma came out of the prison. He adopted a troubled expression at this, but thanked me and said that he'd try to find out more about Kevin's relationships. Pearl had not, apparently, told him about Martine. But maybe she hadn't known.

I took Velma home, where we settled in to our normal routine of waiting and preparing for a possible raid. As usual, we sat in the kitchen – the Duchess all in black, with her hair piled up in a thick bun on the top of her head – listening to the Crazy Gang on the wireless, Nan wearing what looked like most of her clothes against the cold, knitting something or other, while Velma flicked through an old copy of *Picture Post* she'd found in the parlour. Disappointingly, she didn't have much to say about her mother. From what I could gather, Mr Blatt had done most of the talking. Aggie was at work. I smoked. To be honest, my mind was a blank by this time so smoking was all that I did until I finally went to bed at just after ten.

I wake easily – I have done ever since the trenches – so I wasn't worried about not hearing the sirens. But when I came to, at what I later learned was just gone four in the morning, I was convinced that somehow I'd slept through it. And although I couldn't see even the dim glow of light you get through the blackout curtains when a raid's going on outside, I could feel the whole building shaking, which had to mean something. I lit the candle I keep at the side of my bed, then pulled on my trousers. Somewhere above the shaking and the banging a voice was screaming.

I picked up the candle and ran out on to the landing. Strangely, for her, the Duchess was in her bedroom doorway, stock still, her hair hanging loose down to where her knees should have been.

'Nancy's gone downstairs to see who it is,' she said calmly.

'What?'

'Someone at the door, dear. Your sister has gone to find out.'

I ran down the stairs, my candle extinguishing as I did so. War or no war, who the hell went knocking on doors in the small hours of the morning? Looters checking to see whether folk were in or not was the first thing that sprang to mind.

'Nan!' I said, as I burst through the black curtains into the shop.

But the door was opened and shut again by the time I got there and who had been outside was now in. The sheer blackness of her clothing told me immediately who she was.

'I've had to walk from Dagenham,' Sister Teresa said. 'Train couldn't go no further than that.'

In spite of being tired after all that walking, not to mention the energy she must have spent banging on my door and screaming, Sister Teresa was anxious to talk. Nan, whose love of all things Catholic had been tested a bit by the Sister, went back to bed, so it was the Duchess who made tea for the nun and me in the kitchen. Luckily Velma hadn't woken. But she'd had a very busy and emotional day for such a young kid. And although she hadn't said much, it had been easy to tell that the prison and the fact that her mum was in it had frightened her. Who wouldn't it terrify?

'I got a telephone call,' Sister Teresa said, without pre-amble. 'I wrote down what he said after, word for word.' She pushed a piece of paper over the table towards me.

I was still a bit shocked by her appearance, to tell the truth, so my hands shook somewhat when I took it from her. It didn't take long to read, just twenty-two words. After I'd finished reading I looked up and said, 'What secret?'

The Duchess placed a cup and saucer in front of Sister Teresa just as she put her head down and said, 'I can't tell you.'

'Do you know who it was on the phone?' I said. 'Did you recognise the voice?'

'No. Only that it was a man.'

'When did you get it? The call?'

'This afternoon. I left straight away. I told Sister Emerita I had family business again. You know how the trains are – I couldn't risk leaving tomorrow, even in the morning. As it is, I've had a terrible time, on and off trains . . .'

'So what do you want me to do?' I said. I was still, frankly, needled by her outright refusal to talk about the 'secret' mentioned on the paper.

'Nothing, really,' she said. 'But after what's happened to Pearl and Ruby, I'm afraid. It's taken me hours to get here. I just didn't know where else to go.'

'You should go to the police,' I said as I threw the paper back across the table at her.

'No!'

'Why not? If you see some sort of threat in what this bloke said, which you must've done to bother to write it down, you should get some help.'

She looked away. The Duchess, meantime, placed my cuppa on the table and sat down with us.

'I've known there's been something else, a "secret", for a while,' I said, 'and to be truthful, Sister, it's given me the 'ump.'

The nun turned back to me, her eyes a little wet round the edges.

'Because,' I continued, angrily now, 'I was only ever really interested in Kevin Dooley. That I've done what I could for your sisters along the way is lucky for you. But it's not been easy for me. I've done it. My family have gladly looked after Velma—'

'No! I can't!' She began to cry.

'Oh, blimey!' I said. 'Don't—'

'No!'

'Tell my son your secret, my dear.' The Duchess reached out one twisted hand to the nun and smiled. 'He can't help you unless you do. Why indeed should he?'

The two women looked at each other in silence. It was a private moment between them. The same as when a bloke comes across two women gossiping and they stop and stare at him, he has to look away. I looked away now.

I heard the nun sigh and then she said, 'Mr Blatt got Opal adopted to some family he knows, friends of his, because he's her father.'

I looked at her now and shrugged. I had, of course, suspected as much. However, what she said next was something I hadn't even considered.

'Except that he isn't,' Sister Teresa said. 'Mum told him he was to get him to help her after she killed my father.'

'But she must have, you know,' I said, not quite knowing how to approach the subject of sex with a nun, 'had "relations" with Blatt.'

'Oh, yes. But he wasn't Opal's father, or so Mum said.'

'And anyway,' I said, 'Neilson didn't die until eight

years after Opal was born. Did your mum carry on seeing Blatt during that time? How do you know this anyway?'

'Mum told us.'

'When?'

'That night. The night of . . .'

'So did you or your sisters know him?'

'Ruby remembered him. But as you said, Mr Hancock, it had been over eight years before. Mum only saw him for a few months round about when she got, you know, in the family way with our Opal. There were other blokes too, including Neilson. It was her job.'

'So how did she know that Blatt wasn't Opal's father?' I said. 'How could she know that for certain?'

She took a swig from her cup before she replied. 'I don't know,' she said. 'Maybe it was wishful thinking on her part. There was this other fellow, another Jewish geezer, at the same time. He was very young. Not beaten up and wounded by being in the Great War, like Blatt and the rest of them. I think he was a bit of a villain, really. But Mum liked him. It was him my dad hated because he believed that he, this bloke, was Opal's father. Mum would sometimes tease him with it, you know, when he'd been a pig to her.'

'And this is the secret you think this letter-writer knows?' I said.

She looked away briefly, then said, 'Yes.'

I reached across the table and picked up the paper once again. It said: 'I know the secret you and your sisters keep. Meet me at the place you were when Neilson died. Come tomorrow 9 p.m.' All the Reynolds sisters, apart from Opal, had been somewhere else when their mother killed Neilson. Where, I didn't know. In fact, I didn't know much about what had taken place that night. Had the girls come in and found their mother in a state of shock after what she'd done, Neilson's body lying lifeless across their lino? Or had it been more cold-blooded than that? If Victorine had hatched a plan to get herself one of the best lawyers money could buy for free, then she had to have had some sort of grip on what was going on. This didn't seem to square, to me, with the picture of a remorseful woman begging her dead lover's forgiveness on the gallows, if indeed that wasn't just a story. And, anyway, why had whoever it was telephoned Amber/Sister Teresa? If it was blackmail he had in mind, I wondered what form it could possibly take. The nun had no money, as far as I knew, and if the caller's aim was to tell Blatt the truth, if money or information or whatever were not passed over, then what did he think that might achieve? There was no going back on what Blatt had done for Victorine and, being a professional, he was hardly likely to drop Pearl now. That would look bad, suspicious even. And what about what I'd overheard pass between Sister Teresa and Blatt in our parlour? Hadn't they talked about someone 'knowing' something he or she shouldn't? Well, that couldn't possibly be this 'secret', could it? No, it had to be something else . . .

'Do you know whether this Mr Blatt is married with children?' I heard the Duchess say.

'I know he's got a wife,' Sister Teresa said. 'Most of

Mum's blokes usually had wives. That's how that life works.'

'So where were you and your sisters on the night your father died?' I said.

'We went to the park,' the nun said. 'Hyde Park. We often used to go there to play, shouting at courting couples on the Serpentine, running about, you know. Being silly.'

'Wasn't it evening?' I said.

'Yes, but it was summer. Why? Don't you believe me? The police believed us.'

'No, I—'

'We went to the park, Ruby, Pearl and me, and when we come home, I dunno, just as it was getting dark, my dad was dead, my mum had killed him and Opal had slept through it all. End of story.' She looked angry now and, in her anger, not a bit frightening too. All done up in black, her face looming out at me like a moon.

'So do you think that this telephone call might have got anything to do with what has happened to your sisters?' I said.

She sighed. 'I don't know. Seems strange all these terrible things are happening to us all at the same time. Whoever rang me wants something from me at nine' – she looked briefly at her watch – 'tonight.'

'In Hyde Park.'

'Yeah, by the Serpentine,' she said. 'Must be. That's where we were when my dad died. Everyone who knows anything knows that.'

'OK.' I asked the Duchess to leave then, which she did. Probably she'd be all right to listen to talk about men who love other men, but I couldn't have stood the embarrassment. I told Sister Teresa about Kevin Dooley when we were on our own. 'The way Kevin died, could have been coincidence,' I said, even though I didn't really believe that. 'This could all be a coincidence.'

'Yeah, but what about Ruby?'

'I don't know,' I said. And remembering the warning I'd had from the gruff-voiced bloke in Limehouse, I felt anxious about this all over again. 'She shouldn't have run like that after they found Shlomo Kaplan's body.'

Sister Teresa shot me a vicious glare. 'You don't know what it's like,' she said. 'Your mum's never killed no one.'

We sat quietly with our own thoughts for a bit after that.

Eventually, I said, because this was what I really had to know, 'What do you want from me then, Sister? Do you want me to come with you?'

'No!' Again she looked almost fierce. 'No. I have to go on me own. I want, I suppose, well, I wanted somewhere to stay when my train wouldn't go no further and I'd also like it if you'd let the Sisters at Nazareth House know if anything should happen to me. I just want someone to know where I've gone.'

'So you'll go this evening,' I said, 'even though you're afraid?'

'What else can I do? There's no one, is there? Like you said, it ain't really your business.'

'And Mr Blatt?'

'Blatt ain't to know!' She moved in closer towards me and took one of my arms in what proved to be a powerful grasp. 'Never! Opal's got a good family, so I hear. Leave it be!' She let go of my arm and said, 'Just tell my Sisters in Christ I was doing what I felt to be right. They'll understand. They know. And look out for Pearl's kid if you can, if all that goes wrong for her. I know she's got others but they've got family. Not like that poor kid.'

'You speak as if you're about to die,' I said.

'Who knows?' She shrugged. 'There's been such wickedness in my family, Mr Hancock. Who knows who might want to hurt us? Maybe my dad's stories about a son he had by some other woman are true. Maybe that man knows things – although I can't imagine how. How anyone outside could know is – is beyond me.'

'And yet, forgive me,' I said, 'there is still something I feel you're not telling me, Sister. Mr Blatt knows some sort of secret about someone knowing something he shouldn't. I overheard—'

'That's something else,' she said shortly. 'Nothing to bother about.'

'But—'

'It's not got anything to do with this,' she said. 'It's – that's not important.' And then she changed the subject rapidly by asking me for a fag.

I let the nun have my bed for the few hours of darkness that remained. I couldn't sleep anyway. The 'something else' that Blatt knew about was important. But whether or not it had any connection to Kevin Dooley or any of the other strange things that were happening around these women, I didn't know. Whatever else, the nun believed herself to be in danger and in spite of what Blatt had said back in his office about her brooding and fantasising, I wasn't easy about that. Hyde Park is a big place and, after dark, like any big open space in a city, it appears quite creepy. I knew I wouldn't want to be there on my own at night, much less if I knew I was going to be there with someone I felt possessed ill intent towards me.

Chapter Seventeen

Velma, poor little soul, couldn't understand why her aunt didn't want much to do with her any more than I could. But Sister Teresa seemed to have an aversion to the girl that had nothing to do with not liking children. After all, she did work with them. No, it was, I felt, more to do with the distance she and her sisters had maintained for all these years. That thing they did that was 'for the best'.

The kid stood at the back of the shop as I said goodbye reluctantly to her aunt.

'I don't like the idea of you going off on your own to meet this character,' I said.

'You've done enough already,' Sister Teresa said. 'Just look after the kid and . . .'

'So where are you going now?' I said, as I took the nun's hand in mine.

'I've things to do. I – I need to think.'

'And later tonight,' I said, 'if anything should happen . . .'

She shrugged.

'Yes, but what if it all goes wrong? What if—'

'If I disappear or worse? Then tell my Sisters in Christ that I'm sorry for causing them problems. You just keep on, as I said, looking after the kid,' she said. 'And, if you can, help our Pearl. She's never killed her husband. She ain't bad. Not all of us are.'

'I know you're not.' And then I said, 'But, look, what about the blackout? How can you meet someone you don't know in the blackout?'

She shrugged again.

'I mean, where in the park will you go to?'

'I'll walk around the Serpentine,' she said, vaguely waving a hand, as if pushing such details away. 'Ruby, Pearl and me were playing there when it must've happened.'

'And if there's a raid—'

'Well, I'll be going, then.' She cut me off dead. Matter-of-factly and without looking back once, she left the shop and pushed her way into the crowds trying to get a bit of shopping before the next raid. She went towards Canning Town, which meant that she was going west. But soon she'd disappeared. Velma left me too. I heard her tired footsteps clatter out into the yard.

I stood at the door for a bit after that, thinking, but not thinking, troubled by what, if anything, I should do now. Not that there was too much choice because whatever I might be doing for Kevin, for Velma or anyone, I still had to make a living. I went upstairs to get a cuppa and a fag and found Jimmy Pepper sitting at the table with the

Duchess. Nan was at the range, boiling a kettle for tea and frying some bread.

'Smells like nectar, that, Nan,' Jimmy said, as he closed his eyes the better to appreciate it. 'Morning, Frank.'

'Jim.'

I got my baccy and papers off the dresser and sat down. Jimmy is my old oppo Georgie's younger brother. Too little to be in the last lot, luckily for Georgie's mum and dad. They lost three boys, including Georgie, as it was. A carpenter by trade, Jimmy makes our coffins for us with the help of Arthur and Walter who do the labouring. He's not in every day, Jimmy, and hadn't been about that much in recent times on account of his family being bombed out. Not that it had mattered too much with the kind of 'trade' we'd been getting. Taking measurements of a corpse is only something you do when you've got a whole body. But we had a few of those coming up so it was important they got the right boxes and not have to put up with whatever was left in one piece in the store.

The Duchess, Nan, Jimmy and, when she came back inside, Velma had fried bread and tea. I just had tea and a fag. It's my usual breakfast, although sometimes it'll be a pipe rather than a fag. Life of variety! After breakfast, I took the horses out of the stable and began to walk them down towards Beckton. Jimmy said he'd give their stall a look-over while we were out and try to patch up the damage they'd done. I hadn't got round to repairing it, but after the last raid, when they'd been particularly wild with their hoofs, something had to be done.

There are a lot of horsemen over Beckton marshes.

Most of them are gypsies or diddies. Some live in caravans, others in sheds; some still, like Horatio, live elsewhere in some unknown place. I've known Horatio for years. He's a farrier by trade, a Romany, and shoes for all the other geezers down there as well as for the rag-and-bone men, and some other businesses, including mine. He also, for a small consideration, exercises horses. Whenever I need to give the boys a bit of a run I always go looking for Horatio. I like riding with him: he's a real horseman.

The fog was thick that morning – although whether it was just fog or clouds of dust from what had once been houses over Silvertown it was impossible to say. But it got a good cough going in me, Rama and Sita.

'Mr Hancock.' A face as sharp and dark as an ebony pin came out of the grey soup at me, one rough hand stroking its moustache.

'Horatio,' I said. 'Fancy a little gallop?'

The gypsy put out his hand to Rama and patted his muzzle. 'Only if I can ride him,' he said.

'Done.'

Rama is the more spirited of the two and, as a mount, is a bit more fun than his brother Sita. My horses were bred by Horatio's brother, George Gordon. Gypsies often name their kids after military heroes and the like. Horatio is as in Nelson and George Gordon is after the general of the same name, the one who defended Khartoum against the 'Mad' Mahdi. Their names sit strangely with their dark faces and wild black hair.

If anyone had been able to see us through the fog, we must've looked quite a sight, Horatio and me on our galloping black horses. Two refugees from some Oriental land where the sun shines all year long. The ground over the marshes is always wet, winter and summer, so every time Sita's hoofs hit the earth it was in the middle of a spray of mud. I'd be filthy by the time I took them home, but I didn't care. I needed this stretch in the stinking air almost as much as the horses did. I needed the silence of it too. Nothing save the sound of the hoofs on the ground – no sirens, no voices, no crumbling noise as yet another house or school or church collapsed in on itself. Only in such emptiness can my mind be truly still.

We rode over to Gallions, which is a big pub at the end of the Albert Dock on the stretch of water that's known as Gallions Reach. In the old days the lights of Gallions were often the last bright thing of England those going out to the colonies or being transported to Australia would see. It was the first thing my mother remarked on when she sailed down the Thames with my dad all those years ago. 'That's a frightening place,' she'd said. And it can be, especially when it looms out of the fog at you, all dark and top heavy, a bit like pictures you see of the old hulks, the prison ships.

Horatio and I stopped to catch our breath, the horses beneath us stamping and snorting in the cold. Thick white vapour rose from their hot bodies like clouds.

'That's haunted,' Horatio said, as he pointed towards the grim old pile.

'My grandad always used to say that,' I said. Smugglers and pirates, according to Grandad, their spirits trapped on the earth by the killings and other evil deeds they'd committed, tormented for ever by the boozy scene of their crimes.

'You have to let people go, Mr Hancock,' Horatio said, 'or you'll get a haunting and that's no good thing.'

I don't believe in ghosts – only the ones that live in people's minds. But a lot of folk do believe, especially the gypsies. And sometimes what they say I can see some worth in.

'Not that you can always see the ghost,' Horatio said. 'Sometimes it's invisible, but it's there.'

'What do you mean?' I said.

Horatio took his pipe out of his pocket and put the stem between his dark brown front teeth. 'Some people have a lot of misfortune in their lives,' he said. 'They try all sorts to get away from it but they can't. People like this, they smell of fear. Make folk want to get away from them. Haunted, see, just like this pub.'

'So what do you have to do if you want to get rid of a ghost or stop being haunted or whatever?'

'You have to let the spirit go,' Horatio said simply. But then, just for a moment, his face became stern. 'You have to be right with the spirit, though, else it'll carry on hanging on to you. If you've wronged it or you owed it when it was alive then you must put that right with it. You must live a clean life and do no further evil.'

'And if you don't?'

'Then it'll be on your shoulder for the rest of your days and you'll smell the fear, keep turning round to see if it's there. Sometimes ghosts like this can live in families,' he said. 'Where things are not put right the ghost can seek vengeance by following that family around. I suppose you could say they inherit the evil.'

The sins of the fathers – or mothers. All the Reynolds girls did that turning round Horatio had described. Not in reality, of course, but in the way they lived, hidden away in Ruby and Sister Teresa's case and sort of in Pearl's too – concealed among her great big family. And the way they reacted to their recent misfortunes, immediately, in their minds, pinning the blame on an event, and those round it, that had happened when they were all children. Even Sister Teresa's initial denial that Pearl's situation had nothing to do with their mother hadn't rung true, as if she really believed it. Because she didn't and she was going to meet someone who knew 'something' from her past to prove it.

But for a 'haunting' of this size, across seemingly so many people, there had, surely, to be something else too. None of the girls had had any idea about who might be out to discredit them – if, indeed, that was the intention. They'd come up with vague ideas about relatives of Neilson, who might or might not exist, but Blatt, who must've known a thing or two about his client's victim, didn't seem to think that that had any reality to it at all. And as for Sister Teresa's 'secret', that Blatt wasn't Opal's father – I couldn't see how his knowing that now would make any difference. He hadn't adopted the girl and whoever had, presumably loved her now and would love her whether she was his or not. Was it connected to the 'something' these women still weren't telling me, the thing Blatt and the nun had alluded to up in my parlour?

Was it, I wondered, some sort of deeper secret – more secret than anything I'd heard so far? Alone in the fog, I felt like one of Horatio's unquiet ghosts waiting to be released some time. Because if life and particularly undertaking has taught me anything it is this: those who take secrets to the grave are few and far between. The haunted are generally tracked down in the end, often by other haunted types who recognise their plight. All spectres in the mist.

By the time I got back to the shop I'd made up my mind to be at the Serpentine at nine o'clock that night. Whatever she was or had involvement with, I couldn't live with the idea of Sister Teresa going there alone to face someone who might do her harm. Also, I wanted to know what was going on for myself. I had an idea that whatever was going to happen in the park, whatever was going to be said, would have a bearing on a lot of the mysteries that had troubled me so far – maybe even Kevin's death.

It was already long gone dinner-time when the stable was ready to put the horses back into so I told Nan not to bother to heat up what she'd cooked for me. 'I'm going out soon,' I said.

'Where?' she asked.

'I've got a bit of business.' I didn't want to go into what I had planned with either the Duchess or the girls. I didn't want them to worry.

'Who with?'

Part of being a bitter person, as I've observed it in Nan, is to be suspicious of everyone and everything. I know

Aggie can be a bit like this too, but with Ag I always feel she's looking out for me by doing it and not just trying to make me feel bad for being who I can't help being. Nan's persistence was needling me now and I wasn't above showing it.

When I first sighed and then didn't bother to answer her, Nan said, 'So will you be home for your tea?'

'No,' I said tetchily.

'Oh, so if we have a raid tonight I'll have to cope with Mum all alone, will I? Aggie's out at that job of hers—'

'I've been out before when a raid has started!' I said. I was beginning to yell now, which is something I rarely do. 'I was out the other night with the hearse and the horses, for Christ's sake!'

'Yes, I know, and don't blaspheme! But it's better if you're home, Frank. You know Mum can't make the stairs and it's as much as I can do—'

'If Francis needs to go out then that is what he must do.'

We both turned to look at her, the Duchess, smiling, leaning on her stick in the kitchen doorway.

'But, Mum . . .'

'Nancy, if I know Francis is going to be out I can get down to the Anderson at my leisure.'

'Yes, but you don't want to be down there. It's damp.'

'I know.' The Duchess moved painfully to the table and sat down on one of the hard chairs. 'But if I take enough blankets and some warm tea, I will be all right. I know that you're tired, Nancy, and I will try not to be a bother, but please don't take it out on your brother. We all have our crosses to bear, especially Francis.'

Nan put her head down while the Duchess raised her face to me. 'Because Francis has things to do, haven't you, Francis? Things you need to do.'

'Yes, Duchess.'

'I don't know what they are but I imagine they have something to do with the death of that poor man Dooley,' she said. 'You don't like it when death is unresolved, do you, Francis? Like your father, you'll have no truck with lies – whoever is telling them. The dead deserve no less.'

I didn't answer. My mother nursed me for months when I came home from the Great War. She is the only one who even begins to understand me. Nan, put down yet again or so she must've felt, pulled a sour face, which prompted the Duchess to ask her to leave us alone for a minute.

Once Nan had gone, she said to me, 'You know that Agnes thinks you should leave all of this business to the police. She feels it is far more complicated than any of us imagines. She says you're thinking about it far too much. More than is good for you.'

I sighed. Aggie had probably been the one most shocked by how I'd been when I'd come home from the Great War. Before, I'd been her happy-go-lucky big brother – a bit cleverer than most on account of going to the grammar school, not bad-looking in my own way, spoiling my little sister rotten. When I first came home I was so thin nothing fitted me, my skin was the colour of ashes and I didn't even open my mouth to say good morning. I was so frightened of what might fly out of me about the filth and the brutality of the killing – my own included. I kept and keep schtum with difficulty. I'm not good now, I never will be, but back then I was a lunatic, and it was only having to run the business because Dad died that saved me. Aggie says that I came back from the dead at that point, and in a way she's right. But whether I'm working, talking to people or getting involved where maybe I shouldn't, I'm still me inside and that's the thing that runs in a raid and hears voices that gibber and jabber in my skull. Like it or not, that's the real me – now.

'I'll be all right, Duchess.' I took one of her poor little hands in mine and squeezed it gently.

'Well, as long as you will be, Francis,' she said. 'You're very important to a lot of people. Not the least of which to that Miss Jacobs. Very good with young Velma she was the night she came here, very good. Such a nice friend for you to have, Francis.'

Even at forty-seven a bloke can be embarrassed in front of his mother. I felt my face get hot even if it didn't change colour. Later I wondered whether Aggie had confided what she obviously knew about Hannah to the Duchess, but I decided she probably hadn't. The last thing Ag is is disloyal, even if her brother is going with a prostitute. No, the Duchess must have worked out we were more than friends all on her own. Furthermore, she must've approved too – somehow. After all, Hannah had told everyone in the shelter she was a Jew, so it wasn't like the Duchess didn't know that, if nothing else.

* * *

I took note of the time when I left; it was four. After the morning fog, we now had rain and a sky full of dark grey clouds. By half past six it'd be pitch, especially with the blackout in force. There are a lot of stories about cars and buses coming to grief in the blackout, falling into bomb craters and suchlike, so I should've hopped on a bus as soon as I could to get up West. But, much as I felt I didn't have time, I did want someone to know where I was going.

Hannah had just got in from doing a bit of shopping when I fetched up at her place. As she opened the door of her room, the coldness of the damp in the walls hit me like a wet slap in the chops. Dot, who lives directly down below Hannah's room, is very mean with coal and even before the war was known to almost kill herself with cold every winter. So even if Hannah does keep her fire up it's a losing battle in that icy house. On this occasion, however, and in spite of Hannah's natural generosity, there was to be little relief from the ever present damp.

'I ain't got no coal,' she said, pointing to an empty bucket beside her tiny grate, 'but there's newspaper and wood here, for all the good they'll do.'

She gave me one of the bags she'd been carrying, which contained a couple of copies of the *Daily Sketch* and quite a few sticks that looked as if they'd once been painted. It's a big thing to be caught looting, even rubbish like this from bombed-out houses. But how a lot of people would keep warm without such sticks and splinters doesn't bear thinking about.

As I made up the fire, she put away the couple of tins of fish and the loaf she'd bought. Once the fire had caught I told Hannah what I intended to do.

'You shouldn't be going off doing this on your own, Mr H,' Hannah said, once she'd lit herself a fag and sat down at her table. 'Stumbling about in the blackout on your own, anything could happen. There's all sorts about up West. You're not exactly, begging your pardon, a fighting man, are you? You could get beat up or—'

'I handled the Dooleys, sort of,' I said. 'It won't happen. Lightning doesn't strike twice.'

'You don't know that,' she said. 'And, anyway, there could be a raid. You could fall over and hurt yourself in the blackout. This person the nun is meeting could be anyone . . .'

'Yes, yes, but what can I do?' I said. 'That nun could be in danger. And I want to know what's going on too. For my own satisfaction.'

Hannah gave me one of her piercing looks. 'So it's not just finding out who killed Kevin Dooley, then?'

'No. Not just that. Since he died, so many other strange things have happened. I want answers and if there's any chance I'll get some I have to take it.' I put my head down then as if I was ashamed of this admission. But I wasn't. If I was sorry for anything it was that I knew, or rather hoped, that Hannah would worry.

'I s'pose I can't stop you?' Hannah said, after a pause.

'No.'

She sighed, and then, with a flick of her head towards the fire, she said, 'Well, damp that bleeder down a bit and

I'll come with you. Paper and wood don't last like coal anyway.'

'No, Hannah,' I said.

She pointed at me straight in the face. 'Oh, yes,' she said. 'All the pubs up West are full of young tarts on the lookout for new customers. So if you think I'm going to let you go up there on your own you've another think coming!'

'But I thought I was only a customer?' I said, using her own hurtful words to me – hopefully to stop her coming along.

But Hannah, turned away from me now, put on her hat and coat and said, 'You know you're more than that, Francis Hancock.'

I started to speak, but she silenced me with a look. And, stern though it was, I felt that it signalled an end of sorts to our falling out over her sad past.

Journeys on blacked-out buses can be strange, creepy affairs. Unless you get a jolly crowd on board they can seem endless. Inside, the little blue blackout lights give a weird, washed-out tinge to the gloom, which can give you a headache after a bit. While outside there's nothing but blackness, sometimes you can see the occasional shape, a darker black against the grey or black sky. Up front, the bus driver is squinting into the murk, praying that every corner he turns isn't going to be his, and our, last. I looked across at the conductor once; he just scowled back, his eyes shifty with the strain of it all. It made me wonder where Doris's Alfie gets all his good humour from.

Not that I was doing much to lighten the mood. Like almost all our fellow passengers, I wasn't inclined to talk. Poor Hannah tried to bring me out a few times with chatter about the wireless, *ITMA* mainly, and pictures she was keen to go and see, but I couldn't even pretend to be interested in much. Now, looking back, I suppose what we call the undertaker's instinct, that Third Eye, must have been working for me. I had such a dread on me it was almost as if a raid was happening without any noise. Of course, even though I was, hopefully, going to see who Sister Teresa was meeting, that posed no real threat to me personally. Whatever happened, Hannah and I could just walk away. But there was this bad feeling I had in spite of that. Drifting slowly through the ever-darkening streets, our bus full of pale, silent people was, I felt at the time, like some sort of carriage of the damned. Each one of us looked like he had an unquiet ghost on his shoulder. But, then, given such terrible times as these perhaps most of us do.

Hannah and I eventually got off the bus in Regent Street outside Swan and Edgar's at just gone seven thirty. Because Piccadilly was blocked off we had to walk up Regent Street, west along Oxford Street, then either up on the Bayswater Road to enter the park by the north or to the east from Park Lane. It isn't far by anybody's standards, but if you are, well, blind basically, it isn't easy. As we got off the bus I took Hannah's arm and walked on the road side of the pavement, in case a bus or a car should get too close to the kerb. If you're unfortunate you can get knocked down on the pavement these days. But even if you don't get knocked down you can get splashed with muck from the gutters and I didn't want that happening to Hannah.

Although, of course, God knows, I've been out in the blackout before, I'd never been out in it in the West End. Down our way, unless there's a raid on, there are people around, going about their business, kids mucking around in the streets, men going out to their locals, women sitting on their front steps talking about their kids, their lack of money and their aches and pains. Up West, well, it was difficult to tell whether there were more or fewer people on the streets on account of them all being so quiet. Of course, they weren't really silent, but they talked in more muted voices than the folks back home, the clacking of the women's high-heeled shoes all but drowning out their speech.

At the end of Oxford Street we somehow managed to get round Marble Arch without being knocked down by either a car or a bus. Then, on the Bayswater Road, we tried to enter the park by the first gate we came to which, I reckoned, had to be the one just north-west of Speaker's Corner. But it was padlocked up, which, if I'd had any sense, I would've known would happen. It was, by now, as dark as night can get.

I was about to admit defeat and apologise to Hannah for even thinking about doing this mad thing when she took my hand in hers and said, 'Follow me.'

Walking quickly, we went onto Park Lane and then over to Speaker's Corner itself, which was, incredibly, open to both the park and Park Lane and got in through there. It was dead easy.

'How did you know about that?' I asked Hannah, once we were inside. I was, I admit, impressed by what seemed to be her local knowledge.

'Don't worry about it,' she said, as she pushed on in front of me into the darkness of the park.

And it was very, very dark. I, of course, had come quite unprepared for what I was intending. But Hannah, seemingly ready yet again, had not. She put her hand in her pocket, took out a little torch and pointed it down at her watch. It was quarter past eight.

'I think the Serpentine must be over that way,' I said, pointing straight ahead of me, into what looked like a great black field.

'Well, don't make a dash for it yet.' Hannah put a restraining hand on my arm. 'There's trenches been dug in the parks.'

'Oh, yes.' She was right. Back at the beginning of this lot the Government had decided that trench shelters in the parks were a good idea. They could accommodate a lot of people and they were cheap. They also have a tendency to collapse in wet weather, which, if only these Government types had bothered to ask, any old soldier would've known. Now confronted, possibly, with trenches again, I felt my knees start to knock and my breathing came harder and faster than it usually does.

'All right,' I said, after I'd had a minute or two to compose myself. 'Give us the torch. Let's move on very slowly.'

With no light, save the occasional quick flash from the torch, we picked our way carefully as if walking on eggs.

'Not a soul about, is there?' I whispered to Hannah.

I heard her laugh. 'Don't be took in, Mr H,' she said. 'This place is heaving.'

'What?'

'A lot of girls work in the parks,' Hannah whispered. 'Believe me, Mr H, if you shake a load of bushes round here at night you'll as often as not find a girl young enough to be your daughter with one or more gentlemen old enough to be your father!'

'So is that why Speaker's Corner—'

'Can't expect gentlemen to climb over gates, can you?' Hannah said.

'No. Oh, right.' I said. Well, it made sense. If nothing else, the park had to be too big for coppers and other irritations to those 'courting'. 'So is that how you knew to get in through Speaker's Corner?'

'Ask no questions and you'll be told no lies,' Hannah said.

'Oh.'

As we got closer to where I reckoned the Serpentine had to be, I started to sense rather than see movement up ahead. It would have been a bloody miracle if it'd been Sister Teresa and whoever it was she was meeting, but it wasn't them. It was a group of coppers.

As the tallest of the coppers shone his torch up into my face I could see that behind them, between them and the waterway, was a huge roll of barbed wire. Squinting, I put Hannah's little torch into my pocket.

'What's all this, then?' he said, as he turned his light from me to Hannah and back again.

As frequently happens in situations like this I lost my speech. 'I . . . I . . .'

'Do you know this is a restricted area, sir?'

'Er . . .' This was bad. You can get into all sorts of bother if you stray across into military areas now. Looking about as different from a German as a person can get is no defence either.

'Identity cards, please.'

Hannah took hers out of her gas-mask box, which she quite often uses as a handbag. I eventually found mine, after a lot of fumbling, at the back of my wallet.

The copper looked at the cards in silence, then passed them over to one of his fellows, who looked, to me, very young.

'You're a long way from home, Mr Hancock,' the youngster said, 'and you, Miss.'

'Mmm . . . er . . .'

'Do you want to tell us what you're doing in a restricted area? Either of you.'

'Well, it's like this . . .' I heard Hannah begin. Then I listened in silence. We were, apparently, star-crossed lovers – a Jew and a Christian whose mother came, as Hannah put it, 'from the Orient'. 'He's the colour of cardboard if you look at him in the light,' she said. We'd come 'up West' where nobody knew us so we could walk and talk as normal folk without fear or favour. Coming into the park for a 'cuddle', she said, had been our way of rounding off our day out. After all, we were, despite our differences, practically engaged. There wasn't anything immoral going on, she assured them.

In the silence that followed I wondered how long it would take me to lose what was left of my mind behind a door with a lock. Of course, now things half heard from customers, the wireless and on the street came back to me. There was a munitions dump under the Serpentine. Never mind about Hannah's bloody trenches, here we had weapons, barbed wire and coppers. They were, I knew it, going to think that we were spies.

The tallest copper took our cards from the youngster and said, 'Well, Miss, as a load of old cobblers goes, that's probably about one of the best I've ever heard.'

'Oh, no, Officer, but it ain't—'

'Yes, it is, Miss,' he said, 'it's tommyrot.' Then he smiled. 'In fact, it's such a lot of you-know-what that if you are a Nazi spy I'm Benito Mussolini. Mr Hancock here, I must say, makes Funf look like a university professor.'

'Uh . . .'

He handed our cards back to us. I replaced mine in my wallet with shaking fingers.

'A lot of East End girls come up here to earn a bit of bunce,' the copper said, as he looked at Hannah gravely. 'You all think it's the bleeding Promised Land, west of Holborn. But it ain't. There's 'undreds of you and, darling, as I'm sure you know, you ain't going to get any bloke any better than him. And you,' he turned to me, 'have some sense and knock her off down Rathbone Street, like the rest of your lot.'

He was either local or he knew Canning Town well.

'Now, you take these good people up to the Bayswater Road, Constable Barber,' he said, to the youngster at his side, 'and you make sure that they leave this park without having "relations" either near or far from this restricted area.'

'Yes, Sergeant,' the young man said, and then he turned towards us. 'Come on, then, you two,' he said, and started to walk on smartly in front of us. 'Quick as you can.'

As he followed on after us I heard the sergeant say, 'Undertaker, he was. Christ, you'd think he'd have enough to do down that manor. If the docks cop it again tonight he'll be glad I stopped him wasting his energy with her.'

Chapter Eighteen

I'd heard that if you'd got money little had changed in the West End as regards clubs, dancing and drinking. Those who've always had it still do and probably always will. For those of us with rather less, however, a late night on the town with your best girl usually involves a pub. Hannah and I eventually fetched up in one on the corner of Sale Place and Star Street in that area of Paddington, behind Praed Street, they call Tyburnia. We hadn't said a word since the young copper had chucked us out of the park and we didn't speak again until I'd got myself a pint and Hannah a gin and It.

'It's me I'm more cross with rather than you,' Hannah said eventually. 'I should've brought you to your senses with your bleedin' nun meeting some "person" in Hyde Park. Course it was ridiculous! All the parks have got anti-aircraft or allotments or—'

'You said all the parks were given over to "courting",' I said.

'Yes, well, some of them are, in parts. Obviously not up

by that bleedin' river or whatever you call it.' Disgruntled, Hannah lit up a fag and leaned back in her chair. 'So what we gonna do now, then, H? We gonna try and get home and hope there ain't a raid, or we staying here and doing what?'

I shrugged, swigged my pint and began to roll up a fag for myself. The people around us were mainly squaddies home on leave and girls in Hannah's line of business so it might, I knew, get a bit lively later on.

Hannah sipped her gin, being careful not to get any of it on her lipstick. 'I think you should stop running around after other people now,' she said. 'You done what you had to telling the police about Kevin Dooley. Now leave it.'

'Aggie and Nan have said similar things,' I said.

'Yes, and they're right. Caused all sorts of complications. Not least of which between you and me,' Hannah said, referring once again to what my investigations had led me to find out about her family. 'Hyde Park! By the bleedin' water!'

'It's a munitions dump,' I said. 'I remembered.'

'Too bloody late!'

'Yes.'

'And it's not as if that "holy Sister" of yours could meet this whoever at another time. That's a restricted area, that is. No one in their right mind would arrange to meet someone there. Don't make no sense . . .'

Hannah let it trail off into nothing. Sometimes she rants and chatters and she knows she rants and chatters. But not this time.

The noise had gone down a bit now because most of

the squaddies had moved to the other side of the bar to watch a darts match. I smoked and drank and thought how stupid I'd been. This, what I'd been doing, wasn't about Kevin Dooley. It hadn't been about him for a while. It was about those bloody sisters! Not just one of them or each as a separate person, but the Reynolds girls as a whole and what had happened in their lives had taken over, taken *me* over. It – they – were so strange. It was as if, certainly in the case of Ruby and Amber, they'd set out to get themselves into places they thought they should belong – even if, in both cases, they actually didn't. Ruby hid herself away among people she could only guess were her own, and Amber was the strangest nun I'd ever met. There was nothing religious about her. She just wasn't right. Pearl, too, had put up with all sorts from Kevin, as far as I could see, just to keep a roof over her head, but that's not unusual down our way. I wondered what Opal's problem was or even if she had one. If her adoption had been organised by Blatt in the belief that he was her father she probably had a very nice life, thank you. Opal, the spoiled child, her mother's favourite – very privileged compared to her sisters, in all but one respect. Opal, and she alone, had been in the flat when Victorine had killed Neilson and, asleep at the time or not, it had to have had some sort of effect upon the poor girl.

An old biddy, I think maybe the landlord's wife, sat down at the joanna in the corner and started playing something I think was an old Irish tune. Away a bit from the darts match, she was joined by one old boy who danced a slow, stiff jig. It was getting late now and some people were, as they do, starting to feel as if they could relax this evening. I wasn't one of them. I know war doesn't run on any timetable. I know that in reality there are no rules at all. Take what you know and turn it upside-down and maybe you might get a little bit closer to the truth. That's what Ken used to say about the news we got at the front in the first lot. It was designed to make us think the things the generals wanted us to think, not necessarily what was the truth. Propaganda, they called it. And that was when I, too, started to think that maybe I should question what had happened all those years ago in the flat on Praed Street. After all, propaganda, mis-direction, whatever you choose to call it, isn't just the preserve of generals.

'They, the Reynoldses, lived on Praed Street,' I said, as I pulled Hannah after me through the darkened streets. 'It was in their flat on Praed Street that Harold Neilson died.'

Hannah didn't answer because, poor girl, she was all done in by this time.

'The girls, with the exception of little Opal, were out in Hyde Park when it happened. They came home, saw what had happened and Ruby, the eldest, went to get the police. That's what I was told and that's what the jury must have believed when Victorine went on trial. But can we be certain that's how it really happened?'

I always think that the sirens, when they first start up, sound like something living. Not any creature I know, but something with blood and feelings in a lot of pain. As it wailed its way up to full volume, I said to Hannah, 'It's all right, you can go into Paddington, down the tube.'

'Do they use it as a shelter here, then?' Hannah asked.

But I didn't know so I kept quiet. Running now, on to Praed Street, where the great terminus and its station for the underground are, we followed a mass of other folk with similar ideas, who'd suddenly appeared from the doors of their flats and houses. Directly in front of us a woman, a baby in her arms, a toddler being dragged by his hand after her said, 'For Gawd's sake, do come on, Derek!' The poor kid began to cry, adding to the noise that always explodes just before a raid: the sirens, people's voices raised in panic, feet moving quickly over the pavement, crying and shouting, the clanking of metal teacups and other comforts against gas-mask boxes.

'Derek!'

Hannah bent down and scooped up the youngster off the ground. 'You look after your baby – I'll bring him,' she said to the mother, who nodded, probably with relief as much as fear.

When we got to the entrance to the station, I turned to Hannah and was about to speak. But she got in first: 'I s'pose you're going out for a run now, aren't you?'

'I . . . I . . .'

'Derek!' the mother cried yet again, alarmed that Hannah, Derek and I had stopped.

'We're coming, keep your hair on!' Hannah called over to her. Then, looking back at me, she said, 'Just keep yourself safe. Whatever you're thinking about what's happened and who's done which to what, it can wait.'

And then she was off, striding forward like a youngster,

Derek still grizzling gently in her arms. As I pushed my way out into the street again, I wished that I'd kissed her, just in case anything happened. But I hadn't. Praed Street, it seemed, was emptying itself into the station now, hundreds of pairs of eyes passing me in the opposite direction, eyes that looked at me as if I were mad. The noise starting just softly in my head only proved them correct. Only nutters move about in the open in a raid.

As I ran across the road towards the shops with flats above them opposite the station I considered the questions that had been forming in my mind since we'd been in the pub. *What if the Reynolds girls hadn't been out by the Serpentine the night Neilson died? What if they'd been at number 125 Praed Street instead? And what if whoever had telephoned Sister Teresa had known that, as well as the nun herself?*

Turning what I knew on its head. But why not? It would certainly explain why the meeting hadn't taken place and could never have taken place around the Serpentine. After all, if you want to make some sort of dodgy meeting with someone, you make sure it's possible to do so first. The park hadn't been possible. But a flat would be, provided you knew who owned it or could get in somehow. What that might mean, I didn't know. Had Amber and the others seen what their mother had done that night? Did they even help her somehow? Was that, perhaps, the deeper secret they all guarded so zealously?

I moved on towards the flats anyway, even though I couldn't see anything beyond the black bulkiness of the flat roofs and chimneys against what was now a sky crisscrossed by searchlights. The Jerries would be here soon. The terror inside me babbled and screamed as I fought to concentrate on looking for Tony's café. Not that I could see anything much. Once a raid starts, especially in our manor, the sky can light up like Guy Fawkes Night. But just before a raid it's the blackest of blacks as can be imagined. I felt rather than remembered Hannah's little torch in my pocket. Tony's wife had told me they didn't go down the shelter. They'd let me into the building, surely. Then we'd see who was in that old flat of the Reynolds family. Would it be the 'smart lady' Tony had told me about, or would a nun and an unknown man be in there instead?

Totally without bearings, I didn't know whether to move to left or right, so I plumped for one and went left. I turned the torch on a door as the first flash of light came from somewhere over in the east – the Jerries crucifying our manor again. Number 95. I ran to the right and kept going until I thought I might be in the right place: 129 – next to a barber's shop. I'd overshot. I put my finger on the torch button and thought, To hell with bloody Jerry, as I swung the beam along the doorways until I got to what I knew was 125, right next to Tony's café.

I didn't know Tony's surname and so I just banged on the door shouting, 'Tony!' until he came.

By this time, of course, Jerry was in full swing so when Tony did answer the door, in complete blackness, the night was already humming with Nazi bombers.

'Who is it?' the Italian said. 'What do you want?'

I briefly shone my torch up into my face so that he could see me. 'H-Hancock,' I said. 'Remember?'

'Who?'

'F-friend of L-L-Little Ruby,' I said. 'I'm – I'm an undertaker . . .'

Somewhere over the back of Praed Street, Christ knew how near or far, a bomber dropped its load and the earth shook so violently it made me drop the torch on the ground.

'Come in! Come in!' Tony said, as he pulled me roughly inside. 'Why you not in a shelter, Mister? What you doing here?'

The hall was enclosed so Tony pushed the Bakelite switch on the wall, bathing the narrow passageway in a yellowish, almost orange light.

'The – the – the R-R-Reynolds f-f-flat,' I stuttered.

He thought I'd become a gibbering idiot, I could see it in his face. When I'd met him before I hadn't stuttered like this. But there'd been no action going on then.

'Eh?'

'The – the – the – Ruby's old flat . . .'

'Mr Berigliano?'

The voice was female, educated, and came from somewhere near the top of the steep, brown, lino-covered stairway. Looking up, the Italian, frowning, said, 'Miss Green, you not going down the Anderson?'

'No. I've got company. One of my guests doesn't like it down there.'

A pair of high-heeled shoes was what I saw first, black and shiny, then a pair of elegantly shaped legs, which the owner moved with some grace.

'I expect the East End will get it, as usual,' she said. 'Poor things.'

'But there was a bomb over the back somewhere, Miss Green. Didn't you hear it?'

She was a slim young woman, probably in her late twenties, stylishly attired in a sharkskin suit. She looked, and talked, like one of those society girls you see in the *London Illustrated News*. Girls with thick hair and perfect skin who 'come out' at the beginning of the season all the upper crust seem to enjoy so much.

'Yes, I heard it,' she said, and then, smiling a perfect smile, she turned to me. 'Hello.'

I tried to speak, but nothing would come.

'This gentleman know one of the poor girls used to live in your flat, Miss Green,' Tony said. 'You know, the ones I tell you about.'

'Oh, really? How interesting!' Her eyes, which were very dark brown, opened wide.

'I don't know what he do here in a raid,' Tony said, and then, looking at me, he continued, 'You OK, Mister?'

'I – I . . .'

'I think he wants to maybe speak to you about the flat,' Tony said, and then he shrugged.

The sound of anti-aircraft fire from one or more of the batteries across the city punched up into the death-filled sky.

Miss Green's red lips smiled. 'Well, you can't very well go out again in all this,' she said. 'I've got a couple of people over but if you'd like to come up for a cup of tea, I'm sure that would be fine. We all have to pull together, these days, don't we?'

'Th-thank you.'

'My pleasure,' she said, then turned and began to walk back up the stairs, her shiny black hair, cut into a bob, sitting elegantly on her slender white neck. 'Goodnight, Mr Berigliano.'

'Goodnight, Miss Green.'

Tony went back into his flat while I followed the woman upstairs. It seemed I had been wrong about finding anyone other than her and her friends. But I was still compelled to go and look anyway.

'So you know someone connected to that terrible murder, do you?' Miss Green said, as she stopped on the dingy landing and opened the door to her flat.

'Y-yes,' I said. 'Ruby.'

'Oh, one of the daughters of the murderess, I suppose.'

'Y-yes.'

'Come in.'

I followed her into a very white hall – white walls, carpet, ceiling. Half-way down she turned sharply to the left into what was the kitchen saying, as she went, 'The parlour is at the end on the right. Please go in, Mr Hancock. I'll join you in a moment.'

I thanked her and had started to do as she had asked when it occurred to me that she had used my name. How had she known it?

I turned back briefly and found myself looking at a very familiar face. And although I felt fear at the time, I knew that I was also relieved. You always feel like that when you've been proved right about something.

* * *

'What are you doing here?' Sister Teresa whispered angrily, as she led me down the corridor towards where Miss Green had said the parlour was.

'I could ask the same of you,' I replied.

She took me into a room lit by one dull gas lamp, then closed the door behind me.

Although the lighting was old-fashioned, like our own at home, the furniture was something else. Very smart in blacks and whites, like the design of the Troxy Picture Palace in Limehouse. It's called art deco, that style. I only know that because Aggie had a wireless of that design when she was married. That was expensive too.

I didn't sit down on any of the deep leather chairs. 'I bet it wasn't like this when your mother was here,' I said.

'No.' In the silence between her denial and the sound of one or more fire crews over the back, I heard voices from the kitchen. It was only then that I realised I was speaking without stuttering in a raid. I didn't know why then any more than I do now. Maybe it was because I had to. There were things I needed to know, reasons I wanted to understand.

'I went over to the Serpentine earlier,' I said, 'but you weren't there so I came here. Has he arrived yet, the bloke who phoned you?'

'You shouldn't have followed me.'

'I didn't,' I said. 'I told you, I went to the park and *then* I came here, once I'd worked out what could've happened all those years ago. Because this was where he meant to meet you all along, wasn't it, Sister? Because this was where you were when your father died, wasn't it?'

'You were only supposed to tell my Sisters in Christ if I didn't come back!' she snapped.

'I was afraid for you,' I said. 'And, I'll be honest, I was curious.'

'You shouldn't be here, it isn't safe,' the nun said. She turned to face me, full on. Her features were even more drawn than usual, which gave her a ghostly, almost deceased look. 'I never dreamed that anything like this was happening. She should never have gone down to you. She should have left you alone.'

'Who?'

'My sister,' she said.

Between her religious Sisters and her blood relatives, things could get a bit confusing, but I assumed that she meant one of the latter.

'She was expecting Blatt,' the nun said. 'She telephoned him about an hour ago. That's why she went down to you. She thought you might be him.'

'I don't look a bit like Mr Blatt or sound—'

'Yes, I know,' she said. 'But she knows you.'

'Who?'

'My sister,' she said angrily. 'My fucking little sister, you idiot!'

I heard the door open behind me but I didn't look to see who was there.

'Miss Green is your sister?' I said. 'Miss Green is expecting Mr Blatt? So she's, er . . .'

I saw the nun draw breath to reply but before she could do so a voice behind me said, 'That's enough now, Amber. Don't say no more.'

I looked round at her, but I'd known it was Ruby as soon as I'd heard her speak. Not that it had been Ruby, of course, who had opened the door to me. That had been a woman with far more status in life. A woman who had been raised with money.

'So it must've been Opal who let me in,' I began.

'Is that what she told you?'

I looked from a grim-faced Ruby towards the nun, who averted her gaze once again.

'You said your sister, Sister Teresa,' I said. 'You told me your sister opened the door to me. So, in the absence of Pearl, I had to assume that that sister was Opal.'

With the exception of the noises from outside – the gushing of water from the fire hoses, men's voices raised in fear and desperation, the crackling of fires, there was nothing to hear in that room. Both Sister Teresa and Ruby looked down at the floor.

After a bit, what with the yellow gas gloom all around and the thick, almost violent silence, I began to get nervous and I said, 'W-what's going on h-here?'

'It's a family matter,' Ruby said, staring all the time at her more frightened-looking sister. 'You should go now, Mr Hancock.'

'No, he shouldn't!' the nun said. 'Or, rather, we should go with him, Rube. We need to get out of here. Tell people what she's done to you and—'

'You think I'm still not trying to take it in meself?' Ruby said roughly. 'But Mr Hancock here, he don't need to be involved. We can do this ourselves. We always have.'

'But then how will people know?' the nun said.

'There will be a way.'

'How can there be? We can't do nothing, can we? She won't let us and we can't anyway. But this is wrong!' she said. 'It always has been! When Blatt gets here I'm gonna tell him!'

'But he knows,' her sister hissed. 'He would never have bothered to help Mum if she hadn't—'

'No, but Blatt doesn't know that Mum didn't really believe Opal was his child, does he?'

'No. And you're not to tell him neither!' Ruby moved forward as if to hit Sister Teresa and so, I must say bravely, I stepped between them.

'We don't know what he'll do if—'

'She's a killer!' Sister Teresa said, as she backed away from both me and her sister.

'Yeah, well, we've always known that,' Ruby said. 'And that includes Mr Blatt. We've known that for twenty-two bleedin' years, so don't go getting all guilty about it now! We let her get away with it then and—'

'She was a child *then*! Eight! Just a child!'

I felt my heart stop. Just for a moment. But in that moment the woman I'd been introduced to as Miss Green stepped lightly into the open doorway and smiled. 'I don't think my father is coming,' she said, in her very different, very educated accent. Then looking, it felt like through me, to Sister Teresa, she said, 'I told you I knew Mr Hancock, didn't I?'

'You've told us a lot of horrible things, Opal,' the nun replied.

'Oh, yes,' Opal Reynolds said, with a smile. Then her

expression changed and her voice dropped, and even though I'd never seen the face of the person who had threatened me under the railway bridge at Limehouse I recognised the tone of the voice I'd since thought of as that of the gruff geezer. Now the smooth, cool hand 'he' had touched me with made sense. The person 'looking after' the Reynolds girls was their little sister.

'Keep away from the Reynolds women,' she wheezed. 'I'm taking care of them.'

And then Opal, that exquisite, dark-haired woman who had so graciously greeted me and who, I could now see, was carrying a pistol in her cool, smooth hands, laughed. 'I always did enjoy dressing up,' she said. 'I've always been a show-off. I wasn't expecting you, Mr Hancock, but now that you're here it's a bit of a bonus, really.'

'Opal . . .'

'Oh, don't be so wet, Sister bleeding-heart Teresa!' she snapped at the nun, her face suddenly twisting with rage. 'Thanks to all of my lovely sisters he knows rather more than he should so it's good that he's here, where we can see him.'

She looked down at the gun in her hand and then she told me to sit.

'Neilson made Opal do things, dirty things, to him,' Ruby said to me. 'He hated her because she was spoiled and she wasn't his. It was his way of punishing her for that.'

I'd taken up Opal's 'offer' of a seat and was opposite the young woman, watching her gaze at her weapon with what looked like dead eyes.

'She was only a baby.'

'That night, when my father died,' Sister Teresa said, 'he punched Mum in the chest. She couldn't hardly breathe.'

'It took us a good hour to get her right,' Ruby continued, 'by which time he'd been down the pub and had a skinful.'

'You never were in Hyde Park around the Serpentine or otherwise, were you?' I interrupted. 'You all lied.'

'Yes, we had to. We—'

'We wanted her to hit him,' the nun said. 'He was like a sack so we knew it'd be easy. None of us realised she'd be able to knock him down. But then she was angry, wild. She said she wanted to kill him.'

'She said, yes—'

'But once he was out for the count we all just left him,' Sister Teresa said. 'We thought that he'd probably forget about Mum and her hitting him. His drinking had got a lot worse by then. We left him . . .'

'Opal was eight, she was asleep.'

Both women looked towards their younger sister to continue the story. For a moment I wondered whether she'd even heard, but then she spoke, in a dead, flat sort of way. It reflected the absent expression in her deep, dark eyes.

'I took one of Mother's hatpins from her bedroom and I pushed it into his chest several times,' Opal said, more to the gun than to anyone. 'The hatpin is very useful to the prostitute. My mother had used it to threaten men more than once. But Neilson was drunk. I understand, now, that

294

it is unlikely he could have felt anything.'

Her calm made me feel ill. It had been a long time ago but that didn't take away any of the horror of what she had done – not to me.

'Neilson had made her do terrible things,' Ruby said. 'She was eight, younger when he started on her. He deserved no less.'

'But y-your mother . . .' Just very briefly the stuttering had stopped. Now it was back again. Terror, of that madness outside and the threat from what I was coming to see was an unpredictable armed woman inside, was beginning to overwhelm me.

'Mother wanted him dead, which is what I did. I obeyed,' Opal said. 'I gave her what she wanted. I continue to give her what she wants to this day. I owe her that.'

And then she looked up slowly at the two other women in the room, her sisters, and she smiled. 'We're nearly all here now. All except Pearl. But my father will fix that. It isn't beyond repair, you know.'

I saw that Sister Teresa was about to say something but then she appeared to change her mind and sat back, tense.

'Have you worked it all out for yourself, Mr Hancock?' Opal Reynolds said, as she lifted the pistol and pointed it at my head.

Inside my brain everything rattled and throbbed and I felt my feet slip anxiously against the carpet as if they wanted to be on the move. Between all those feelings and a mouth as dry and dumb as a corpse's I could only take things in. I was beyond reacting now.

'I got us all back together again, Mr Hancock,' she said,

with another of her smiles, 'the Reynolds sisters, just as my mother wanted. Here in our old home, which my father recommended my adoptive parents buy for me. A nice little flat in London. Every girl should have one, you know.' And then, moving the pistol still closer to my head, she said, 'Miss Green is such a respectable woman, isn't she? Not even that dreadful old bitch Pia downstairs has made the connection between her and Opal. Miss Green wouldn't even think about trying to pull on Pia's son's cock, would she? Only nasty, spoiled little Opal would think of doing something like that.'

When everything disappeared I must've thought, inasmuch as I could think, that I'd either died or completely lost my reason. But I don't remember anything much except that in a sense, I suppose, I entered a kind of hell for a while. Even now I've only impressions of what might have happened in the hours that followed. There were voices – not loud or unpleasant – urgent and, against all the thuds and bangs from outside, like a sort of soup of sound that swam sickeningly in my head. In fact, if I wasn't sick, then I certainly felt as if I might be in that room of black and yellow where everything was diluted, bleeding into my brain. 'It's a long way to Tipperary' was all that kept on going inside my head. 'It is really a hell of a long way to Tipperary.'

Chapter Nineteen

'**H**e didn't know you. You should never have let him in,' Blatt said.

His face, which was less than a foot from mine, appeared larger than I had remembered it.

'You've got to get him out of here!' The voice came from underneath my head, from the throat of the nun. 'You've got to stop this.'

I was lying, most strangely, across Sister Teresa's chest. Half propped up, my eyes attempting to focus on first Blatt and then the really very pretty Opal.

'Oh, Amber, don't be such a silly!' the latter said. 'My dear old dad won't do anything to stop me getting what I want.'

'Mr Blatt,' the nun began, only to be curtailed by the rough voice of her older sister.

'Don't!' Ruby Reynolds said. 'Whatever's on your mind, just keep it!'

Something muttered between Blatt and Opal passed me by, except that at the end of whatever it was he said, 'Well, he'll have to go now anyway.'

'Yes,' Opal said. 'If he's got this far, he has to. That was my intention at least.'

'What do you mean?' I heard myself say. 'What are you saying?'

Now able to focus more or less normally I saw both Blatt and Opal in front of me. The solicitor turned. 'It's safe now, old chap,' he said. 'We can take you home soon.'

Underneath my head I felt the nun's heart beat faster. 'The all-clear . . .' Well, of course it must have gone. If it hadn't I wouldn't have been able to speak. Or would I? Nothing was certain in this place. But, then, if the all-clear had gone, Hannah could be leaving the station . . . I needed to get back to her – she'd be worried. I made as if to get up, but strong hands pushed me back into the nun's lap.

'You wait until we're ready, Mr Hancock,' Ruby Reynolds said. 'Don't you say nothing else now. You passed out, probably had all sorts of silly dreams, you did. Just let us take you home.'

'I know the East End quite well now,' Opal said, with a laugh in her voice. 'I can find the places you all go to down there with my eyes shut.'

For just a second I saw a glance of fear whiz, almost like a quickly passed Lucifer in the trenches, from Blatt to Ruby to Sister Teresa.

I'd be lying if I said I'd never been so frightened in my life. Of course I had. What I'd never felt before was in the middle of something so unknown. I'd passed out and done God knows what besides, but at this point I remembered that Opal had said she'd killed Neilson. It was fantastic to me that a child should do such a thing, but that was what she had said. There was more too – although I wasn't to understand all about that for a bit.

I saw Ruby go to leave the room, only to be stopped by Blatt. 'Just get your coat,' he said. 'We need to get this fellow home before his family start to worry.'

Ruby picked up her coat and hat from the back of a chair and put them on. I watched intently as she secured the feathered hat to her thick black wig with a pin decorated with butterflies. The action made me feel quite queasy.

I remember wondering whether Opal knew what she'd said to me. I wondered whether I'd just dreamed the whole bloody thing. Or maybe what was happening now was the dream. I don't often think too much about what other people might be thinking and seeing but I did wish at this point that I wasn't so alone. If only Hannah had been with me, or Ken. They would've known what was going on; they would have understood what was real.

As it happened, reality – in other words that which was deliberate and thought out – was precisely what I missed. I was surrounded by them in the car, all talking at me, unravelling it in front of me. Why didn't I try to jump out? Maybe it was because I was so mesmerised by it. I am, after all, an undertaker: death is my business. I have an interest.

'You see, the important thing about me,' Opal said, as she draped one arm across my shoulders, 'is that I remember everything. I remember killing Harold Neilson, I remember Mum telling me and the rest of the girls never to tell anybody and I remember her saying that we must stick together. That was important.' She looked across at Sister Teresa, who was sitting on the other side, on my left, her face pushed up against the car window, looking out into the darkened streets beyond. 'That was the last thing she ever said to me,' Opal said. 'But my sisters chose . . .'

'You went for adoption,' the nun said, 'to those Green people.'

'Yes, but I knew who my family really were, didn't I? I've never forgotten a thing. I knew about my sisters and my father. Mother and Father Green, my adoptive parents, Mr Hancock, are friends of my father. Dad would come over every week to see me – not with his wife. She is never to know. That is understood. Some secrets are really very good. It's all right to be a different person with different people. I like that. I love my dad. He saved me. I think that people would not have understood what I did to Harold. It was best I didn't go to court. I didn't want that and my dad gives me everything I do want, you know.'

Blatt, who was driving, turned briefly and smiled at her. Yes, he would give her everything, wouldn't he? With no nippers from his wife, she was his only kid: he'd do anything for her. What would he do, I wondered, if Sister Teresa told him he might not be Opal's dad? I felt, by instinct I suppose you'd say, that I didn't want to find that out.

I don't know what kind of car we were in, only that it

was big. When coppers and wardens stopped it periodically to tell Blatt about an obstruction or to direct him another way, they acted very respectfully, as if they either knew him or recognised that the car was quality. But someone like Blatt wouldn't have driven anything cheap. Usually, or when I'd seen him before, he'd had a driver. That he didn't have one now was something else that was setting off warning sirens in my head. It made me remember that Opal might well know where I lived – she certainly seemed, at least some of the time, to know where I went. Every muscle in my body was rigid and that included the ones of my throat. I couldn't speak.

'I helped Pearl and Ruby when I knew they were in trouble,' Opal continued, 'and to free them so we could all be together again. I worked very hard, planning my disguises, voices and hair to make that happen.'

'Pearl's in prison for something you did!' Sister Teresa said. 'You haven't helped her at all! Or Ruby. And what about me? What surprises you got up your sleeve to make me grateful to you, to bring us all back together? Gonna burn Nazareth House to the ground, are you?'

'Amber!' Even in the early-morning gloom I could see that Ruby's face was red with fury as she tipped her head in my direction. 'Shut up, for Christ's sake!'

'Oh, I think he's worked it out now!' the nun shouted back. Then, turning to me, she said, 'But if you ain't, Mr Hancock, we all lied to keep her secret all these years. Not for her but because Mum told us to. "She's only a baby," Mum said. "She didn't know what she was doing. It's wrong to put a kiddie up in court." Stupid Mum! She knew all right! She killed Pearl's husband and Ruby's fellow.'

'Oh, bleedin' clever telling him!' Ruby said.

'Yeah? Like it fuckin' matters now!'

Blatt chimed in with something else at this point, and then Opal spoke, but I didn't take much notice of either of them. I kept thinking, Opal killed Kevin Dooley and Shlomo Kaplan. How did she do that? Her reasons, to free her sisters so they could be with her, to fulfil some sort of obligation to her mother, I could understand if not appreciate. Barmy I may be, but I'm not that mad. But how had she killed Kevin Dooley during that night of fire and fights and sex? And then I remembered that voice she'd put on to warn me off and I began to feel cold.

I cleared what I could from my throat and said, 'So did you pretend to be, you know, a bloke, so you could, you know, Kevin Dooley . . .'

'I dressed as a boy so no one would ever be able to identify me. I am a criminal. I naturally think about things like that and I'm good at changing my appearance,' Opal said, with a smile. 'Kevin wasn't strictly homosexual, Mr Hancock, but I knew he wasn't too fussy about who french-polished his cock either. That's why he was so easy to get to know. He didn't love Pearl. I observed him for some weeks and saw him with women and several boys who got on their knees in front of him for the price of a pint. I just did likewise.'

'Oh, God help us!' Sister Teresa said.

'Don't be such a prig!' Opal snapped. 'One does what

one does to survive, as well you know. I had to get close to him to kill him. I was very good. He said so. He shut his eyes, as men do when they're having sex, as Harold always did, and then I stabbed him.'

'How did you know what Kevin liked and what he didn't?' I said. 'How did you find him?'

'Oh, Daddy had found Pearl and Ruby for me some time ago. He is a solicitor, you know,' Opal said, almost playfully. And then she added, with more menace than I can convey on mere paper, 'But it was I who took the decision to free them at this time. The bombing was propitious. I couldn't have my family subjected to violence. The things my sisters put up with! Not that I told Daddy about it until it was over.' She laughed. 'And you did your bit too, Mr Hancock. Daddy had searched for Amber for some time, but with no success. You know that those nuns lied to him when he asked them about her? But you . . .'

'I only left Nazareth House for Pearl,' the nun said bitterly. 'Because I thought she was in trouble.'

'You're a good Reynolds girl, then, aren't you?' Opal said, still smiling.

The car fell silent then. I was stunned. She'd killed her sisters' partners to fulfil some ancient promise and Blatt, unwittingly at the beginning certainly, had helped her. But things hadn't worked out the way she'd wanted them to with Pearl. So now her 'daddy' had to try to free that sister to 'be together again' with Opal and all because of me and my little firelit meeting with the dying Kevin Dooley. What had he done, I wondered, immediately after she'd stabbed him? Had he tried to hit her? And if she had been dressed up as a boy how had he known she was a woman? He'd said that *she* stabbed him. I wanted to ask her then but my throat had closed with fear again, fear at what might lie ahead of me now. This wasn't the first time I'd thought I might be cashing in my chips that night but it was the first time I felt it had to be a dead cert. Knowing what I now did, they were never going to run the risk of letting me tell anyone else.

I think we must have been near to Aldgate before anyone spoke again. Sister Teresa turned towards me and said, 'I'm very sorry, Mr Hancock.'

'What for?' I said hoarsely, even though I knew full well what for.

But neither she nor anyone else attempted an answer so, once again, I was left with my thoughts – or, rather, the lack of them.

Going east it got worse – the devastation, the sight of shadowy figures walking like madmen among the rubble. Men and women in negative against the fires from the incendiary bombs, people without features or identity – people who could just vaporise without a trace. It's what Opal had counted on – the anonymity of a people at war. I don't know whether I was more disgusted or afraid just then. I know I couldn't look at any of them – not Blatt the adoring father whistling at the wheel, not that creature still holding a pistol beside me, not those others, conspirators in their own mother's death. And yet Ruby, at least, had had feelings for Shlomo Kaplan. Had she forgotten them? Was this younger sister whom everyone,

304

it seemed to me, was falling over themselves to protect more important to her than he had been? And what of Pearl? She was in prison because of what Opal had done.

'So what about Pearl, Mr Blatt?' I said. I could hear my voice shaking, but I had to find out. 'How are you going to save her from the gallows for your little girl, eh?'

'I wouldn't worry about that if I were you,' he said.

Once again the feeling that I was going to die, that they were going to kill me, knocked the side of my heart like a kick from a horse. I looked across at Sister Teresa, hoping maybe for some help from that direction. But what could she do? These women were up to their necks in crimes and the lies that grow up and get nurtured around them. And that included the nun. What, I wondered, as we turned into somewhere very familiar, was it about this Opal that had them all protecting her with such passion? When I stumbled out of the car and on to the grass, Blatt, an old Webley Mark IV revolver, probably from his army days, jammed into my ribs, let me in on at least part of it.

'We all let Opal down one way or another,' he said, as he took my arm between his fingers and pulled me after him. 'If Victorine had told me I had a daughter before the Neilson affair, I would have been able to look after them all. I would have done that. If her sisters had been able to protect her against Neilson, maybe he wouldn't have done those dreadful things to her. And if I'd had the courage to adopt her myself when her mother died . . .' He shrugged. 'But there was always Julia to consider – that's my wife. She couldn't have children . . .'

'So you condone her murderous actions?'

'He led her to us,' I heard Sister Teresa mutter, as she, too, stumbled out of the car and on to a moss-covered tombstone. 'Using his position to give her what she wanted. I couldn't even hide in my convent! This nightmare has come for me!' Then, suddenly raising her voice, she shouted, 'You knew what she was like! We all knew what she was like!'

'Ssssh!' Ruby hissed. 'For Christ's sake, Amb!'

'I didn't and don't condone her actions, Mr Hancock,' Blatt said, as he pushed me, really rather gently, in front of him. 'But one's blood is one's blood and I will, of course, do everything I can to protect my daughter and help her to repay the debt she feels she owes to her mother.'

'But that's bonkers . . .'

'I don't really think that a man who runs around during raids talking to imaginary people can make that sort of judgement, do you?' Blatt said.

I felt my face redden, even though I only half understood what he was saying. The one thing I've always known is that, barmy as I might be, I don't talk to people who aren't real. I know that.

'I wish she hadn't done what she has, but there's no going back now,' Blatt continued. 'Now we all just have to see it through and . . .'

'And if one day she feels she can't forgive you for not getting her mother off?' I asked. 'What then?'

'What indeed?' Blatt said. There was a look almost of resignation on his face. Was he saying he would, because she was his daughter, let Opal take even his life? I'm not a father, but I do know about loving people. I would draw the line, though. I wouldn't kill for the Duchess, not even for Hannah. I've done too much of that already.

After a bit, I looked across the ranks of gravestones at the almost gay figure of Opal Reynolds in front of me. Here in St Mary Magdalene's churchyard where, for me at least, all of this had started, there she was, skipping across the grass just ahead of me – I didn't know where she was headed to at the time. In the place where the bare-knuckle fight had happened? Near to where poor old Kevin Dooley had met such a terrible and strange end? As if in answer to some of the questions that were going on in my head, she turned and said, 'I met Kevin Dooley in the public lavatories almost opposite the Boleyn pub in Plaistow. He'd been thrown out. He was very drunk. I said I'd take him somewhere quiet for some french-polishing – for a price.' She laughed. 'He was desperate for it, drunk and ghastly. But, then, Kevin was a brute. I'd been watching what he did to Pearl for some time. He beat her, and what about all those children, eh? She had to be rid of him. He deserved to die like that, slowly. They bleed to death inside when you use a pin, but I expect you know—'

'Yes, I do.'

'If everything had gone to plan, I would have cared for Pearl and her children afterwards,' Opal said. 'But suddenly there you are, Mr Hancock. Now, look, it can't be a hatpin for you . . .'

'You know that Pearl loved Kevin, don't you?' I said

wildly, trying to buy myself time. Perhaps somebody, somehow, would come.

Opal's face dissolved into a sneer. 'She can't have,' she said. 'He was appalling.'

'But she did,' I continued. 'Whatever he later became, Kevin saved her from a life of destitution after Velma's father died. She was grateful to him. And, anyway, love is blind, don't you—'

'Kevin Dooley liked to be pleasured,' she interrupted. 'He liked to do it with his big blonde sister-in-law, Martine, up against walls, and he also liked to pick up anything he could find in or outside pubs. Although no "iron" as I believe you call homosexuals around here, I knew he'd go for my "boy". It was fun. He was so drunk, it was simple and, dressed as a boy – which is, anyway, a great challenge – I could so easily hide my identity, essential if one is to do these things where one might be observed. Of course I showed him I was a girl just after I plunged the pin into his chest. He was staggering by then so I took off my shirt. The shock on his face! It was hilarious! Even better than when I killed the old Orthodox Jew, although not as exciting as Harold's death. But that was why I went back to the hatpin. It's so appropriate, historically.'

'Opal,' Blatt said, 'let us not talk about it any more.'

'Oh, but I want to,' I said. I knew we were getting very near now to some sort of conclusion here in this graveyard. Opal Reynolds, at least in Kevin Dooley's case, might be a bit keen on doing things in what she saw as appropriate ways. I didn't like to think too much about what she had in mind for me. 'I want to talk about Shlomo Kaplan actually,' I said. 'I want to know why he had to die. He hadn't done—'

'Oh, yes, he had!' Opal spat. 'He was a beast! All men are ultimately beasts! The stories going around about him were ghastly. And that wig?' She laughed. 'I couldn't have Ruby going around in that wig. Those sort of Jews are just not acceptable, are they?'

I looked back at Ruby who, even through the gloom, I could see was almost totally without expression.

'Of course I put one on myself, a big black one, when I went to Spitalfields to get the old bastard,' Opal said. 'But that was just some fun. Wearing one makes you more believable as one of them. That's why the old man answered the door to me even though there was a raid on, because he thought I was one of his own. He wanted to help me.'

'Ruby,' I said, 'all of that about Shlomo was—'

'You mustn't hurt Mr Hancock. You mustn't!' I heard the nun butt in anxiously.

Ruby Reynolds, her wig still firmly on her head, looked at me coldly and said, 'He knows it all. We can't have him hanging about.'

'You like this place, don't you, Mr Hancock?' Opal, laughing now, stopped in front of a large rectangular monument that was leaning at about a forty-five-degree angle. St Mary's, I knew, hadn't taken any hits from the Jerries as yet, but I also knew that it was old and damaged.

'Ruby, you loved Shlomo,' I said, my voice quavering a little now.

'Yes, but I love my sister,' Ruby replied. 'I care for her, like she's cared for me.'

'She tricked you out of that synagogue.'

'Yes, and I used you to do it.' Opal laughed.

I turned to her. 'You think that killing me here is sort of right for me, don't you?'

'His family'll come looking for him!' I heard Sister Teresa cry as she, and I, saw Opal raise her pistol towards my head.

'She's right, you know,' I said. 'Someone like me will be missed and people did know where I was going last night.'

'What people?'

'Well . . .' I clammed up tight. I didn't want to say anything about Hannah. In fact, I didn't want to say anything about anyone close to me if I was going to be dead as a dodo in a very short space of time. I didn't want this madwoman going about looking for them.

'Well, if you did tell people you were going up to the West End it won't do you or them any good,' Opal said. 'If you hadn't interfered, Mr Hancock, poor Pearl wouldn't be in Holloway now. She'd be with the rest of us. You've done enough mucking up.' She pointed her weapon towards the broken monument and said, 'Let's get on, shall we?'

'What do you mean?' I said.

'I want you to get in there,' she said.

I could see that where the monument had come away from its base there was a gap. You can't usually see the soil underneath these things even when they do move and sink a bit over the years, but this was a sorry example: not only could I look into the hole underneath it, I could see what I knew were probably broken shards of wood sticking up too. 'You want me to climb on top of some poor person's coffin?' I said. 'No.'

'Don't worry,' Opal said spitefully. 'He won't feel anything and you won't know that you're there for long.'

'No,' I said. 'Shoot me here, if you must, but I'm not getting in there.'

I'd survived the trenches. I wasn't going to die in my worst nightmare. I wasn't going to be buried alive.

Blatt, his voice almost filled with fear of her, began, 'Opal, I don't think this is really—'

'Daddy, it's perfect,' she replied. 'I'm dressing up Mr Hancock in a coffin. You know we have to kill him and no one will think to look in an existing grave. Once it's done we can cover him up with what is left of the coffin and some leaves and dirt and . . .' Even though I couldn't see them, I could feel the horror in some of the faces of those standing behind me. 'Now, look, we're all in it together this time, aren't we?' Opal said. 'We're all as guilty as hell already and we know it.'

'But you can't bury him alive!' The nun was crying now.

'Oh, goodness, no!' Opal said, laughing softly. 'I know he's an undertaker but even I'm not that ambitious. We'd need to have shovels and overalls to do that properly. No, once he's in I'll shoot him. Can't have any mess even here – it might attract attention. I've thought it all through. Ruby, would you mind lifting those pieces of wood up so that Mr Hancock can join . . .' she took a torch out of her pocket and flashed it briefly at one of the inscriptions on the side of the monument '. . . Frederick Godfrey?'

Ruby Reynolds took off her hat and coat, laid them down on the ground beside the monument and set to her gruesome task with a will. She was, I felt at that moment, the only one who was totally with Opal.

'You know that this is all your own fault, don't you, Mr Hancock?' Opal said, as she looked at me without a shred of compassion in her cold, hard eyes.

'Never your fault is it, Miss?' I said. 'Always some excuse, isn't there? You were a child, your victim is a bad lot, it's just a game . . .'

'Yes, well, it is.'

'You killed Neilson because your mum wanted him dead and because he was cruel to you and I can sort of understand that,' I said. 'But because you were so young your mind made it into a kind of a game. I think you killed Kevin Dooley and Shlomo Kaplan for your own pleasure, to delight in your own cleverness and to bind what was over and past, your family, to you whether they liked it or not. I don't think it's got too much to do with your poor mother now. I think it's about what's in your head. But that isn't anything I can easily understand, thank Christ!'

'Oh, that's enough!' she said. 'What do you know about what I've been through and how I feel? Get in there and die.'

I was pushed from behind, with some force, by Blatt. Stumbling, I fell on my knees in front of a hole. Cleared now of coffin wood, I could just make out the wisps of rotting grave clothes that still clung to what was left of

312

Frederick Godfrey. I felt my entire body heave and I screamed and, I'm ashamed to say, I wet myself at the same time. Thank God Hannah couldn't see me like this! Although the thought of never seeing her again made me cry even harder. I think it must have been Blatt who eventually silenced me with a punch to the side of the head.

Chapter Twenty

Even though I knew I was going to die anyway, I couldn't lie face down on top of poor old Frederick. There is a word 'liquefaction', that fails to do justice to what happens to the soft tissues of a person after burial, but suffice to say it isn't pleasant. What is also far from nice is the way that old bones crack and splinter as you lower yourself on to them. I kept on saying, 'Sorry, sorry,' over and over as I did as this monster asked me, pushing me down, my cheek bleeding on to things I didn't want to think about. But I still felt bad for Frederick. In fact I think that in spite of the horror of it – the stench, the darkness, the terrifying callousness of those above me on the grass – I was more angry than afraid at this point. What I was being made to do was totally at odds with who I am. Hancock hides away with the dead, looks after them, makes sure above all that they get where they want and need to be. Not this desecration! Not this total disregard for the little we have left that is decent in these terrible times.

'If there's a hell, you're on your way there, Opal Reynolds,' I said.

'You first, though, eh?' She laughed.

Lying down now I felt something hard and cold press itself into my left-hand temple. Just like I'd done in the trenches I wished I could pray, but I knew I'd be fooling myself so I shut my eyes instead. It was dark but even so I didn't want to run the risk of seeing myself pass away. I was back in the mire and the mud and I was crying now for the shame of having ended up like this – desecrating a grave, my clothes covered in blood and piss, dying in the way I'd spent four years dreading. Why, I thought as I lay there with that gun against my head, had I lived through the Great War just to come to this? What had been the point of it? Maybe this was all some sort of punishment for passing poor old Kevin Dooley by? Now perhaps I'd know how he'd felt dying violently at the hands of this madwoman.

From up above there was a grunt and then a woman's muffled voice said something that made no sense to me at the time.

'No, you.'

And then the gun moved away from my head. For a while I lay, unable to move, locked in to Frederick and a fear of what I might find if I raised my head from his. But then I heard screaming so I had to move. But when I opened my eyes, I realised that Opal Reynolds had gone.

Blatt was cradling his girl in his arms, her legs spread out almost obscenely across the grass. Clutching, clawing almost at her chest, Opal Reynolds's movements reminded me of Kevin Dooley's on his last night on this earth. Looking at me, or so I thought, she said, 'I loved you.'

'No, you never loved anyone. I loved Shlomo and you killed him. Showing off as usual, having a laugh with your dressing-up clothes. You killed the man I loved!'

Ruby, one hand still clutching the butterfly hatpin she had thrust into her sister's heart, put her other hand on my arm and asked me if I was all right.

'We need to get a doctor,' I said. 'For her.'

'No.'

'But . . .'

Ruby Reynolds looked at me with fury in her eyes. 'You know,' she said, 'my little sister came to look after me when she turned up at Princelet Street? Even talked about going out of London to hide me. Fed me some cock-and-bull story about how she found me. I was grateful – she was so sympathetic about Shlomo. Then, suddenly, there's Amber, she's got her too now, and she tells us both tonight about Shlomo and about Pearl's husband. Said we had to face up to it together – like we did in the old days. Christ! She waited all those days to tell me! Knowing what she'd done to me! I thought she'd changed. I hoped, I kidded myself. But no more . . .'

The gun was on the grass now and I suppose I could've picked it up and used it to underwrite my argument. But I didn't because although Ruby Reynolds seemed content to watch her sister die slowly in front of her eyes she didn't try to stop me when I started to go off in search of help. I began walking out of there, past the weeping nun, the man holding the dying young woman in his arms, bits of poor old Frederick trailing after me as I went.

'You know, I should've done this twenty-two years ago,' I heard Ruby say, 'but you were a child then and I'm no natural killer, even of grown-up people. I'm a good person!'

'I know – which was why I got rid of that man who was hurting you!' I heard her sister gasp. 'I did it to save you!'

'Shlomo never hurt me. That was just a story,' Ruby replied, 'a lie his son spread because he didn't want us marrying. You shouldn't believe stories. But you wanted to believe it, didn't you, Opal? It fitted in with what you wanted to do.'

'Bring us all back tog—'

'No! You wanted to bash his head in! Or did you try to stab him first but he got the better of you? You killed him knowing what the coppers would think about me because of that past we've all created together. You wanted me to be a murderer just like you!'

I turned in time to see Ruby bend down and pick something up off the ground. I knew what it was and began to move back slowly towards the little group on the ground. Blatt, I knew, also had a gun.

'No,' Ruby said, as she held out the weapon in front of her, pointing it towards Opal's chest. 'No, it wasn't about us or Mum or anything other than you. Killing Harold was fun, wasn't it? I saw you, remember?'

'Ruby!'

'Please don't kill my child!' Blatt, his revolver nowhere

in sight as far as I could see, wept pathetically. 'Please, please, let us get a doctor.'

'No!'

Sister Teresa ran forward and attempted to grab hold of Ruby's arm, but she threw her off on to the grass.

'You're dying, Opal. You're too dangerous to live. Mum and all of us made a big mistake when we protected you. We killed Harold, too, in a way because of you. You've ruined our lives and now I will be a murderess just like you! So you get what you wanted, as usual. But I don't care. We all died a long time ago – the night you killed Neilson.'

'Well, why should I have to live with it all on my own?' Although shaky, her words were loud and, by the light of the first streaks of dawn in the sky, I could see her face quite clearly. It looked much older than when I'd first seen it, white and spattered with mud and blood. 'Nothing was going to happen to you or to Pearl,' she said. 'I just wanted to frighten you, to make you feel the way I had felt—'

'You felt nothing!' Ruby screamed.

I looked around to see whether anyone else was about, but no one was so I began to edge a little closer to Ruby.

'Mum took the gallows for you!' Ruby carried on. 'You ain't suffered! You did it because you're a spoiled, selfish little whore! Mum spoiled you, them people who adopted you spoiled you and you, 'she pointed the gun at Blatt, 'you who've kidded yourself you're her father—'

'Ruby!'

'No, Amber,' she said. 'Mum told us she was never sure.

It's the truth and you know it! She could be anyone's. She could've been Neilson's. All we do know about her is that even when she was tiny she was selfish and vain and spoiled, and we all made excuses and protected her. But she's a monster.'

'Ruby,' Blatt began, 'please—'

'I'll hang for her.' Ruby held out the gun straight in front of her and said, 'And for you too, Mr Blatt.'

'No!'

'I loved Shlomo. I belonged in Spitalfields. But you ruined all that – you and that thing you call your daughter. You can go with her now – my present to you!'

And then, before I could even think, fire exploded out of the end of the pistol. Ruby shot Opal and Blatt behind her too, three times in one go and then three more at closer range. The last time, she shot her sister straight in the face. I couldn't move. Christ, I kept on thinking, Christ, please help me!

But no one came. Not even Sister Teresa moved from where she was beside Ruby. She wasn't crying any more, I noticed. Just like a statue, a nun with a lowered head – you see monuments like that on some Catholic graves. She looked down at the two corpses in front of her, totally and completely calm. It was so quiet that when dawn came I heard a little bit of birdsong. I hadn't heard that for ages.

'You should go and get a copper if you can, Mr Hancock,' Ruby said, after we'd all been motionless for a while.

'Er, um, er . . .'

She smiled. 'Don't worry,' she said. 'I won't go nowhere now.'

'Ah . . .'

I looked her in the eyes and she added, 'I meant what I said about being prepared to hang for her. I ain't done nothing what didn't need doing here.'

'But I thought you loved her,' I heard the nun say through what sounded like an almost closed throat. 'Ruby?'

'I did. I wanted to,' Ruby said. 'But as soon as she told me about Shlomo, after all that time I'd spent pouring my heart out to her for those few days, I hated her. My love for him was bigger than her, see. And at that moment I knew what I had to do. I just needed to wait for the right time. Are you going to get a copper, then, Mr Hancock?'

'Oh, er, y-yes, I, er...'

And so I left and about ten minutes later I returned with two coppers. Both the women were in exactly the same positions as I'd left them. Not a hair had moved in my absence.

Even by wartime standards the coppers were horrified by what they saw in that churchyard, not to mention my own grisly appearance.

'Blimey, H,' said one of the older sergeants, Jack Webster, who knew me and the family a bit. 'Fancy her trying to plant you! An undertaker! Bloody funny in a way, though, ain't it?'

And we laughed. Covered with bits of coffin plus stuff I didn't want to think too hard about, stinking of the toilet, my own mirth was hysterical to say the least. But it was funny in the way that really horrible things are – after the event. Getting an undertaker to lie down in a grave! That Opal Reynolds had had some neck. The boys down at East Ham would be telling that one to frighten the new lads for years.

Of course, both Sister Teresa and I had to give statements. Hers took longer than mine, she having more of a history with her sisters, but I waited for her anyway. After all, she'd need somewhere to stay for a few days while the coppers made, as Sergeant Webster had put it, 'further enquiries'. One of the young constables went to the shop to let the Duchess and the girls know I was all right. I knew they'd probably be worried by then especially with the telephones down yet again. I thought about Hannah, too, and hoped that she'd got home from Paddington all right. She had to be worried about me. I'd have to go and see her when I could. I needed to see her.

Once Sister Teresa was free to go, we were offered a lift home in one of the police cars. Looking and feeling the way I did, I had no choice but to accept. Not that I would've chosen to walk after what I'd been through.

As soon as we were both in and settled, Sister Teresa said to me, 'I'm so sorry, Mr Hancock. If I'd known it was Opal who telephoned me, putting on a voice, I would never have come to you and got you involved. I never dreamed it was her. I thought it was someone who'd found out what she'd done, what we all did that night Neilson died.'

'You had to go to protect her?' I said.

'Yes. I knew whoever called meant to meet me at Praed Street. Anyone who thought us girls was in the park when Neilson died couldn't know anything about who really killed him. I knew that if I went to the flat and there was no one there, everything was all right. That Opal killed Neilson is and always had been the only real secret here. But there she was and that was when she told me and Ruby what she'd done. I did think you might go to the park, Mr Hancock, but I never thought you'd come up to the flat. Why did you do that?'

'Well, partly because the Serpentine is an ammunition dump,' I said. Sister Teresa, obviously unaware of this fact, looked sheepish. 'And partly because I had this idea you girls might have been there when your father died. I wasn't sure, of course, but I knew that something wasn't right because of the way you talked about that incident. You, Sister, were so keen for me to believe your version of events about Neilson's death that in the end I just couldn't. There was too much fear from you, Pearl and Ruby, too, and it was, strangely to me, centred around your mum and Neilson all the time. There had to be something amiss.'

A really quite old-looking constable got into the driver's seat and off we went.

'So you went straight to the flat on Praed Street?' I continued.

'Yes.'

'And Ruby was already there?'

'Opal'd gone out to Spitalfields to get Ruby, as you know,' Sister Teresa said. 'Got her out using that note supposed to be from you. She was outside when Ruby left, all dressed up again. Thought she was a boy at first, Ruby did, in that get-up. Mr Blatt helped Opal all the way. Got her names, addresses, found out what Ruby and Pearl were like and what they were doing. She watched them and you.'

'I know,' I said. 'But I don't think that Mr Blatt knew exactly what she was going to do with the information that he gave her, do you?'

Sister Teresa shrugged. 'No. But once she'd done it, of course, he must have twigged. Although whether he really knew or not beforehand, none of us'll find out now. She was his only child.'

'If she was.'

'Who can tell?' For the first time in ages, the nun smiled softly, then shook her head sadly and said, 'So many stories, Mr Hancock. Who's to know what might be true?'

I looked at her, frowning.

'Mum told some right whoppers,' Sister Teresa said. 'Girls on the game do, they have to. Blokes want to hear some things, don't they? Begging your pardon, but men as go with such women like to hear they're different and special and good,' here she lowered her voice to little above a whisper, lest the constable should hear, 'at "it", you know. Girls get into the habit of lying to make men happy.'

I tried to smile but I think it came out as a sort of frozen death-mask. Yes, I knew what the good Sister was talking about all right. I may not be typical, but I am a bloke. I know what goes on.

'Blatt could've been Opal's dad,' Sister Teresa said. 'But, then, her dad could've just as easily been that young Jewish bloke, that gangster Mum was going with, the one she really fancied. Or it could've been Neilson. That's a bad thought, isn't it? Meant she killed her own father. Meant he hated and abused his own daughter. I know she don't – didn't look like me, but . . . Then again Mum was on the game, it could've been anyone.' She looked me hard in the eyes and said, 'I like to think we don't know and can't tell who her father was.'

'Why's that?'

'Because I don't want to know anyone whose child can stab a bloke and smile. There's bad blood somewhere in there.'

'Is that what Opal did?' I said. 'She smiled?'

'When we found her, she was giggling,' the nun said, her face now quite old-looking in the thin autumn light. 'Sticking the hatpin in him, blood all over her, laughing.'

'Yes, but—'

'Oh, she knew what she was doing all right,' Sister Teresa said. 'You can say what you like about the unknowingness of kiddies but . . . I've only ever seen real evil once and it was on my sister's eight-year-old face.'

It was a minute or two before I took that in. For a nun to protect someone she knows, or claims to know, is evil seemed like a nonsense to me and I said so.

'It comes back to stories again, I suppose,' Sister Teresa said. 'Opal was Mum's little angel. We all lied for her. Mum died for her – we had to make her worthwhile if only for that. Her going to the Greens and having Blatt spend

324

all his money on her was to make her as near to perfect as a person could get. And I didn't take holy orders because I wanted to hide from the world, you know. Someone had to do penance for my sister. But you can't make someone like that better whatever you do, can you?'

'No,' I said. 'You can't.'

The car pulled up outside the shop and Sister Teresa said, 'You know, when we all split up it was so we'd never talk, not even among ourselves. Even when I knew that Pearl and Ruby might be in trouble, all I could think about was how we was going to keep Opal's secret through it all. It's why I never wanted to get to know Pearl's kid. Didn't want to let nothing slip, didn't want to see something I might not like in her eyes. I mean, who knows where Opal got her character from? Maybe our mum . . .'

A view obviously not shared by Pearl Dooley, who must have told Father Burton the truth about her sister Opal, I now realised. It seemed Pearl hadn't believed that any bad blood had come down from her mother. And maybe that was true but Victorine, in pitting her man and her child against each other in the way that she had, hadn't done either of them any favours. She hadn't deserved to hang for what her daughter had done but she was guilty in part, I felt, all the same.

'Velma is a very nice girl,' I said. 'There's nothing bad about her.'

'Maybe not.'

I got out of the car as Doris came running out of the shop, shouting behind her, 'It's him, Mrs H! He's here!'

Closely followed by Nan, Doris said, looking at me properly, 'God help us, Mr H, you look like a bleedin' Guy! Christ, what a pong!'

'I've had a bit of a night of it, one way or another, Doris,' I said, and then I bent into the car to retrieve Sister Teresa from the back seat.

'You know, I think that Mum knew all along in a way,' she said, as she took my hand and swung her feet out on to the pavement, 'about Opal. She loved jewels, Mum. It's why we're all called after them. But Opals are unlucky, aren't they?'

'So it's said.'

'Well, it's right, then, ain't it? Bad jewels for bad blood,' she said, and smiled again. 'Bloody silly superstition. Ain't Christian, you know.'

I choked up a small and very dry laugh.

Chapter Twenty-one

Hannah was, I'd recently discovered, a dab hand at putting on her makeup with only a candle and a fragment of mirror to judge the effect by. I had to hold the mirror while she put it on, mind, but that didn't in any way detract from my admiration for her skill.

'Can't go out on a date looking like Gawd knows what, can I?' she said, as she pinned her hair on to the top of her head in a big yellow roll.

'No,' I said, as I watched her study her face critically in the mirror.

'Hold it up!' she said, as she moved the mirror and my hands several inches higher. 'There, that's better.'

It was two weeks now since the deaths of Opal Reynolds and Leonard Blatt. Of course, a lot of other people, some known some unknown, had also died in that time, but it was those two who had had the most impact on me and mine. Except to pick up instructions, I hadn't been able to be indoors for the first week after it happened. I'd worked, of course, but if I wasn't either conducting a funeral or out the back with the deceased or the horses I was pounding the streets and what was left of the open spaces of West Ham. Sometimes alone but sometimes with Ken, I walked and ran myself almost to a standstill that first week. As Hannah said at the end of it when I went to her, desperate, in the middle of one long, strangely silent night, 'It wasn't dying, it was burying alive that frightened you, wasn't it? Like being back in the mud in Flanders.'

I'd hugged her almost to the point of crushing the poor girl. She knew, of course she did. Our age group does. She'd had a brother out in Passchendaele. He'd loved her and written to her, in spite of their parents' disapproval, mainly about the mud, and then nothing. So they had no children left now, Hannah's parents. That glum old couple she'd taken me to see that night in Spitalfields. One really dead and the other as good as. How sad they'd let their beliefs kill their love. It's so rare in this world.

When she'd finished putting her face on, as she calls it, Hannah took the piece of mirror from me and said, 'You know that when I come out of Paddington that night after the all-clear and you weren't there I was convinced you had to be dead.'

I started to say something wisecracky about how it would take more than bombs and girls with guns to kill me, when Hannah put one of her fingers over my lips. 'Because, see, I knew that you'd come back for me,' she said.

'Well, yes, love, you know I would.'

'You're the only one that ever has,' she said, and then

she turned away very quickly. 'Listen to me, soppy old cow.'

But I could see there were tears in her eyes and it caused me to have a few in mine too. Love isn't a word I'd use either about or to Hannah, it frightens her, but it is what I feel for her. I know what she is and what she does – why she's in this life too. Dumped by her boyfriend, rejected by her parents. Women don't do too well alone, don't do too well unless they've got money, and, as she'd told me herself, Hannah didn't think she deserved any better than the streets anyway. Poor girl. I give her money, of course I do, but not very often, not now. She'd rather I take her out once in a while. Bad as me, really, she is, out and about and happy to be so with the dead.

Hannah went over to the sink and picked up a little bottle of scent from beside one of the taps. 'How's Velma?' she said, as she dabbed a little behind each ear and on her wrists.

'Happy now she's got her mum back,' I said. Pearl had finally been released from Holloway two days before, and she and Velma had had a tearful reunion in our parlour. Now they knew who had killed Kevin Dooley, the police and Pearl's new solicitor had got her out. The new brief, a Mr Dobson, had also managed to persuade the coppers that Pearl's defence about going to Dot Harris for an abortion was a story she'd made up because she was frightened. No one believed this, including me, but with no evidence that didn't matter. Dot certainly wasn't going to argue with it. But Pearl was out and that was the main thing.

'So what about the Dooleys?' Hannah asked, as the smell of Californian Poppy began to get inside my nostrils. 'Pearl back there, is she?'

'She's been,' I said. I'd taken her over to Canning Town and seen for myself how hard it had been for Vi Dooley and her son Johnny to admit they'd been wrong about her. 'Picked up the rest of the kids.'

'What, and took them back to yours?' Hannah's eyes widened with surprise.

I laughed. All those kids in our place! 'No,' I said. 'Sister Teresa took her and all of them down to Southend with her.'

'To the convent?'

'To start with, yes,' I said. 'Pearl'll have to work and then who knows?'

If Sister Teresa carries on doing what she's doing I'll be very surprised. By her own admission, and just like Pearl, in her way she had hidden in the first safe place she could find. For Pearl that was marriage, any marriage, and children. For Amber it was the veil, doing penance for a crime that wasn't even hers. Thinking back on it, which I've done almost all of the time these past couple of weeks, I reckon it was only ever Ruby who had found any peace in her life. Had Opal not ruined it, she would have been happy among the Jews with Shlomo as her husband. Gerald would've got used to it eventually, and Ruby would've been a contented congregant at the Great Synagogue on Brick Lane with all the other frummers. Fred Bryant says she'll almost certainly hang for the murder of her sister and Blatt, and you don't have to be a copper to realise that's on the cards. But when I'm called to give evidence I will do my best to try to give the court some idea of the strain and grief she was suffering, of the cruelty that had been done to her. However, as Sister Teresa said to me the night after it had happened, 'Ruby ain't going to try to get out of it, Mr Hancock. She did what she thought was right. She's prepared, as she said, to hang for it.'

But it still isn't a comfortable thought, so for a moment I frowned.

Hannah, seeing this look flash across my face, said, 'I hope you're not going to have a face like that on all through the picture.'

'No.' Then I smiled. 'How can I with Deanna Durbin up on the screen and you on my arm?'

Hannah shook her head in mock irritation. 'Come on, then,' she said, as she went over to the door and opened it. 'Let's get out of here before the Jerries turn up.'

I stood up and followed her out into the hall.

Epilogue

When someone you know dies the world changes, or so some people say. In many ways, however, it remains the same and I don't know which is more hurtful: the change or the endless sameness of it all.

I'm standing here now, back in the graveyard where the bare-knuckle fight took place, next to where Kevin Dooley died, where I was nearly buried in the monument that the woman I'm looking at now is leaning against. I know she's scared, of the bombs crashing to the ground all over the manor as well as of me because, as happens sometimes, I can't help laughing. Sometimes in the trenches I'd laugh for hours without a break.

But I know it's a measure of her desperation that she's followed me up here. 'Johnny's chucked us out,' she said, as she grabbed hold of my sleeve that first time over by the gate. 'You helped Pearl. Help me. I'll do anything you want.'

And then, poor cow, she'd opened her blouse and shown herself to me. She's a well-built woman, Martine

Dooley, and I can easily appreciate what a man might see in her. But not me. I can't take to a woman whose face shows open disgust every time she looks at you. I started to stutter I wasn't interested and then she began to laugh, which is why I'm howling myself now.

So she, Martine, is silent and I am behaving like a madman. It's nearly winter now and the Nazis have all but blasted us back to the start of creation here in West Ham. Everyone has lost someone, many of whom I've buried. The business goes from strength to strength.

Here I sit, Francis Hancock – undertaker, wog – out of his tiny mind, looking at that still broken monument that Opal Reynolds put me into.

Wishing, madly, I could climb inside one last and final time.

19 Princelet Street –
Europe's First Museum
of Immigration and Diversity

Although the characters in this book are fictional, most of the locations are real and many of them are still in existence. Sadly, not all of these old buildings are in the best of condition. The building referred to in this book as the 'Princelet Synagogue' is one of them. Originally the home of a Huguenot silk merchant, 19 Princelet Street is a magical place which possesses a beautiful Victorian East European Synagogue built over its rear garden.

The Spitalfields Centre charity is working to preserve this building and give it new life as a place of education and a museum of immigration. It will be a celebration of the rich diversity that exists amongst the people who have settled into the area and of the tradition of giving refuge that Britain can so rightly be proud of.

This delicate, vulnerable and evocative building is close to my heart both as a place and as a symbol of cross-cultural tolerance and understanding. However, in order to properly preserve this international site of conscience, a Grade II* Listed building of national importance as a permanent exploration of issues of immigration, exile and identity, the charity needs money. If you would like to help save the house and make the museum a reality, then please send your contribution to The Spitalfields Centre, 19 Princelet St, London, E1 6QH. The Spitalfields Centre

is a registered charity number 287279, www.19princelet
street.org.uk.

Thank you.
Barbara Nadel.

Glossary

Abyssinia (slang)	'I'll-be-seeing-you'
Anderson	type of World War II domestic air-raid shelter
billet	housing for military personnel. Used by old soldiers to describe their home
buckshee (slang)	free
bunce (slang)	something good, usually money
frum (Yiddish)	religious, observant. 'Frummer' – a religious person
Funf	stupid German spy character in the popular wartime radio show *ITMA*
gelt (Yiddish)	money
goy (Yiddish)	a gentile. Plural 'goyim'
gyppo (slang)	gypsy
Hassidic Jews	very observant; otherwise known as the 'Pious Ones'

Jewish Free School	in Bell Lane, Stepney until bombed in 1941. Gave Jewish pupils a largely secular, English-language education
karzy	lavatory
mensch (Yiddish)	gentleman
mug (slang)	face
nipper (slang)	child
oppo (naval slang)	short for 'opposite number', a pal, a chum
phut (Hindi)	to break down, go wrong
Ratcliff	southern part of Stepney
sappers	military engineers
schlep (Yiddish)	to drag
schtum (Yiddish)	quiet
shikseh (Yiddish)	a gentile woman or girl
sort (slang)	a good man
Torah	Jewish law and scriptures